THE LANGUAGE OF THORNS

MIDNIGHT TALES AND DANGEROUS MAGIC

LEIGH BARDUGO

ILLUSTRATED BY SARA KIPIN

{Imprint}
MAKE YOUR MARK

NEW YORK

[Imprint]
MAKE YOUR MARK

A part of Macmillan Publishing Group, LLC
175 Fifth Avenue, New York, NY 10010

Library of Congress Control Number: 2017937768

Our books may be purchased in bulk for promotional, educational, or business use.
Please contact your local bookseller or the Macmillan Corporate and Premium Sales Department
at (800) 221-7945 ext. 5442 or by e-mail at MacmillanSpecialMarkets@macmillan.com.

"The Too-Clever Fox," "The Witch of Duva,"
and "Little Knife" were previously published on Tor.com.

Book design by Natalie C. Sousa
Illustrations by Sara Kipin
Imprint logo designed by Amanda Spielman

First edition, 2017

ISBN 978-1-250-12252-0 (hardcover)
1 3 5 7 9 10 8 6 4 2

ISBN 978-1-250-16708-8 (special edition)
1 3 5 7 9 10 8 6 4 2

ISBN 978-1-250-16709-5 (special edition)
1 3 5 7 9 10 8 6 4 2

ISBN 978-1-250-17392-8 (international edition)
1 3 5 7 9 10 8 6 4 2

ISBN 978-1-250-12253-7 (ebook)

fiercereads.com

In fairy tales, clever thieves are rewarded for their ingenuity,
but purloin this book and be hounded forever by a gingerbread golem
who will hide your keys and spoil all your dinner parties
by talking about the boring dream she had last night.

For Gamynne—
THE BABE WITH THE POWER

Zemeni

AYAMA AND THE THORN WOOD

1

Ravkan

THE TOO-CLEVER FOX

51

THE WITCH OF DUVA

79

LITTLE KNIFE

117

Kerch

THE SOLDIER PRINCE

143

Fjerdan

WHEN WATER SANG FIRE

191

AUTHOR'S NOTE

278

Ayama
and the
Thorn Wood

IN THE YEAR THAT SUMMER STAYED too long, the heat lay upon the prairie with the weight of a corpse. The tall grass withered to ash beneath the unforgiving sun, and animals fell dead in the parched fields. That year, only the flies were happy, and trouble came to the queen of the western valley.

We all know the story of how the queen became a queen, how despite her tattered clothes and lowly position, her beauty drew the notice of the young prince and she was brought to the palace, where she was dressed in gold and her hair was woven with jewels and all were made to kneel before a girl who had been nothing but a servant bare days before.

That was before the prince became a king, when he was still wild and reckless and hunted every afternoon on the red pony that he'd done the work of breaking himself. It pleased him to rile his father by choosing a peasant bride instead of marrying to forge a political alliance, and his mother was long dead, so he went without sage counsel. The people were amused by his antics and charmed by his lovely wife, and for a time the new couple was content. His wife gave birth to a round-cheeked princeling, who gurgled merrily in his crib and grew more beloved with every passing day.

But then, in the year of that terrible summer, the old king died. The reckless prince was crowned and when his queen grew heavy with their second child, the rains ceased. The river burned away to a dry vein of rock. The wells filled with dust. Each day, the pregnant queen walked the battlements at the top of the palace, her belly swollen, praying that her child would be wise and strong and handsome, but praying most of all for a kind wind to cool her skin and grant her some relief.

The night their second son was born, the full moon rose brown as an old scab in the sky. Coyotes surrounded the palace, howling and clawing at the walls, and tore the insides from a guard who had been sent to chase them away. Their frenzied baying hid the screams of the queen as she looked upon the creature that had slipped squalling from her womb. This little prince was shaped a bit like a boy but more like a wolf, his body covered in slick black fur from crown to clawed foot. His eyes were red as blood, and the nubs of two budding horns protruded from his head.

The king wasn't eager to start a precedent of killing princes, but such a creature could not be raised in the palace. So he called upon his most learned ministers and his greatest engineers to build a vast maze beneath the royal compound. It ran for mile after mile, all the way to the market square, doubling back on itself again and again. It took years for the king to complete the labyrinth, and half the workmen tasked

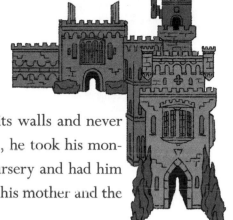

with its construction were lost within its walls and never heard from again. But when it was done, he took his monstrous son from the cage in the royal nursery and had him placed in the maze that he might trouble his mother and the kingdom no more.

In that same summer of the beast's birth, another child came into the world. Kima was born into a far poorer family, one with barely enough land to feed themselves from its crops. But when this child took her first breath, it was not to cry but to sing, and when she did, the skies opened and the rains began to fall, putting an end to the long drought at last.

The world turned green that day, and it was said that wherever Kima went you could smell the sweet scent of new growing things. She was tall and lithe as a young linden tree, and she moved with a grace that was almost worrying—as if, being so light upon her feet, she might simply blow away. She had smooth skin that glowed brown like the mountains in that honeyed hour before the sun sets, and she wore her hair unbound, in a thick halo of black curls that framed her face like a flower blooming.

No one in the town could dispute that Kima's parents had been blessed when she was born, for she was surely meant to marry a rich man—maybe even a prince—and bring them

3

good fortune. But then, barely a year later, their second daughter came into the world, and the gods laughed. For as this new child aged, it became clear that she lacked all the gifts that Kima possessed in such abundance. Ayama was clumsy and apt to drop things. Her body was solid and flat-footed, short and round as a beer jug. While Kima's voice was gentle and calming as rain, when Ayama spoke it was like the glare of noon, harsh enough to make you wince and turn away. Embarrassed by their second daughter, Ayama's parents bid her speak less. They kept her at home, busy with chores, only letting her make the long walk to the river and back to wash clothes.

So as not to trouble Kima's rest, their parents made a pallet for Ayama on the warm stones of the kitchen hearth. Her braids grew untidy and her skin soaked up ash. Soon, she looked less brown than gray as she crept timidly from shadow to shadow, afraid of causing offense, and in time, people forgot that there were two daughters in the house at all, and thought of Ayama only as a servant.

Kima often tried to talk to her sister, but she was being prepared to be a rich man's bride, and no sooner would she find Ayama in the kitchen than she would be called away to school or to her dancing lessons. During the days Ayama worked in silence, and at night she crept to Kima's bedside,

held her sister's hand, and listened to their grandmother tell stories, lulled by the creak of Ma Zil's ancient voice. When the candles burned low, Ma Zil would poke Ayama with her cane and tell her to get back to the hearth before her parents woke to find her bothering her sister.

Things went on this way for a long while. Ayama toiled in the kitchen, Kima grew more beautiful, the queen raised her human son in the palace against the cliff and put wool in his ears late at night when the howls of his younger brother could be heard far below. The king waged a failing war to the east. People grumbled when he levied new taxes or took their sons to be soldiers. They complained about the weather. They hoped for rain.

Then on a clear and sunny morning, the town woke to the rumble of thunder. Not one cloud could be seen in the sky, but the sound shook the roof tiles and sent an old man tottering into a ditch, where he waited two hours before his sons fished him out. By then, everyone knew that no storm had caused the awful din. The beast had escaped the labyrinth, and it was his roar that had boomed off the valley walls and made the mountains shudder.

Now the people stopped fretting over their taxes and their crops and the war, and instead worried they might be snatched from their beds and eaten. They barred their doors and sharpened their knives. They kept their children inside and their lanterns burning all through the night.

But no one can live in fear forever, and as the days passed without incident, the people began to wonder if perhaps the beast had done them the courtesy of finding some other valley to terrorize. Then Bolan Bedi rode out to tend to his herds and found his cattle slain and the grass of the western fields soaked red with blood—and he was not the only one. Word of the slaughter spread, and Ayama's father walked out to the far pastures for news. He returned with horrible tales of heads torn from newborn calves, and sheep slit open from neck to groin, their wool turned the color of rust. Only the beast could have managed such devastation in a single night.

The people of the western valley had never seen their king as much of a hero, what with his losing wars, his peasant wife, and his taste for comforts. But now they bristled with pride as he took command and vowed to protect the valley and deal with his monstrous son once and for all. The king assembled a vast hunting party to travel into the wild lands where his ministers suspected the beast had taken refuge, and ordered his own royal guard to serve as escort. Down the main road they marched, a hundred soldiers kicking up dust from their boots, and their captain led the way, his bronze gauntlets flashing. Ayama watched them pass from behind the kitchen window and marveled at their courage.

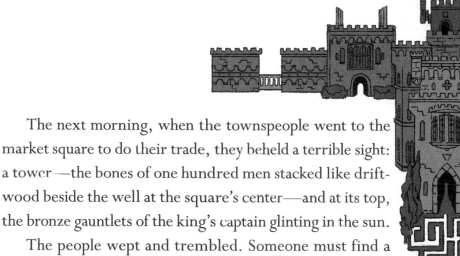

The next morning, when the townspeople went to the market square to do their trade, they beheld a terrible sight: a tower—the bones of one hundred men stacked like drift-wood beside the well at the square's center—and at its top, the bronze gauntlets of the king's captain glinting in the sun.

The people wept and trembled. Someone must find a way to protect them and their herds. If no soldier could slay the beast, then the king must find a way to appease his younger son. The king ordered his cleverest minister to travel into the wild lands and forge a truce with the monster. The minister agreed, went to pack a bag, and then ran as fast as he could from the valley, never to be seen again. The king could find no one brave enough to travel to the wild lands and negotiate on his behalf. In desperation, he offered three chests of gold and thirty bolts of silk to anyone bold enough to serve as his emissary, and that night there was much talk in the houses of the valley.

"We should leave this place," said Ayama's father when the family gathered for the evening meal. "Did you see those bones? If the king cannot find a way to placate the monster, no doubt it will come and devour us all."

Ayama's mother agreed. "We will travel east and make a new home on the coast."

But Ma Zil was sitting by the fire on her low stool, chewing a jurda leaf. The old grandmother had no wish to make a long journey. "Send Ayama," she said, and spat into the fire.

There was a long pause as the flames hissed and crackled. Despite the heat of the cookstove where she stood toasting millet, Ayama shivered.

Almost as if she knew it was her part to protest, Ayama's mother said, "No, no. Ayama is a difficult girl, but my daughter nonetheless. We will go to the sea."

"Besides," said her father. "Look at her dirty smock and messy braids. Who would believe Ayama could be a royal messenger? The beast will laugh her right out of the wild lands."

Ayama didn't know if monsters could laugh, but there was no time to think on it, because Ma Zil spat into the fire again.

"He is a beast," said the old woman. "What does he know of fine clothes or pretty faces? Ayama will be the king's royal messenger. We will be rich and Kima will be able to catch a better husband to provide for us all."

"But what if the beast devours her?" asked kind Kima, with tears in her lovely eyes. Ayama was grateful to her sister, for though she wanted desperately to object to her grandmother's plan, her parents had spent so long teaching her to hold her tongue that speech did not come easily.

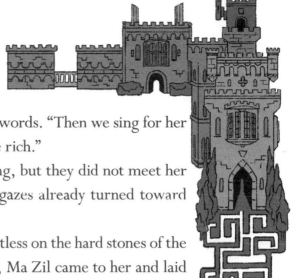

Ma Zil waved away Kima's words. "Then we sing for her a bone song and we will still be rich."

Ayama's parents said nothing, but they did not meet her eyes, their thoughts and their gazes already turned toward the king's piles of gold.

That night, as Ayama lay restless on the hard stones of the hearth, unable to sleep for fear, Ma Zil came to her and laid a calloused hand upon her cheek.

"Don't worry," she said. "I know you are frightened, but after you have earned the king's reward, you will have servants of your own. You need never scrub a floor or scrape stew from an old cookpot again. You will wear blue summer silks and eat white nectarines, and sleep in a proper bed."

Ayama's brow still creased with worry, so her grandmother said, "Come now, Ayama. You know how the stories go. Interesting things only happen to pretty girls; you will be home by sunset."

This thought comforted Ayama, and as Ma Zil sang a lullaby, she fell into dreams, snoring loudly—for in sleep, no one could quiet her voice.

Ayama's father sent word to the king, and though there was much scoffing at the thought of such a girl making the endeavor, the only condition the king had set for his messenger was courage. So Ayama became the king's emissary and was told to travel into the wild lands, find the beast, and hear his demands.

Ayama's hair was oiled and rebraided. She was given one of Kima's dresses, which was too tight everywhere and had to be hemmed so that it did not drag in the dust. Ma Zil tied a sky-blue apron at her granddaughter's waist and sat a wide hat with a band of red poppies upon her head. Ayama tucked the little axe she used for chopping wood into the pocket of her apron, along with a dry hermit cake and a copper cup for drinking—if she was lucky enough to find water.

The townspeople moaned and dabbed at their eyes and told Ayama's parents how brave they were; they marveled at how fine Kima looked despite her tearstained cheeks. Then they went back to their business, and away went Ayama to the wild lands.

Now it's fair to say that Ayama's spirits were a bit low. How could they not be when her family had sent her to die for the sake of a bit of gold and a good marriage for her sister? But she loved Kima, who slipped Ayama pieces of honeycomb when their parents weren't looking and who

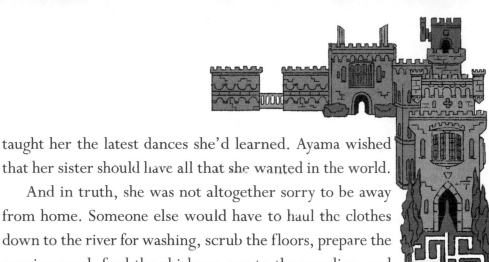

taught her the latest dances she'd learned. Ayama wished that her sister should have all that she wanted in the world.

And in truth, she was not altogether sorry to be away from home. Someone else would have to haul the clothes down to the river for washing, scrub the floors, prepare the evening meal, feed the chickens, see to the mending, and scrape last night's stew from the pot.

Well, she thought, for she had learned to keep silent even when alone. *At least I do not have to work today, and I will see something new before I die.* Though the sun beat down mercilessly on Ayama's back, that thought alone made her walk with a happier step.

Her cheer did not last long. The wild lands were nothing but parched grasses and barren scrub. No insects buzzed. No shade broke the relentless glare. Sweat soaked the fabric of Ayama's too-tight dress, and her feet felt like heated bricks in her shoes. She quivered when she saw the bleached bones of a horse's carcass, but after another hour she started to look forward to glimpsing a clean white skull or the staves of a rib cage splayed like the beginnings of a basket. They were at least a break in the monotony and a sign that something had survived here, if only for a while.

Perhaps, she thought, *I will just drop dead before I ever reach the beast and I have nothing to fear at all.* But eventually, she saw a black line on the horizon, and as she drew closer, she realized she had reached a shadowy wood. The gray-bark trees were tall and so thick with thorn-covered brambles that Ayama could see nothing but darkness between them. She knew that this was where she would find the king's son.

Ayama hesitated. She did not like to think of what might await her in the thorn wood. She could well be minutes from her last breath. *At least you will take it in the shade*, she considered. *And really, is the wood much worse than a garden overgrown with pricklers? It is probably very dull inside and will do nothing more than bore me to tears.* She gathered Ma Zil's promise around her like armor, reminded herself that she was not destined for adventure, and found a gap in the iron vines to slip through, hissing as the thorns pricked her arms and slashed at her hands.

With shaking steps, Ayama passed through the thicket and into the wood. She found herself in darkness. Her heart thumped a jackrabbit beat and she wanted to turn and run, but she had spent much of her life in shadows and knew them well. She forced herself to stillness as the sweat cooled on her skin. In a few short minutes, she found that the wood was dark only compared to the brightness of the wild lands she'd left behind.

As her eyes adjusted, Ayama wondered if perhaps the heat

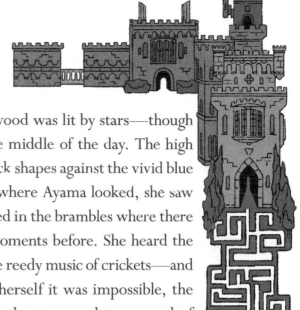

had muddled her mind. The wood was lit by stars—though she knew very well it was the middle of the day. The high branches of the trees made black shapes against the vivid blue of the twilight sky, and everywhere Ayama looked, she saw white quince blossoms clustered in the brambles where there had been only thorns mere moments before. She heard the sweet call of night birds and the reedy music of crickets—and somewhere, though she told herself it was impossible, the burble of water. The light from the stars caught on every leaf and pebble, so that the world around her seemed to glow silver. She knew she must stay cautious, but she could not resist slipping off her shoes to feel the ground, cool and mossy beneath her aching feet.

She forced herself to leave the surety of the thicket at her back and walk. In time, she came to the banks of a stream, its surface so bright with starlight it was as if someone had peeled the rind from the moon like a piece of fruit and laid it in a gleaming ribbon upon the forest floor. Ayama followed its winding path deeper and deeper into the wood until at last she arrived at a quiet glade. Here the trees sparked with fire-flies and the sky was the cloudy purple of a ripe plum. She had reached the heart of the wood.

The stream fed a wide pool bordered by ferns and smooth stones, and when Ayama saw the clear, sweet water, she could not help but hurry to kneel beside it. The poppies on her hat had long since wilted, and her throat was dry as an old husk. She took her little copper cup from her apron and plunged it into the water, but as she lifted it to drink, she heard a thunderous roar and felt the cup knocked from her hand. It sailed across the glade and Ayama nearly toppled into the pool.

"Stupid girl!" said a voice that rumbled like an avalanche off the mountain. "Do you wish to become a monster?"

Ayama cowered on the grass, her hands pressed to her mouth to stop the scream that wanted to slip free. She could sense more than see the massive shape of the monster prowling back and forth in the dark.

"Answer me," he demanded.

Ayama shook her head and somehow found her voice, though it sounded brittle as chalk to her ears. "I was only thirsty," she said.

She heard a sharp growl and felt the ground tremble as the beast stalked toward her. He reared up on his hind legs, looming over her, blocking out the stars. He had the body of a black wolf and yet the bearing of a man. Around the thick fur of his ruff he wore a lariat of gold and rubies, and the twisting horns that rose from his head were marked with ridges that glowed as if lit from within by secret fire. But most

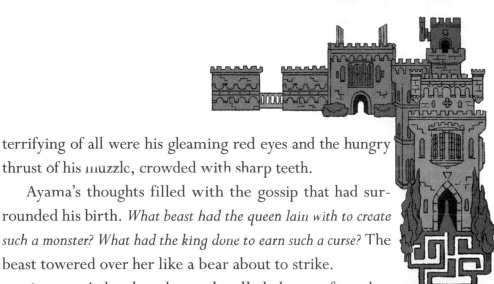

terrifying of all were his gleaming red eyes and the hungry thrust of his muzzle, crowded with sharp teeth.

Ayama's thoughts filled with the gossip that had surrounded his birth. *What beast had the queen lain with to create such a monster? What had the king done to earn such a curse?* The beast towered over her like a bear about to strike.

A weapon! she thought, and pulled the axe from her apron.

But the beast only smiled—there was no other word for it, his lips pulling back to reveal black gums and the terrible points of his long teeth.

"Strike me," he dared her. "Cleave me in two."

Before Ayama could even think to comply, he snatched the axe from her hands with one thick-clawed paw and dragged the blade across his chest. It did not leave any mark. "No blade can pierce my hide. Do you think my father didn't try?"

The monster lowered his huge head and sniffed deeply at Ayama's neck, then snorted. "He sends a peasant, covered in ash and stinking of kitchen fires. You are not even fit to eat. Perhaps I will skin you and offer you to the other creatures of the thorn wood to goad them with offense."

Ayama had grown very used to being insulted, so much so that she hardly noticed it anymore. But she was miserably tired, and miserably sore, and so frightened that the very bones in her body were quaking. Perhaps this was why she stood, opened her mouth, and in the piercing voice that had vexed her parents bitterly said, "So much for the terrifying beast. His weak teeth require soft-limbed ladies."

Ayama wanted to grab the words back, but the beast merely laughed, and such a human sound coming from his monstrous body raised the hair on Ayama's arms.

"You're as thorny as the wood," he said. "Tell me, why does the king command a stub of a serving girl to trouble me?"

"The king chose me to—"

In a breath, the beast's mirth vanished. He threw back his head and howled, the sound shaking the leaves on the trees and sending white and pink petals fluttering from the branches. Ayama stumbled backward and covered her head with her arms, as if she could hide herself within them. But the beast leaned down so close she could smell the strange animal scent of his pelt and feel the warm gust of his breath when he spoke.

"There is but one rule in my wood," he growled. "Speak truth."

Ayama thought of trying to explain her family and the offer of the chests of gold and silk, but the truth was far simpler than all of that. "No one else would come."

"Not the king's brave soldiers?"

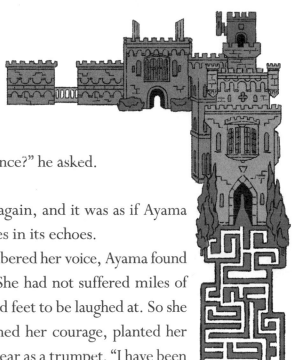

She shook her head.

"Not the perfect human prince?" he asked.

"No."

The beast's laugh rang out again, and it was as if Ayama could hear the grinding of bones in its echoes.

But now that she had remembered her voice, Ayama found she was eager to use it again. She had not suffered miles of thirst and boredom and blistered feet to be laughed at. So she pushed her fear aside, summoned her courage, planted her flat feet, and said, blaring and clear as a trumpet, "I have been sent to ask you to stop slaughtering our herds."

The beast left off his laughing. "Why should I?"

"Because we are hungry!"

"What do I care for your hunger?" he snarled, pacing the glade. "Did you care for my aching belly when I was a child left alone in the labyrinth? Did you use that loud voice to petition the king for mercy then, little messenger?"

Ayama twisted the strings of her apron. She had been but a child herself at the time, but it was true that she had never heard her parents or a single resident of the valley spare a sympathetic word for the beast.

"No," said the monster, answering his own question. "You did not. Let the good king feed you from his royal herds if he worries so much for his people."

It was possible the king should do just that, but it was not Ayama's place to say so. "I have been sent to bargain with you."

"The king has nothing I want."

"Then perhaps you might show mercy freely."

"My father never taught me mercy."

"And can you not learn?"

The beast stopped his prowling and turned very slowly toward Ayama, who did her best not to tremble even as his bloody eyes fastened upon her. His smile was sly.

"I have a bargain for *you*, little messenger, not the king. Tell me a tale that can make me feel more than anger, and if you manage it, I may let you live."

Ayama did not know what to make of such an offer. It might be a trick or simply an impossible task. The beast might be feeling generous or he might just be full after his last meal and in need of some idle entertainment. Then again, Ayama had spent much of her life neither speaking nor being spoken to. She supposed it was possible the beast might simply long for conversation.

She cleared her throat. "And you will cease troubling our herds?"

The beast snorted. "If you do not bore me. But you are already boring me."

Ayama took a steadying breath. It was very hard to think with such a creature looming over her.

18

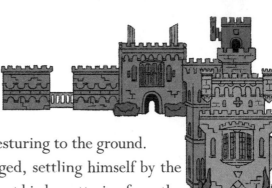

"Would you sit?" she said, gesturing to the ground.

The beast growled but obliged, settling himself by the water with a great thump that sent birds scattering from the dark trees.

Ayama sat down on the ground a good distance away and arranged her apron around her, tucking her shoes back onto her feet. She closed her eyes to shut out the sight of the beast curled beside the stream, already licking his chops.

"You're stalling," he said.

"I'm only trying to make sure I tell the story right."

He laughed a low, ugly laugh. "Speak truth, little messenger."

Ayama shivered, for she was not sure which of Ma Zil's stories were true and which were false. Besides, the prospect of dying made it hard to think of anything at all. But just because no one bothered to listen to Ayama didn't mean she had nothing to say. In fact, she had plenty. And if it was true that the beast was happy to be spoken to, then perhaps it was also true that Ayama was glad to be heard.

THE FIRST TALE

"Once there was a boy who ate and ate but could not get full. He consumed flocks of geese without stopping to rid them of their feathers. He drank whole lakes, consumed all the fish within them, and belched out the rocks. He filled his mouth with a dozen eggs in a single bite, then had one thousand head

19

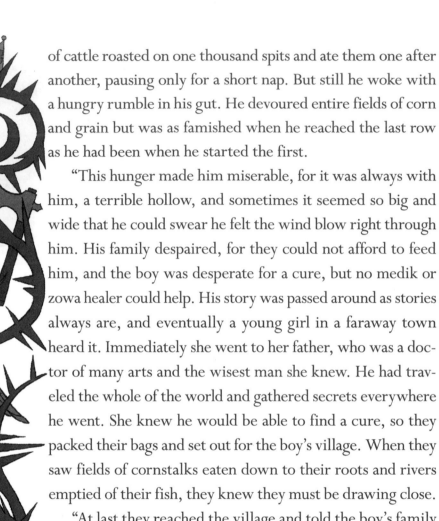

of cattle roasted on one thousand spits and ate them one after another, pausing only for a short nap. But still he woke with a hungry rumble in his gut. He devoured entire fields of corn and grain but was as famished when he reached the last row as he had been when he started the first.

"This hunger made him miserable, for it was always with him, a terrible hollow, and sometimes it seemed so big and wide that he could swear he felt the wind blow right through him. His family despaired, for they could not afford to feed him, and the boy was desperate for a cure, but no medik or zowa healer could help. His story was passed around as stories always are, and eventually a young girl in a faraway town heard it. Immediately she went to her father, who was a doctor of many arts and the wisest man she knew. He had traveled the whole of the world and gathered secrets everywhere he went. She knew he would be able to find a cure, so they packed their bags and set out for the boy's village. When they saw fields of cornstalks eaten down to their roots and rivers emptied of their fish, they knew they must be drawing close.

"At last they reached the village and told the boy's family they'd come to offer their help. The boy was not hopeful, but he let the doctor look into his eyes and ears and when the doctor asked to peer down his throat, the boy tipped his head back obligingly.

"'Aha!' said the wise doctor, once he'd gotten a look at the boy's gullet. 'When your mother carried you in her womb, did she sleep with her window open?' The boy's mother said that she had, for it had been a very hot summer that year. 'Well then,' said the doctor, 'it is simple. In her sleep, your mother swallowed a bit of night sky, and all of that empty is still inside you. Just eat a bit of the sun to fill the sky and you will feel empty no longer.'

"The doctor claimed that it was simple. The boy was not so sure. There was no tree or ladder high enough to reach the sun, and soon he fell even deeper into despair. But the doctor's daughter was as smart as she was kind, and she knew that every night the sun sank low enough to touch the sea and turn the water gold. So she built them a little boat and they sailed west together. They traveled many miles, and the boy ate two whales along the way, and at last they reached the golden place where the sun met the sea. The girl took a white ash ladle from her pocket and scooped up a bit of the sun from the water. When the boy drank it down—"

The beast released a rumbling growl and Ayama jumped, for she'd been so caught up in the story and the pleasure of being listened to that she'd almost forgotten where she was.

"Let me guess," snarled the beast. "The miserable boy swallowed a gulp of the sea and ever after that he was a

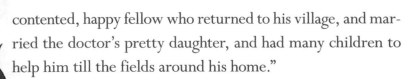

contented, happy fellow who returned to his village, and married the doctor's pretty daughter, and had many children to help him till the fields around his home."

"What nonsense!" said Ayama, hoping the trembling of her voice did not betray her. "Of course that's not how the story ends."

It was not nonsense. The story ended just as the beast had said, at least every time Ayama had heard it told. Still, she could admit that it had always left her feeling a bit melancholy and dissatisfied, as if a false note had been played. But what ending might appease the beast? Because Ayama had been hushed so often, she had become a very good listener, and she remembered the one rule of the thorn wood. The story needed an ending that was true.

Ayama collected her thoughts, then gathered up the thread of the tale and let it unspool anew.

"It's true that the boy drank sun from the white ash ladle," she said. "And, yes, it's true that he no longer required a herd of cattle for his breakfast or a lake to wash it down. He did indeed marry the doctor's pretty daughter and worked each day to till his fields. But despite all this, the boy found he was still unhappy. You see, some people are born with a piece of night inside, and that hollow place can never be filled—not with all the good food or sunshine in the world. That

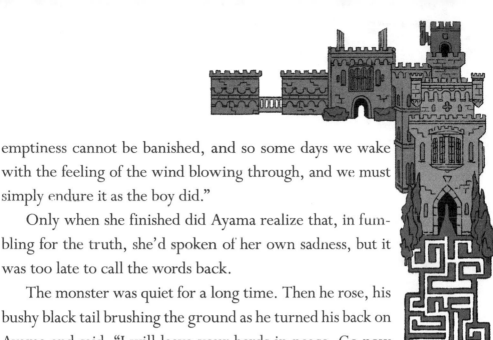

emptiness cannot be banished, and so some days we wake with the feeling of the wind blowing through, and we must simply endure it as the boy did."

Only when she finished did Ayama realize that, in fumbling for the truth, she'd spoken of her own sadness, but it was too late to call the words back.

The monster was quiet for a long time. Then he rose, his bushy black tail brushing the ground as he turned his back on Ayama and said, "I will leave your herds in peace. Go now and do not return."

And because the wood demanded truth, she knew his vow was good.

Ayama could scarcely believe her luck. She leapt to her feet and hurried from the glade, but as she bent to pick up her axe and her copper cup, the beast said, "Wait."

He was little more than a shape in the dark now, and she could make him out only by the red gleam of his eyes and the glow of the carved ridges on his horns.

"Take a sprig of quince blossoms with you and make sure not to drop it as you pass through the wild lands."

Ayama did not stop to question his command, but plucked a slender branch and ran back along the stream. She did not slow until she had pushed her way through the cruel thorns of the thicket and felt the sun on her face once more.

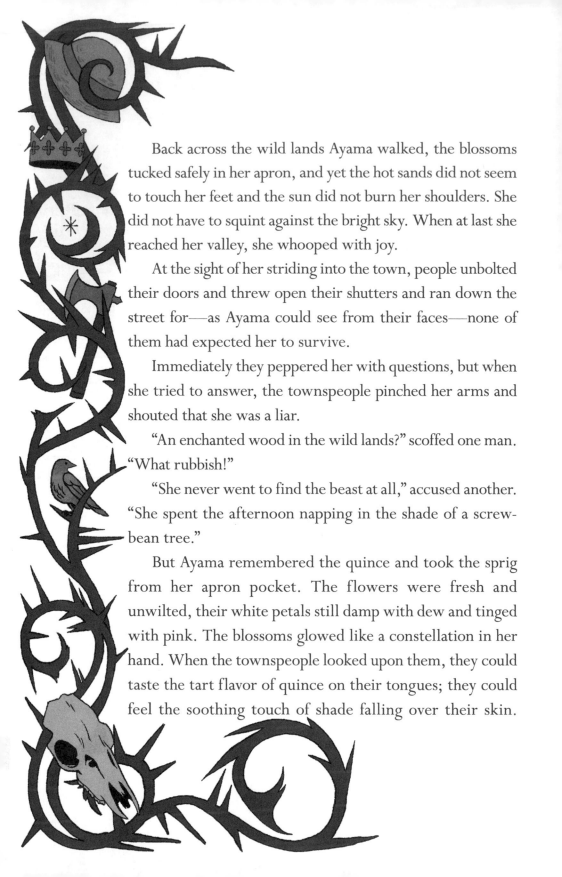

Back across the wild lands Ayama walked, the blossoms tucked safely in her apron, and yet the hot sands did not seem to touch her feet and the sun did not burn her shoulders. She did not have to squint against the bright sky. When at last she reached her valley, she whooped with joy.

At the sight of her striding into the town, people unbolted their doors and threw open their shutters and ran down the street for—as Ayama could see from their faces—none of them had expected her to survive.

Immediately they peppered her with questions, but when she tried to answer, the townspeople pinched her arms and shouted that she was a liar.

"An enchanted wood in the wild lands?" scoffed one man. "What rubbish!"

"She never went to find the beast at all," accused another. "She spent the afternoon napping in the shade of a screw-bean tree."

But Ayama remembered the quince and took the sprig from her apron pocket. The flowers were fresh and unwilted, their white petals still damp with dew and tinged with pink. The blossoms glowed like a constellation in her hand. When the townspeople looked upon them, they could taste the tart flavor of quince on their tongues; they could feel the soothing touch of shade falling over their skin.

These were no ordinary flowers. Now the people listened as Ayama stood with the sprig clasped in her fist and told them of the beast's promise, and when she had finished, they led her all the way to the palace, murmuring in wonder, forgetting that the girl they now looked upon with awe still had the marks of their pinching fingers on her arms.

The king gazed down from his throne with cold eyes when Ayama spoke of the beast's vow, but he could not deny the magic of the quince that bloomed sweet and strange in Ayama's hands, its petals only now beginning to turn red.

"Such a marvel!" said the king's handsome human son, smiling brightly. "And what a brave girl to attempt such a task. Her pockets shall be weighted with jewels and all shall sing songs of her courage."

Ayama returned his smile, for it was impossible not to bloom in the prince's sunny regard. But what she really wanted was a glass of water.

The queen took the flowers from Ayama, eyes sparkling with what might have been tears. "You must do as you promised," she told her husband.

So the king called for three chests of gold and thirty bolts of silk to be brought to Ayama's family.

That night, Ayama's parents rejoiced, and Kima kissed her

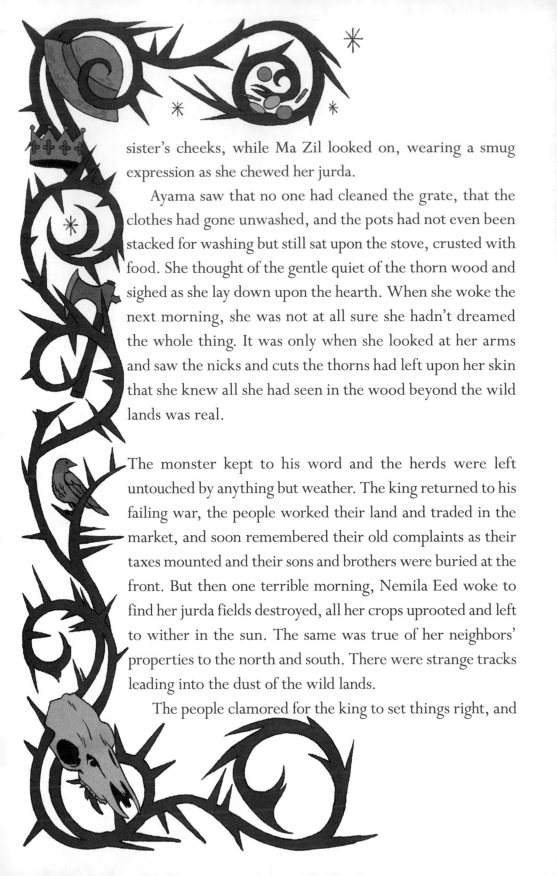

sister's cheeks, while Ma Zil looked on, wearing a smug expression as she chewed her jurda.

Ayama saw that no one had cleaned the grate, that the clothes had gone unwashed, and the pots had not even been stacked for washing but still sat upon the stove, crusted with food. She thought of the gentle quiet of the thorn wood and sighed as she lay down upon the hearth. When she woke the next morning, she was not at all sure she hadn't dreamed the whole thing. It was only when she looked at her arms and saw the nicks and cuts the thorns had left upon her skin that she knew all she had seen in the wood beyond the wild lands was real.

The monster kept to his word and the herds were left untouched by anything but weather. The king returned to his failing war, the people worked their land and traded in the market, and soon remembered their old complaints as their taxes mounted and their sons and brothers were buried at the front. But then one terrible morning, Nemila Eed woke to find her jurda fields destroyed, all her crops uprooted and left to wither in the sun. The same was true of her neighbors' properties to the north and south. There were strange tracks leading into the dust of the wild lands.

The people clamored for the king to set things right, and

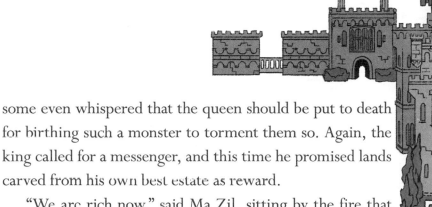

some even whispered that the queen should be put to death for birthing such a monster to torment them so. Again, the king called for a messenger, and this time he promised lands carved from his own best estate as reward.

"We are rich now," said Ma Zil, sitting by the fire that night. "But just think how fine it would be to live in a grand house where Kima could receive suitors. Then she would be sure to make a good marriage. Ayama, wouldn't you like to wear white furs in the winter and eat sweet persimmons and sleep in a proper bed?"

Ayama was not at all sure she would survive a second meeting with the beast, and she couldn't very well enjoy persimmons and soft cushions if she'd been eaten. But her grandmother laid a rough palm upon her cheek and swore that no harm would befall her. And if Ayama was honest, some small part of her wanted to return to the wood. Her family was rich now and had many servants, but they'd gotten so used to ordering Ayama about that they'd forgotten how to treat her as a daughter. She still slept in the kitchen and scrubbed the pots and watched as the bolts of silk were cut for Kima's gowns, and her mother's hair was dressed by a dainty maid who wore a flowered pinafore. People tipped their hats to her in the street now, but they never stopped to talk or ask how Ayama was faring. The beast might shout and snarl, and he

might well devour her, but he'd at least been interested enough to listen to her speak.

So when dawn came, Ayama took her little copper cup and the axe that she used to chop wood, and tucked them into her apron. She placed her wide hat upon her head and once more set out for the wild lands.

The journey through the dust and brush was just as long and wearying the second time. When at last Ayama reached the iron-colored trees of the thorn wood, her throat was dry as burnt bread and her feet ached from walking. She pushed eagerly through the thicket, and as soon as she felt the silver light of the stars upon her shoulders, she heaved a contented sigh.

Only then did she remember to be afraid. After all, the beast might be hungrier. Or angrier. He might have forgotten the mercy he'd found when he'd let Ayama pass safely from the wood before. But she was here now and there was nothing to be done about it. Ayama followed the silver stream, letting the soft leaves and damp soil cool her feet, and tried not to think of the beast eating her in one bite—or worse, two.

At last she came to the glade. This time, the beast did not lurk in the shadows, but was pacing as if he had been waiting.

"Well, then," he said in his rumbling voice when he saw

her. "They must not value you much if they expect you to escape a second time."

Since the wood demanded truth, Ayama supposed he was right, but now she found it far easier to speak in return. "You must stop destroying our crops."

"Why?"

"We will have no cotton or flax to spin when the winter comes."

"What do I care for winter? No season touches this wood. Did anyone think of winter when I shivered in my father's labyrinth? Let the king feed and clothe you from his stores."

This time she could acknowledge it was not such a bad idea, and so she said, "Do not behave as a tyrant and then tell me to scold a tyrant to behave. Show mercy and mercy you may be shown."

"My father never taught me mercy."

"And can you not learn?"

It was hard to tell, but it seemed the beast might have smiled.

"You know the only bargain I will make, little messenger." The beast settled beside the stream in a heap of black fur and golden claws. "Tell me a tale that can make me feel more than anger, and perhaps if it pleases me, I may let you live."

This was the invitation Ayama had been waiting for, and

she realized that in all the silent days and nights since she'd left the wood, she'd been storing up words to offer the king's son. Ayama sat down by the banks of the stream and began to speak.

THE SECOND TALE

"Once there was a woman with a mournful bearing who came to a village, and there she met a man who longed for a wife, and so they were married. They had two fine children, a boy and a girl, but as these children grew older, they became difficult and disobedient. They were often sickly and this made them sulky and tired, and they were a great trial to their mother, Mama Tani. All the women in the village felt sorry for Mama Tani, whose bearing had become even sadder, but who bore her children's complaining and sickness with great dignity.

"All that changed when an evil spirit came into Mama Tani's house and began to make trouble for the whole family. The spirit smashed Mama Tani's treasured pots of cream and the bottled tinctures she used to keep her skin smooth. It broke her husband's plow so that he had to stay home and was always underfoot. But it was the children the spirit most liked to prey upon, as if lured by their bad behavior. When they tried to sleep, the spirit would rattle the windows and shake the bed so that they could find no rest. When they tried to

eat, the spirit broke their bowls and spilled their supper on the floor."

The beast growled, and Ayama saw that he'd drawn very close indeed. Though her heart hopped in a frightened rhythm, she sat as still as she could.

"Let me guess," said the beast. "The children cried and prayed and said they would be good forevermore, and so the spirit departed and Mama Tani was the envy of all the women in the village, and this is a lesson to ungrateful children everywhere."

That was certainly the way that Ayama had been taught the story, but she had thought a lot about how she would tell the tale when it belonged to her.

She straightened her apron and said with all the authority her loud voice could muster, "What nonsense! Of course that's not how the story ends." *Speak truth*, she reminded herself. Then she wound the story tight and let it unspool anew.

"No, one day when their parents weren't home, instead of crying when the spirit rattled and roared like an angry wind around the house, the children sat quietly and held each other's hands. Then they sang a lullaby like the ones their mother had sung when they were younger, and sure enough, after a long while, the spirit quieted—and after a longer while, the spirit spoke. Except it was not one spirit, but two."

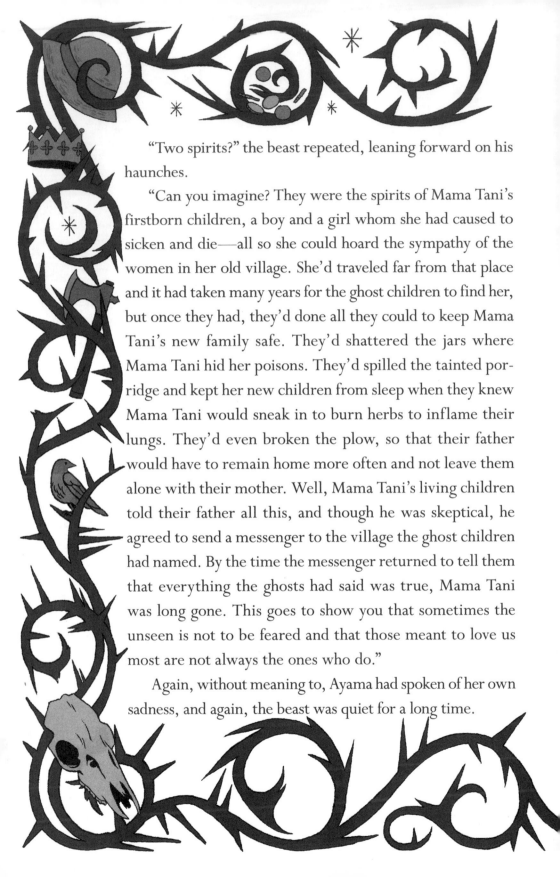

"Two spirits?" the beast repeated, leaning forward on his haunches.

"Can you imagine? They were the spirits of Mama Tani's firstborn children, a boy and a girl whom she had caused to sicken and die—all so she could hoard the sympathy of the women in her old village. She'd traveled far from that place and it had taken many years for the ghost children to find her, but once they had, they'd done all they could to keep Mama Tani's new family safe. They'd shattered the jars where Mama Tani hid her poisons. They'd spilled the tainted porridge and kept her new children from sleep when they knew Mama Tani would sneak in to burn herbs to inflame their lungs. They'd even broken the plow, so that their father would have to remain home more often and not leave them alone with their mother. Well, Mama Tani's living children told their father all this, and though he was skeptical, he agreed to send a messenger to the village the ghost children had named. By the time the messenger returned to tell them that everything the ghosts had said was true, Mama Tani was long gone. This goes to show you that sometimes the unseen is not to be feared and that those meant to love us most are not always the ones who do."

Again, without meaning to, Ayama had spoken of her own sadness, and again, the beast was quiet for a long time.

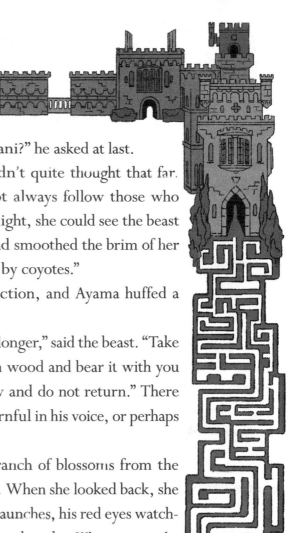

"What happened to Mama Tani?" he asked at last.

Ayama had no idea. She hadn't quite thought that far. "Who can say? Bad fates do not always follow those who deserve them." Even in the dim light, she could see the beast frown. She cleared her throat and smoothed the brim of her hat. "But I believe she was eaten by coyotes."

The beast nodded in satisfaction, and Ayama huffed a little sigh of relief.

"I will trouble your fields no longer," said the beast. "Take a sprig of quince from the thorn wood and bear it with you through the wild lands. Go now and do not return." There might have been something mournful in his voice, or perhaps it was just his growl.

Ayama plucked a slender branch of blossoms from the thicket and left the glade behind. When she looked back, she saw the beast still sitting on his haunches, his red eyes watching her, and for a moment, Ayama thought, *Why not stay a bit longer? Why not rest awhile here? Why not tell another story?*

Instead she made her way out of the wood and back across the hot plains. She tucked the sprig of quince flowers into her braids, and it was as if she carried the cool leaves and the shade of the wood with her.

This time when she reached the town, the people saw the white blossoms in her hair and did not pinch Ayama or shout

33

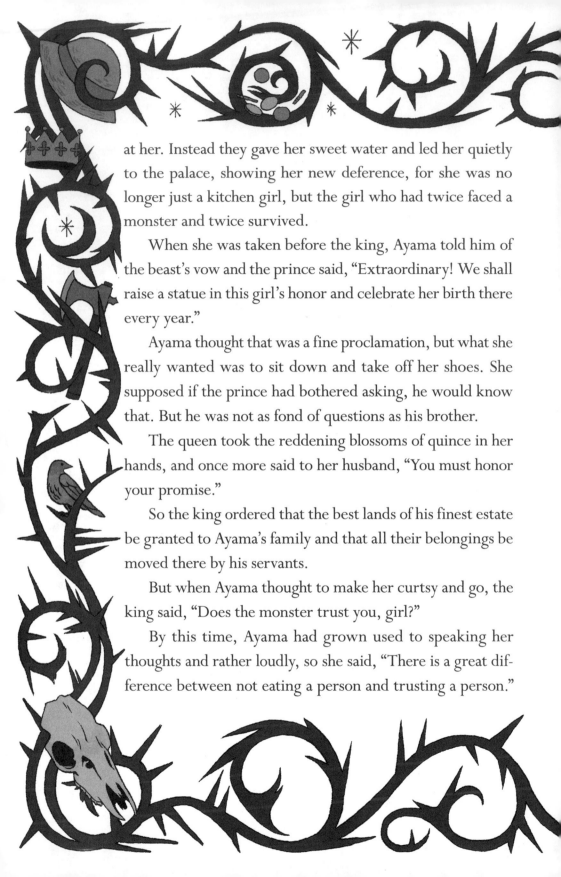

at her. Instead they gave her sweet water and led her quietly to the palace, showing her new deference, for she was no longer just a kitchen girl, but the girl who had twice faced a monster and twice survived.

When she was taken before the king, Ayama told him of the beast's vow and the prince said, "Extraordinary! We shall raise a statue in this girl's honor and celebrate her birth there every year."

Ayama thought that was a fine proclamation, but what she really wanted was to sit down and take off her shoes. She supposed if the prince had bothered asking, he would know that. But he was not as fond of questions as his brother.

The queen took the reddening blossoms of quince in her hands, and once more said to her husband, "You must honor your promise."

So the king ordered that the best lands of his finest estate be granted to Ayama's family and that all their belongings be moved there by his servants.

But when Ayama thought to make her curtsy and go, the king said, "Does the monster trust you, girl?"

By this time, Ayama had grown used to speaking her thoughts and rather loudly, so she said, "There is a great difference between not eating a person and trusting a person."

Besides, she thought it would be better for everyone if the beast were left to himself in the thorn wood.

But as had been the case for most of Ayama's life, despite the strength of her voice, the king either did not listen or did not hear.

"You will take a knife into the thorn wood," he commanded. "You will slay this beast so that we may all live in peace and safety. If you do this, then you will marry my son, the prince, and I will grant your family title so none but those who bear my own name shall be higher in the land."

The prince looked somewhat startled but did not object.

"No blade can pierce your second son's skin," Ayama protested. "I have seen it for myself."

As the queen wrung the silk of her skirt in her lap, the king called for a servant and an iron-colored box was brought forward.

The king lifted the lid and drew a strange knife from it. Its handle was bone but its blade was the same murky gray as the box—and the thorn wood. "This blade was crafted by a powerful zowa maker and wrought from the very thorns of the quince tree. Only it can kill him."

The queen turned her face away.

Ayama hoped her family would speak and say she need

not return to the thorn wood, for they had a fine home and Kima already had a rich dowry. But no one spoke, not even Ma Zil, who had promised that adventures only happened to pretty girls.

Ayama did not want to take the knife, but she did. It was light as a dry seedpod. It seemed wrong that death should feel like nothing in her hands.

"Return with the beast's heart and all will pay you homage and you will want for nothing in this life," said the king.

Ayama had no wish to be a princess. She had no wish to slay the beast. But for a girl who had spent her life ignored and unwanted, this was no small offer.

"I will agree to this," she said finally. "But if I do not return, Kima must wed the prince, and my family must still receive their reward."

She could see the king did not like the terms of this trade. Though he wanted the beast dead, he'd thought to make her risk her life cheaply. But in the end, what choice did he have? He agreed to Ayama's demands and she tucked the knife into her apron.

All her family's belongings were carried to their splendid new home. Her father cried out with happiness and her mother turned in circles in the garden, looking out at the fields that went on and on, as if she could scarcely believe that

all of it was now hers. Only Kima clutched Ayama's hand and said, "Sister, you do not have to go. We are rich now thanks to your bravery. We have land and servants. No prince is worth your life."

Ayama supposed it depended on the prince.

Ma Zil said nothing.

That night, Ayama slept poorly. Her new bed felt too soft after the hard stones of the old hearth. She rose before dawn, when the rest of the house was still asleep, put on her sky-colored apron, and settled her hat upon her head. Into her pocket, she tucked her axe and her copper cup. Then Ayama touched her fingers once to the jagged blade of the knife, slipped it into her apron, and for the last time, she set out across the wild lands.

Perhaps because her dread was so great, the trek through the barren plains seemed to last no time at all. Too soon she was plunging through the iron-colored thicket and into the shade of the wood. Starlight fell upon her skin, so sweet and cool and welcoming she might have wept for it. She told herself that once the beast was dead, she could return to the wood, that she might bring Kima, or simply come here on her own whenever she grew weary. But she wasn't sure that was true. Would the thorn wood still stand without the beast? Had it always been here or had it come into being just to

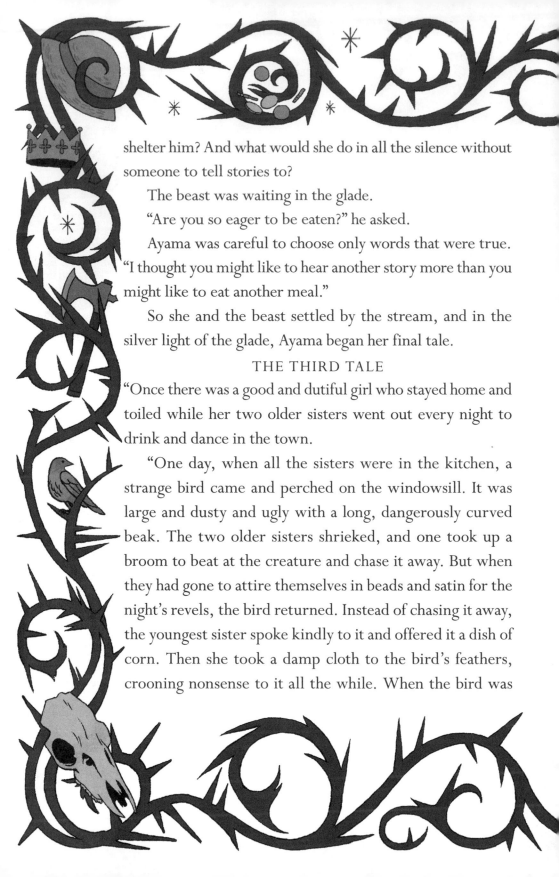

shelter him? And what would she do in all the silence without someone to tell stories to?

The beast was waiting in the glade.

"Are you so eager to be eaten?" he asked.

Ayama was careful to choose only words that were true. "I thought you might like to hear another story more than you might like to eat another meal."

So she and the beast settled by the stream, and in the silver light of the glade, Ayama began her final tale.

THE THIRD TALE

"Once there was a good and dutiful girl who stayed home and toiled while her two older sisters went out every night to drink and dance in the town.

"One day, when all the sisters were in the kitchen, a strange bird came and perched on the windowsill. It was large and dusty and ugly with a long, dangerously curved beak. The two older sisters shrieked, and one took up a broom to beat at the creature and chase it away. But when they had gone to attire themselves in beads and satin for the night's revels, the bird returned. Instead of chasing it away, the youngest sister spoke kindly to it and offered it a dish of corn. Then she took a damp cloth to the bird's feathers, crooning nonsense to it all the while. When the bird was

finally clean, she could see it had plumage of iridescent gold and that its beak shone like topaz. It flapped its great wings and flew away, but returned every night that week once the older sisters were gone to their parties, and sang pretty songs while the youngest did her work.

"On the seventh day, the bird waited until the older sisters had left to prepare for their fun, then flew in through the kitchen window. All at once there was a great flapping of wings and a sound like trumpets. There in the kitchen, where the bird had been mere moments before, the girl now beheld a handsome prince dressed in robes of gold.

"'Come away with me to my palace by the sea,' said the prince, 'and all will pay you homage and you will want for nothing in this life.' And as you may know, when you have had very little and worked very hard, that is no small offer.

"So the girl put her hand in the prince's and away they flew to his palace by the sea. But once they arrived, the girl found that the king and queen were not so happy with his choice of a peasant bride. So the queen set three challenges for the girl—"

The beast snarled and Ayama jumped, for she hadn't realized that he'd lain down quite so close to her, his snout nearly touching her knee. His lips were pulled back in a sneer.

"What a foolish story you've brought me this time," he complained. "She will accomplish the three tasks and wed the handsome prince. What joy for them both."

"Nonsense!" said Ayama straightaway, for she'd thought on this story quite a long time as she'd walked through the wild lands, and how the ending she'd been told as a child had seemed far more enchanting before she'd actually met and spoken to royalty. "Of course that's not how it ends. No. Do you remember the girl's older sisters?"

The beast gave a grudging nod and settled his great head on his forepaws.

"It's true they were selfish and silly in many ways," said Ayama. "But they also loved their youngest sister dearly. As soon as they found her missing and a golden feather on the chair, they guessed what had happened, for they had seen plenty of the world. They saddled their horses and rode all day and all night to reach the palace by the sea, then pounded on the doors until the guards let them in.

"When the sisters entered the throne room, making a racket and demanding that their sister return home to them, the prince insisted that they were just jealous sorts who wanted to be princesses themselves, and that they were wicked girls who liked to drink and dance and be free with their favors. In fact, the sisters did like all those things, and it was precisely

because they'd seen so much and done so much that they knew better than to trust handsome faces and fine titles. They pointed their fingers and raised their loud voices and demanded to know why, if the prince loved their sister so, he should let her be made to perform tasks to prove her worth. And when he did not answer, they stomped their slippered feet and demanded to know why, if the prince was worthy of their sister, he should bend so easily to his parents' will. The prince had no answer but stood there stammering, still handsome, but perhaps a bit less so now that he had nothing to say.

"The sisters apologized for not doing their share of the chores and promised to take the girl to parties so she wouldn't have to settle for the first boy who flew in through her window. The younger sister saw the wisdom in this bargain, and they all returned home together, where their days were full of work made easier in the sharing, and their nights were full of laughter and carousing."

"And what lesson am I to learn from this story?" asked the beast when she was done.

"That there are better things than princes."

Now Ayama stood and the beast knelt before her, his big shaggy head bowed, his horns glowing. "Do you have no more stories for me, little messenger?"

"Only one," said Ayama, the jagged knife in her hand,

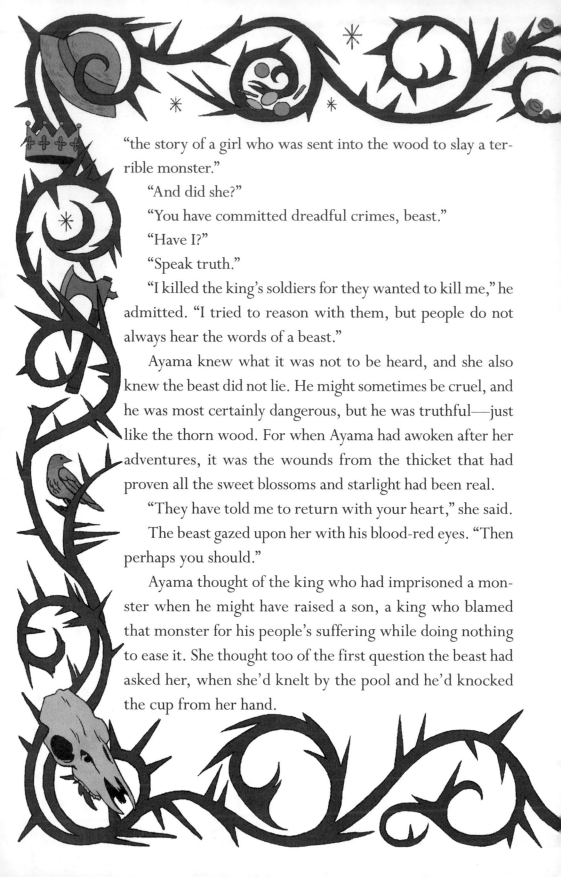

"the story of a girl who was sent into the wood to slay a terrible monster."

"And did she?"

"You have committed dreadful crimes, beast."

"Have I?"

"Speak truth."

"I killed the king's soldiers for they wanted to kill me," he admitted. "I tried to reason with them, but people do not always hear the words of a beast."

Ayama knew what it was not to be heard, and she also knew the beast did not lie. He might sometimes be cruel, and he was most certainly dangerous, but he was truthful—just like the thorn wood. For when Ayama had awoken after her adventures, it was the wounds from the thicket that had proven all the sweet blossoms and starlight had been real.

"They have told me to return with your heart," she said.

The beast gazed upon her with his blood-red eyes. "Then perhaps you should."

Ayama thought of the king who had imprisoned a monster when he might have raised a son, a king who blamed that monster for his people's suffering while doing nothing to ease it. She thought too of the first question the beast had asked her, when she'd knelt by the pool and he'd knocked the cup from her hand.

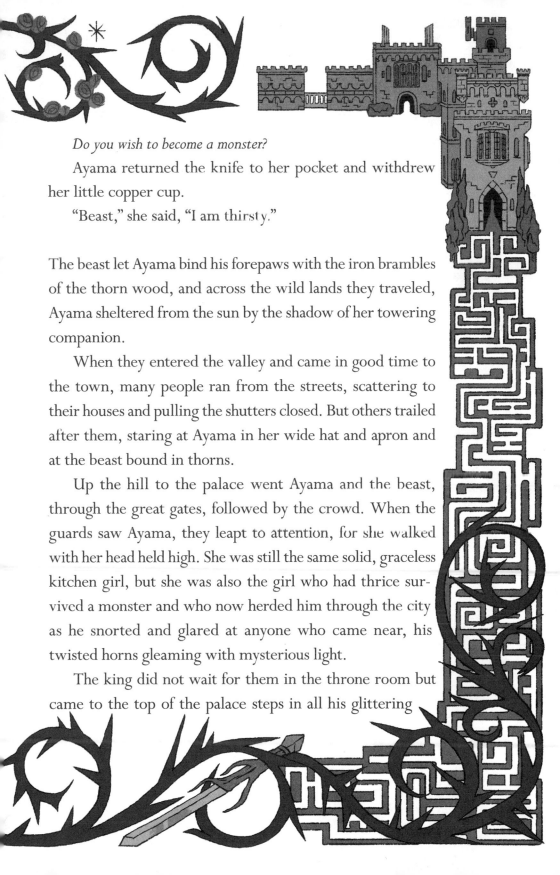

Do you wish to become a monster?

Ayama returned the knife to her pocket and withdrew her little copper cup.

"Beast," she said, "I am thirsty."

The beast let Ayama bind his forepaws with the iron brambles of the thorn wood, and across the wild lands they traveled, Ayama sheltered from the sun by the shadow of her towering companion.

When they entered the valley and came in good time to the town, many people ran from the streets, scattering to their houses and pulling the shutters closed. But others trailed after them, staring at Ayama in her wide hat and apron and at the beast bound in thorns.

Up the hill to the palace went Ayama and the beast, through the great gates, followed by the crowd. When the guards saw Ayama, they leapt to attention, for she walked with her head held high. She was still the same solid, graceless kitchen girl, but she was also the girl who had thrice survived a monster and who now herded him through the city as he snorted and glared at anyone who came near, his twisted horns gleaming with mysterious light.

The king did not wait for them in the throne room but came to the top of the palace steps in all his glittering finery and, with the queen and the beautiful young prince beside him, looked down at Ayama and the monster.

"Why do you bring this beast to my door?" the king demanded to know. "I told you to return with his heart."

"And so I have," said Ayama in her loud, clear voice that echoed like a horn of war over the listening crowd. "His heart is mine and mine is his."

"You think to love a monster?" the king asked, and now there were murmurs and snickers all around her. "Even a wretch like you might hope for better."

But Ayama was used to insults and paid the king's words no mind.

"I will love an honest monster before I swear loyalty to a treacherous king." She raised the thorn knife and pointed it at the king's chest. "When your wars were failing and the valley was in disquiet, it was you who slaughtered our herds and mowed down our fields just so that we would fear a false villain, instead of seeing that a fool sat the throne."

"You speak treason!" roared the king.

"I speak truth."

"And can this ugly beast not speak for himself?"

The beast looked upon his father and said, "A man like you is owed no words. I trust Ayama to tell my story."

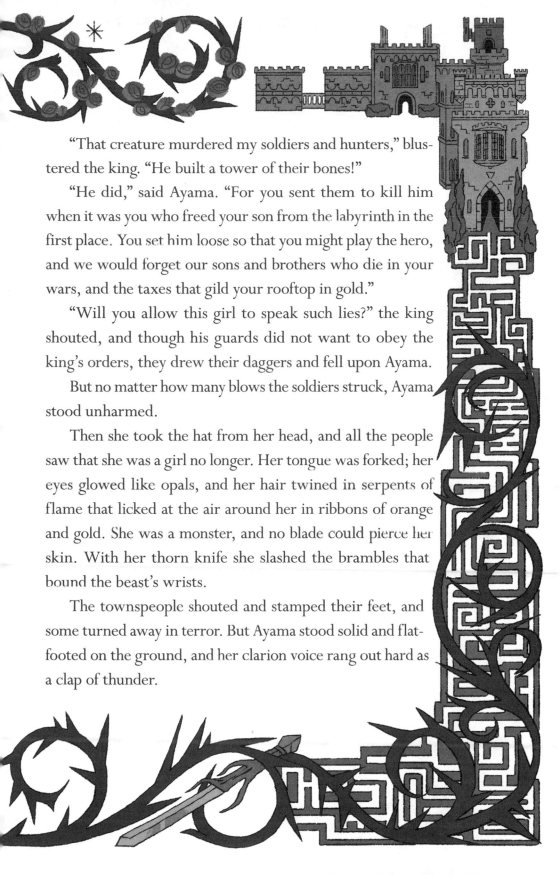

"That creature murdered my soldiers and hunters," blustered the king. "He built a tower of their bones!"

"He did," said Ayama. "For you sent them to kill him when it was you who freed your son from the labyrinth in the first place. You set him loose so that you might play the hero, and we would forget our sons and brothers who die in your wars, and the taxes that gild your rooftop in gold."

"Will you allow this girl to speak such lies?" the king shouted, and though his guards did not want to obey the king's orders, they drew their daggers and fell upon Ayama.

But no matter how many blows the soldiers struck, Ayama stood unharmed.

Then she took the hat from her head, and all the people saw that she was a girl no longer. Her tongue was forked; her eyes glowed like opals, and her hair twined in serpents of flame that licked at the air around her in ribbons of orange and gold. She was a monster, and no blade could pierce her skin. With her thorn knife she slashed the brambles that bound the beast's wrists.

The townspeople shouted and stamped their feet, and some turned away in terror. But Ayama stood solid and flat-footed on the ground, and her clarion voice rang out hard as a clap of thunder.

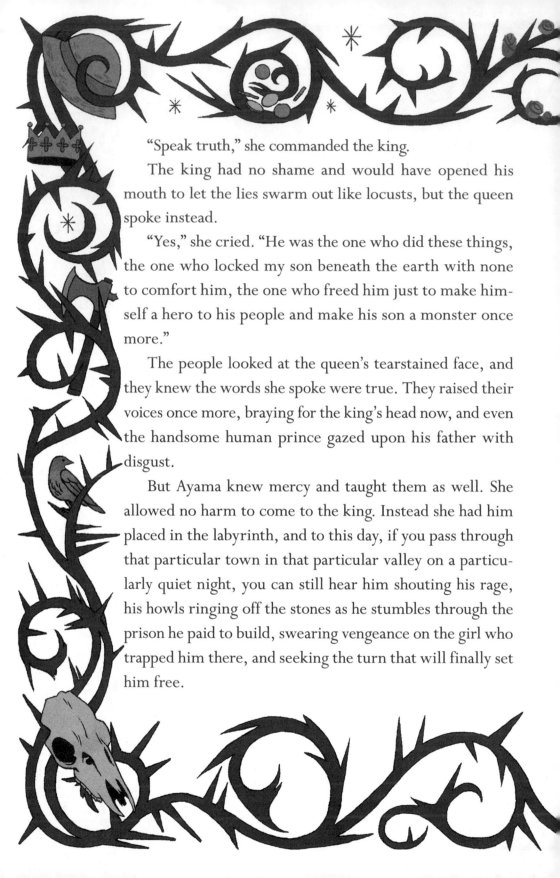

"Speak truth," she commanded the king.

The king had no shame and would have opened his mouth to let the lies swarm out like locusts, but the queen spoke instead.

"Yes," she cried. "He was the one who did these things, the one who locked my son beneath the earth with none to comfort him, the one who freed him just to make himself a hero to his people and make his son a monster once more."

The people looked at the queen's tearstained face, and they knew the words she spoke were true. They raised their voices once more, braying for the king's head now, and even the handsome human prince gazed upon his father with disgust.

But Ayama knew mercy and taught them as well. She allowed no harm to come to the king. Instead she had him placed in the labyrinth, and to this day, if you pass through that particular town in that particular valley on a particularly quiet night, you can still hear him shouting his rage, his howls ringing off the stones as he stumbles through the prison he paid to build, swearing vengeance on the girl who trapped him there, and seeking the turn that will finally set him free.

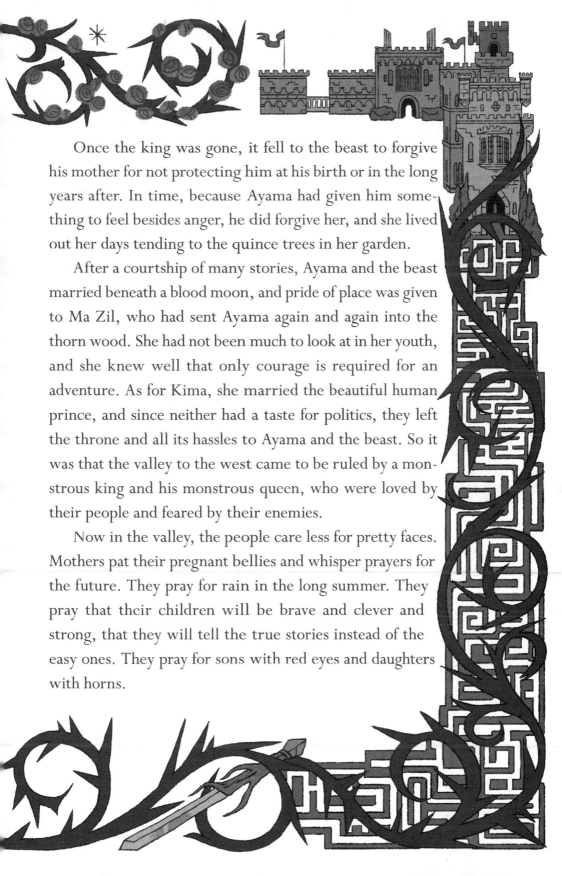

Once the king was gone, it fell to the beast to forgive his mother for not protecting him at his birth or in the long years after. In time, because Ayama had given him something to feel besides anger, he did forgive her, and she lived out her days tending to the quince trees in her garden.

After a courtship of many stories, Ayama and the beast married beneath a blood moon, and pride of place was given to Ma Zil, who had sent Ayama again and again into the thorn wood. She had not been much to look at in her youth, and she knew well that only courage is required for an adventure. As for Kima, she married the beautiful human prince, and since neither had a taste for politics, they left the throne and all its hassles to Ayama and the beast. So it was that the valley to the west came to be ruled by a monstrous king and his monstrous queen, who were loved by their people and feared by their enemies.

Now in the valley, the people care less for pretty faces. Mothers pat their pregnant bellies and whisper prayers for the future. They pray for rain in the long summer. They pray that their children will be brave and clever and strong, that they will tell the true stories instead of the easy ones. They pray for sons with red eyes and daughters with horns.

THE TOO-CLEVER FOX

THE FIRST TRAP THE FOX ESCAPED

was his mother's jaws.

When she had recovered from the trial of birthing her litter, the mother fox looked around at her kits and sighed. It would be hard to feed so many children, and truth be told, she was hungry after her ordeal. So she snatched up two of her smallest young and made a quick meal of them. But beneath those pups, she found a tiny, squirming runt of a fox with a patchy coat and yellow eyes.

"I should have eaten you first," she said. "You are doomed to a miserable life."

To her surprise, the runt answered. "Do not eat me, Mother. Better to be hungry now than to be sorry later."

"Better to swallow you than to have to look upon you. What will everyone say when they see such a face?"

A lesser creature might have despaired at such cruelty, but the fox saw vanity in his mother's carefully tended coat and snowy paws.

"I will tell you," he replied. "When we walk in the wood, the animals will say, 'Look at that ugly kit with his handsome mother!' And even when you are old and gray, they will not talk of how you've aged, but of how such a beautiful mother gave birth to such an ugly, scrawny son."

51

She thought on this and discovered she was not so hungry after all.

Because the fox's mother believed the runt would die before the year was out, she didn't bother to name him. But when her little son survived one winter and then the next, the animals needed something to call him. They dubbed him Koja—handsome—as a joke, and soon he gained a reputation.

When he was barely grown, a group of hounds cornered him in a blind of branches outside his den. Crouching in the damp earth, listening to their terrible snarls, a lesser creature might have panicked, chased himself in circles, and simply waited for the hounds' master to come take his hide.

Instead Koja cried, "I am a magic fox!"

The biggest of the hounds barked his laughter. "We may sleep by the master's fire and feed on his scraps, but we have not gone so soft as that. You think that we will let you live on foolish promises?"

"No," said Koja in his meekest, most downtrodden voice. "You have bested me. That much is clear. But I am cursed to grant one wish before I die. You only need name it."

"Wealth!" yapped one.

"Health!" barked another.

"Meat from the table!" said the third.

"I have only one wish to grant," said the ugly little fox, "and you must make your choice quickly, or when your master arrives, I will be obliged to bestow the wish on him instead."

The hounds took to arguing, growling and snapping at one another, and as they bared their fangs and leapt and wrestled, Koja slipped away.

That night, in the safety of the wood, Koja and the other animals drank and toasted the fox's quick thinking. In the distance, they heard the hounds howling at their master's door, cold and disgraced, bellies empty of supper.

Though Koja was clever, he was not always lucky. One day, as he raced back from Tupolev's farm with a hen's plump body in his mouth, he stepped into a trap.

When those metal teeth slammed shut, a lesser creature might have let his fear get the best of him. He might have yelped and whined, drawing the smug farmer to him, or he might have tried gnawing off his own leg.

Instead Koja lay there, panting, until he heard the black bear, Ivan Gostov, rumbling through the woods. Now, Gostov was a bloodthirsty animal, loud and rude, unwelcome at feasts. His fur was always matted and filthy, and he was just as likely to eat his hosts as the food they served. But a killer might be reasoned with—not so a metal trap.

Koja called out to him. "Brother, will you not free me?"

When Ivan Gostov saw Koja bleeding, he boomed his laughter. "Gladly!" he roared. "I will liberate you from that trap and tonight I'll dine on free fox stew."

The bear snapped the chain and threw Koja over his back. Dangling from the trap's steel teeth by his wounded leg, a lesser creature might have closed his eyes and prayed for nothing more than a quick death. But if Koja had words, then he had hope.

He whispered to the fleas that milled about in the bear's filthy pelt, "If you bite Ivan Gostov, I will let you come live in my coat for one year's time. You may dine on me all you like, and I promise not to bathe or scratch or douse myself in kerosene. You will have a fine time of it, I tell you."

The fleas whispered amongst themselves. Ivan Gostov was a foul-tasting bear, and he was constantly tromping through streams or rolling on his back to try to be rid of them.

"We will help you," they chorused at last.

At Koja's signal, they attacked poor Ivan Gostov, biting him in just the spot between his shoulders where his big claws couldn't reach.

The bear scratched and flailed and bellowed his misery. He threw down the chain attached to Koja's trap and wriggled and writhed on the ground.

"Now, little brothers!" shouted Koja. The fleas leapt onto

the fox's coat, and despite the pain in his leg, Koja ran all the way back to his den, trailing the bloody chain behind him.

It was an unpleasant year for the fox, but he kept his promise. Though the itching drove him mad, he did not scratch, and even bandaged his paws to better avoid temptation. Because he smelled so terrible, no one wanted to be near him, yet still he did not bathe. Whenever Koja got the urge to run to the river, he would look at the chain he kept coiled in the corner of his den. With Red Badger's help, he'd pried himself free of the trap, but he'd kept the chain as a reminder that he owed his freedom to the fleas and his wits.

Only Lula the nightingale came to see him. Perched in the branches of the birch tree, she twittered her laughter. "Not so clever, are you, Koja? No one will have you to visit and you are covered in scabs. You are even uglier than before."

Koja was untroubled. "I can bear ugliness," he said. "I find the one thing I cannot live with is death."

When the year was up, Koja picked his way carefully through the woods near Tupolev's farm, making sure to avoid the teeth of any traps that might be lurking beneath the brush. He snuck through the hen yard, and when one of the servants opened the kitchen door to take out the slops, he slipped right into Tupolev's house. He used his teeth to pull back the covers on the farmer's bed and let the fleas slip in.

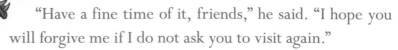

"Have a fine time of it, friends," he said. "I hope you will forgive me if I do not ask you to visit again."

The fleas called their good-byes and dove beneath the blankets, looking forward to a meal of the farmer and his wife.

On his way out, Koja snatched a bottle of kvas from the pantry and a chicken from the yard, and he left them at the entrance to Ivan Gostov's cave. When the bear appeared, he sniffed at Koja's offerings.

"Show yourself, fox," he roared. "Do you seek to make a fool of me again?"

"You freed me, Ivan Gostov. If you like, you may have me as supper. I warn you, though, I am stringy and tough. Only my tongue holds savor. I make a bitter meal, but excellent company."

The bear laughed so loudly that he shook the nightingale from her branch in the valley below. He and Koja shared the chicken and the kvas and spent the night exchanging stories. From then on, they were friends, and it was known that to cross the fox was to risk Ivan Gostov's wrath.

Then winter came and the black bear went missing.

The animals had noticed their numbers thinning for some time. Deer were scarcer, and the small creatures too—rabbits and squirrels, grouse and voles. It was nothing to

remark upon. Hard times came and went. But Ivan Gostov was no timid deer or skittering vole. When Koja realized it had been weeks since he had seen the bear or heard his bellow, he grew concerned.

"Lula," he said, "fly into town and see what you can learn."

The nightingale put her little beak in the air. "You will ask me, Koja, and do it nicely, or I will fly someplace warm and leave you to your worrying."

Koja bowed and made his compliments to Lula's shiny feathers, the purity of her song, the pleasing way she kept her nest, and on and on, until finally the nightingale stopped him with a shrill chirp.

"Next time, you may stop at 'please.' If you will only cease your talking, I will gladly go."

Lula flapped her wings and disappeared into the blue sky, but when she returned an hour later, her tiny jet eyes were bright with fear. She hopped and fluttered, and it took her long minutes to settle on a branch.

"Death has arrived," she said. "Lev Jurek has come to Polvost."

The animals fell silent. Lev Jurek was no ordinary hunter. It was said he left no tracks and his rifle made no sound. He traveled from village to village throughout Ravka, and where he went, he bled the woods dry.

"He has just come from Balakirev." The nightingale's pretty voice trembled. "He left the town's stores bloated with deer meat and overflowing with furs. The sparrows say he stripped the forest bare."

"Did you see the man himself?" asked Red Badger.

Lula nodded. "He is the tallest man I've ever seen, broad in the shoulders, handsome as a prince."

"And what of the girl?"

Jurek was said to travel with his half sister, Sofiya. The hides he did not sell, Jurek forced her to sew into a gruesome cloak that trailed behind her on the ground.

"I saw her," said the nightingale, "and I saw the cloak too. Koja . . . its collar is made of seven white fox tails."

Koja frowned. His sister lived near Balakirev. She'd had seven kits, all of them with white tails.

"I will investigate," he decided, and the animals breathed a bit easier, for Koja was the cleverest of them all.

Koja waited for the sun to set, then snuck into Polvost with Lula at his shoulder. They kept to the shadows, slinking down alleys and making their way to the center of town.

Jurek and his sister had rented a grand house close to the taverns that lined the Barshai Prospekt. Koja went up on his hind legs and pressed his nose to the window glass.

The hunter sat with his friends at a table heaped with

rich foods—wine-soaked cabbage and calf stuffed with quail eggs, greasy sausages and pickled sage. All the lamps burned bright with oil. The hunter had grown wealthy indeed.

Jurek was a big man, younger than expected, but just as handsome as Lula had said. He wore a fine linen shirt and a fur-lined vest with a gold watch tucked into his pocket. His inky blue eyes darted frequently to his sister, who sat reading by the fire. Koja could not make out her face, but Sofiya had a pretty enough profile, and her dainty, slippered feet rested on the skin of a large black bear.

Koja's blood chilled at the sight of his fallen friend's hide, spread so casually over the polished slats of the floor. Ivan Gostov's fur shone clean and glossy as it never had in life, and for some reason, this struck Koja as a very sad thing. A lesser creature might have let his grief get the best of him. He might have taken to the hills and high places, thinking it wise to outrun death rather than try to outsmart it. But Koja sensed a question here, one his clever mind could not resist: For all his loud ways, Ivan Gostov had been the closest thing the forest had to a king, a deadly match for any man or beast. So how had Jurek bested him with no one the wiser?

For the next three nights, Koja watched the hunter, but he learned nothing.

Every evening, Jurek ate a big dinner. He went out to one of the taverns and did not return until the early hours. He liked to drink and brag, and frequently spilled wine on his clothes. He slept late each morning, then rose and headed out to the tanning shed or into the forest. Jurek set traps, swam in the river, oiled his gun, but Koja never saw him catch or kill anything.

And yet, on the fourth day, Jurek emerged from the tanning shed with something massive in his muscled arms. He walked to the wooden frames, and there he stretched the hide of the great gray wolf. No one knew the gray wolf's name, and no one had ever dared ask it. He lived on a steep rock ridge and kept to himself, and it was said he'd been cast out of his pack for some terrible crime. When he descended to the valley, it was only to hunt, and then he moved silent as smoke through the trees. Yet somehow, Jurek had taken his skin.

That night, the hunter brought musicians to his house. The townspeople came to marvel at the wolf's hide, and Jurek bade his sister rise from her place by the fire so that he could lay the horrible patchwork cloak over her shoulders. The villagers pointed to one fur after another, and Jurek obliged them with the story of how he'd brought down Illarion the white bear of the north, then of his capture of the two golden lynxes who made up the sleeves. He even described catching the seven little kits who had given up their tails for the cloak's grand collar. With every word Jurek spoke, his sister's chin sank lower, until she was staring at the floor.

Koja watched the hunter go outside and cut the head from the wolf's hide, and as the villagers danced and drank, Jurek's sister sat and sewed, adding a hood to her horrible cloak. When one of the musicians banged his drum, her needle slipped. She winced and drew her finger to her lips.

What's a bit more blood? thought Koja. The cloak might as well be soaked red with it.

"Sofiya is the answer," Koja told the animals the next day. "Jurek must be using some magic or trickery, and his sister will know of it."

"But why would she tell us his secrets?" asked Red Badger.

"She fears him. They barely speak, and she takes care to keep her distance."

"And each night she bolts her bedroom door," trilled the nightingale, "against her own brother. There's trouble there."

Sofiya was only permitted to leave the house every few days to visit the old widows' home on the other side of the valley. She carried a basket or sometimes pulled a sled

61

piled high with furs and food bound up in woolen blankets. Always she wore the horrible cloak, and as Koja watched her slogging along, he was reminded of a pilgrim going to do her penance.

For the first mile, Sofiya kept a steady pace and stayed to the path. But when she reached a small clearing, far from the outskirts of town and deep with the quiet of snow, she stopped. She slumped down on a fallen tree trunk, put her face in her hands, and wept.

The fox felt suddenly ashamed to be watching her, but he also knew this was an opportunity. He hopped silently onto the other end of the tree trunk and said, "Why do you cry, girl?"

Sofiya gasped. Her eyes were red, her pale skin blotchy, but despite this and her gruesome wolf hood, she was still lovely. She looked around, her even teeth worrying the flesh of her lip. "You should leave this place, fox," she said. "You are not safe here."

"I haven't been safe since I slipped yowling from my mother's body."

She shook her head. "You don't understand. My brother—"

"What would he want with me? I'm too scrawny to eat and too ugly to wear."

Sofiya smiled slightly. "Your coat is a bit patchy, but you're not so bad as all that."

"No?" said the fox. "Shall I travel to Os Alta to have my portrait painted?"

"What does a fox know of the capital?"

"I visited once," said Koja, for he sensed she might enjoy a story. "I was the queen's personal guest. She tied a blue ribbon around my neck and I slept upon a velvet cushion every night."

The girl laughed, her tears forgotten. "Did you, now?"

"I was quite the fashion. All the courtiers dyed their hair red and cut holes in their clothes, hoping to emulate my patchy coat."

"I see," said the girl. "So why leave the comforts of the Grand Palace and come to these cold woods?"

"I made enemies."

"The queen's poodle grew jealous?"

"The king was offended by my overlarge ears."

"A dangerous thing," she said. "With such big ears, who knows what gossip you might hear."

This time Koja laughed, pleased that the girl showed some wit when she wasn't locked up with a brute.

Sofiya's smile faltered. She shot to her feet and picked up her basket, hurrying back down the path. But before she

63

disappeared from view, she paused and said, "Thank you for making me laugh, fox. I hope I will not find you here again."

Later that night, Lula fluffed her wings in frustration. "You learned nothing! All you did was flirt."

"It was a beginning, little bird," said Koja. "Best to move slowly." Then he lunged at her, jaws snapping.

The nightingale shrieked and fluttered up into the high branches as Red Badger laughed.

"See?" said the fox. "We must take care with shy creatures."

The next time Sofiya ventured out to the widows' home, the fox followed her once more. Again she sat down in the clearing, and again she wept.

Koja hopped up on the fallen tree. "Tell me, Sofiya, why do you cry?"

"You're still here, fox? Don't you know my brother is near? He will catch you eventually."

"What would your brother want with a yellow-eyed bag of bones and fleas?"

Sofiya gave a small smile. "Yellow is an ugly color," she admitted. "With such big eyes, I think you see too much."

"Will you not tell me what troubles you?"

She didn't answer. Instead she reached into her basket and took out a wedge of cheese. "Are you hungry?"

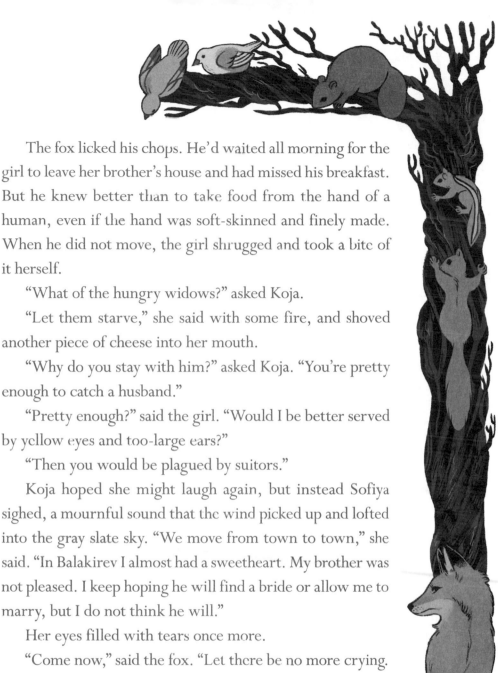

The fox licked his chops. He'd waited all morning for the girl to leave her brother's house and had missed his breakfast. But he knew better than to take food from the hand of a human, even if the hand was soft-skinned and finely made. When he did not move, the girl shrugged and took a bite of it herself.

"What of the hungry widows?" asked Koja.

"Let them starve," she said with some fire, and shoved another piece of cheese into her mouth.

"Why do you stay with him?" asked Koja. "You're pretty enough to catch a husband."

"Pretty enough?" said the girl. "Would I be better served by yellow eyes and too-large ears?"

"Then you would be plagued by suitors."

Koja hoped she might laugh again, but instead Sofiya sighed, a mournful sound that the wind picked up and lofted into the gray slate sky. "We move from town to town," she said. "In Balakirev I almost had a sweetheart. My brother was not pleased. I keep hoping he will find a bride or allow me to marry, but I do not think he will."

Her eyes filled with tears once more.

"Come now," said the fox. "Let there be no more crying. I have spent my life finding my way out of traps. Surely I can help you escape your brother."

"Just because you escape one trap, doesn't mean you will escape the next."

So Koja told her how he'd outsmarted his mother, the hounds, and even Ivan Gostov.

"You are a clever fox," she conceded when he was done.

"No," Koja said. "I am the cleverest. And that will make all the difference. Now tell me of your brother."

Sofiya glanced up at the sun. It was long past noon.

"Tomorrow," she said. "When I return."

She left the wedge of cheese on the fallen tree, and once she was gone, Koja sniffed it carefully. He looked right and left, then gobbled it down in one bite and did not spare a thought for the poor hungry widows.

Koja knew he had to be especially cautious now if he hoped to loosen Sofiya's tongue. He knew what it was to be caught in a trap. Sofiya had lived that way a long while, and a lesser creature might choose to live in fear rather than grasp at freedom. So the next day he waited at the clearing for her to return from the widows' home, but kept out of sight. Finally, she came trundling over the hill, dragging her sled behind her, the wool blankets bound with twine, the heavy runners sinking into the snow. When she reached the clearing, she hesitated. "Fox?" she said softly. "Koja?"

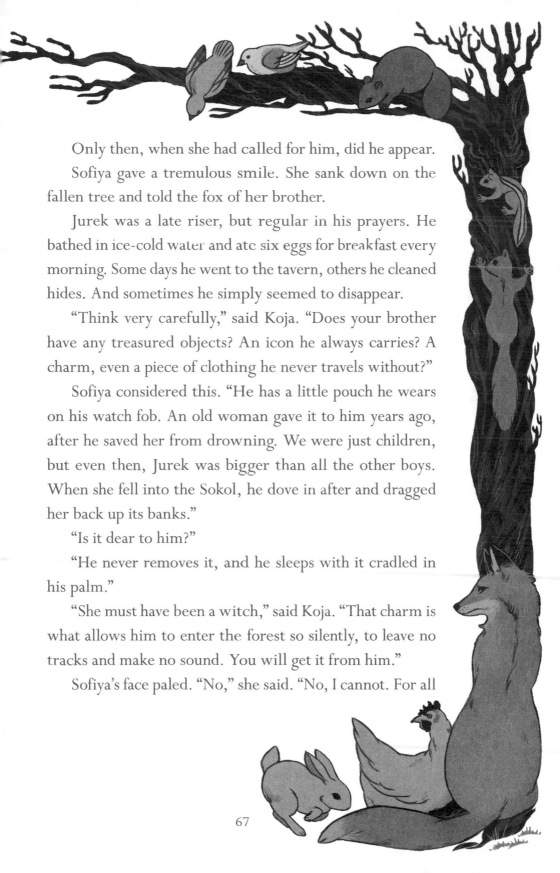

Only then, when she had called for him, did he appear.

Sofiya gave a tremulous smile. She sank down on the fallen tree and told the fox of her brother.

Jurek was a late riser, but regular in his prayers. He bathed in ice-cold water and ate six eggs for breakfast every morning. Some days he went to the tavern, others he cleaned hides. And sometimes he simply seemed to disappear.

"Think very carefully," said Koja. "Does your brother have any treasured objects? An icon he always carries? A charm, even a piece of clothing he never travels without?"

Sofiya considered this. "He has a little pouch he wears on his watch fob. An old woman gave it to him years ago, after he saved her from drowning. We were just children, but even then, Jurek was bigger than all the other boys. When she fell into the Sokol, he dove in after and dragged her back up its banks."

"Is it dear to him?"

"He never removes it, and he sleeps with it cradled in his palm."

"She must have been a witch," said Koja. "That charm is what allows him to enter the forest so silently, to leave no tracks and make no sound. You will get it from him."

Sofiya's face paled. "No," she said. "No, I cannot. For all

his snoring, my brother sleeps lightly, and if he were to discover me in his chamber—" She shuddered.

"Meet me here again in three days' time," said Koja, "and I will have an answer for you."

Sofiya stood and dusted the snow from her horrible cloak. When she looked at the fox, her eyes were grave. "Do not ask too much of me," she said softly.

Koja took a step closer to her. "I will free you from this trap," he said. "Without his charm, your brother will have to make his living like an ordinary man. He will have to stay in one place, and you will find yourself a sweetheart."

She wrapped the cables of her sled around her hand. "Maybe," Sofiya said. "But first I must find my courage."

It took a day and a half for Koja to reach the marshes where a patch of dropwort grew. He was careful digging the little plants up. The roots were deadly. The leaves would be enough to manage Jurek.

By the time he returned to his own woods, the animals were in an uproar. The boar, Tatya, had gone missing, along with her three piglets. The next afternoon their bodies were spitted and cooking on a cheery bonfire in the town square. Red Badger and his family were packing up to leave, and they weren't the only ones.

"He leaves no tracks!" cried the badger.

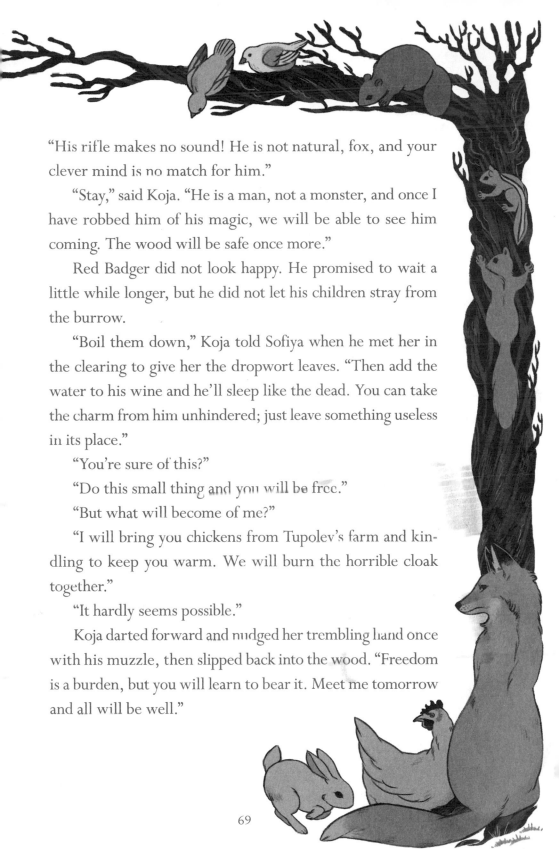

"His rifle makes no sound! He is not natural, fox, and your clever mind is no match for him."

"Stay," said Koja. "He is a man, not a monster, and once I have robbed him of his magic, we will be able to see him coming. The wood will be safe once more."

Red Badger did not look happy. He promised to wait a little while longer, but he did not let his children stray from the burrow.

"Boil them down," Koja told Sofiya when he met her in the clearing to give her the dropwort leaves. "Then add the water to his wine and he'll sleep like the dead. You can take the charm from him unhindered; just leave something useless in its place."

"You're sure of this?"

"Do this small thing and you will be free."

"But what will become of me?"

"I will bring you chickens from Tupolev's farm and kindling to keep you warm. We will burn the horrible cloak together."

"It hardly seems possible."

Koja darted forward and nudged her trembling hand once with his muzzle, then slipped back into the wood. "Freedom is a burden, but you will learn to bear it. Meet me tomorrow and all will be well."

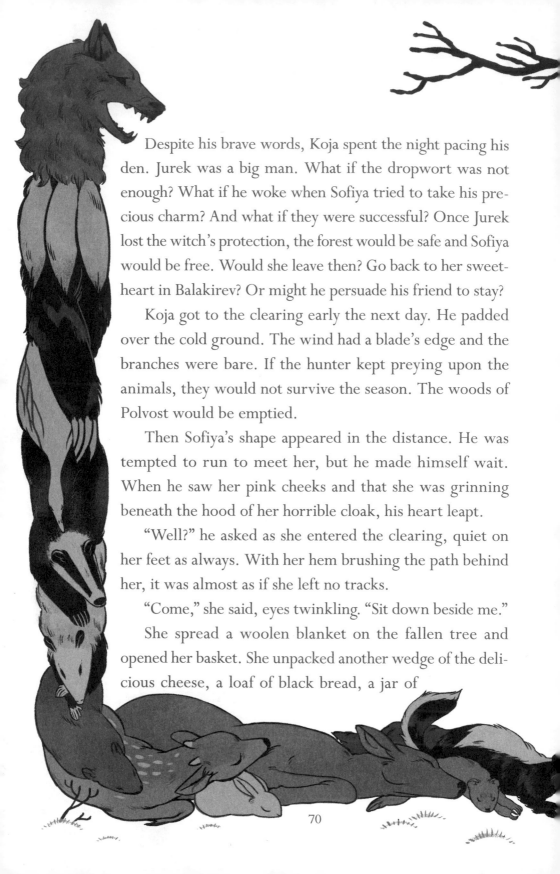

Despite his brave words, Koja spent the night pacing his den. Jurek was a big man. What if the dropwort was not enough? What if he woke when Sofiya tried to take his precious charm? And what if they were successful? Once Jurek lost the witch's protection, the forest would be safe and Sofiya would be free. Would she leave then? Go back to her sweetheart in Balakirev? Or might he persuade his friend to stay?

Koja got to the clearing early the next day. He padded over the cold ground. The wind had a blade's edge and the branches were bare. If the hunter kept preying upon the animals, they would not survive the season. The woods of Polvost would be emptied.

Then Sofiya's shape appeared in the distance. He was tempted to run to meet her, but he made himself wait. When he saw her pink cheeks and that she was grinning beneath the hood of her horrible cloak, his heart leapt.

"Well?" he asked as she entered the clearing, quiet on her feet as always. With her hem brushing the path behind her, it was almost as if she left no tracks.

"Come," she said, eyes twinkling. "Sit down beside me."

She spread a woolen blanket on the fallen tree and opened her basket. She unpacked another wedge of the delicious cheese, a loaf of black bread, a jar of

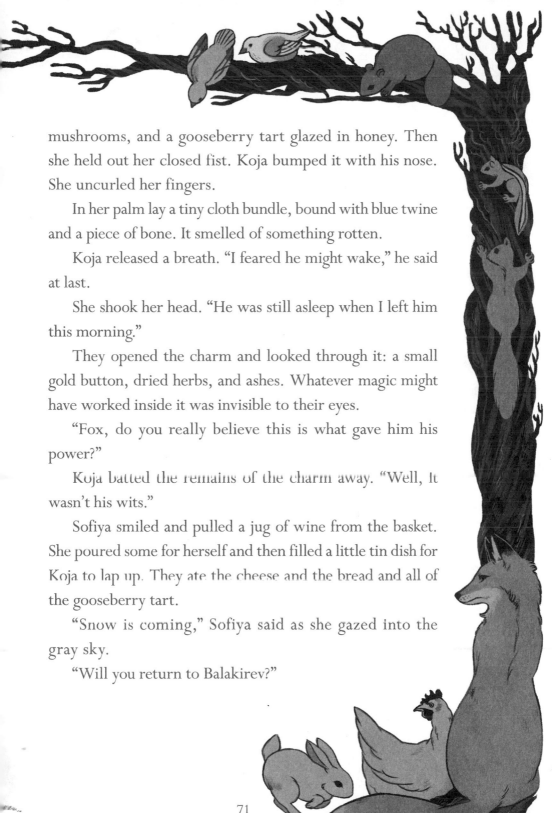

mushrooms, and a gooseberry tart glazed in honey. Then she held out her closed fist. Koja bumped it with his nose. She uncurled her fingers.

In her palm lay a tiny cloth bundle, bound with blue twine and a piece of bone. It smelled of something rotten.

Koja released a breath. "I feared he might wake," he said at last.

She shook her head. "He was still asleep when I left him this morning."

They opened the charm and looked through it: a small gold button, dried herbs, and ashes. Whatever magic might have worked inside it was invisible to their eyes.

"Fox, do you really believe this is what gave him his power?"

Koja batted the remains of the charm away. "Well, it wasn't his wits."

Sofiya smiled and pulled a jug of wine from the basket. She poured some for herself and then filled a little tin dish for Koja to lap up. They ate the cheese and the bread and all of the gooseberry tart.

"Snow is coming," Sofiya said as she gazed into the gray sky.

"Will you return to Balakirev?"

71

"There is nothing for me there," Sofiya said.

"Then you will stay to see the snow."

"Long enough for that." Sofiya poured more wine into the dish. "Now, fox, tell me again how you outsmarted the hounds."

So Koja told the tale of the foolish hounds and asked Sofiya what wishes she might make, and at some point, his eyes began to droop. The fox fell asleep with his head in the girl's lap, happy for the first time since he'd gazed upon the world with his too-clever eyes.

He woke to Sofiya's knife at his belly, to the nudge of the blade as it began to wiggle beneath his skin. When he tried to scramble away, he found his paws were bound.

"Why?" he gasped as Sofiya worked the knife in deeper.

"Because I am a hunter," she said with a shrug.

Koja moaned. "I wanted to help you."

"You always do," murmured Sofiya. "Few can resist the sight of a pretty girl crying."

A lesser creature might have begged for his life, given in to the relentless spill of his blood on the snow, but Koja struggled to think. It was hard. His clever mind was muddled with dropwort.

"Your brother—"

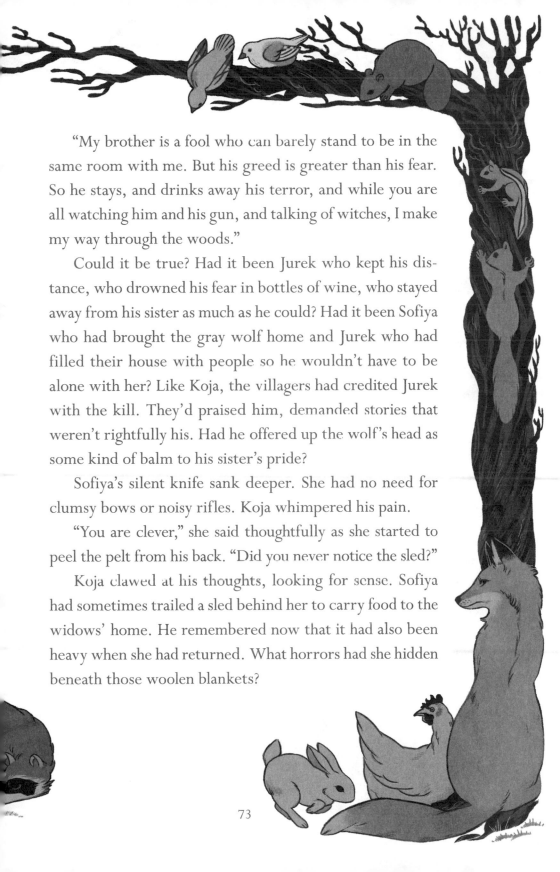

"My brother is a fool who can barely stand to be in the same room with me. But his greed is greater than his fear. So he stays, and drinks away his terror, and while you are all watching him and his gun, and talking of witches, I make my way through the woods."

Could it be true? Had it been Jurek who kept his distance, who drowned his fear in bottles of wine, who stayed away from his sister as much as he could? Had it been Sofiya who had brought the gray wolf home and Jurek who had filled their house with people so he wouldn't have to be alone with her? Like Koja, the villagers had credited Jurek with the kill. They'd praised him, demanded stories that weren't rightfully his. Had he offered up the wolf's head as some kind of balm to his sister's pride?

Sofiya's silent knife sank deeper. She had no need for clumsy bows or noisy rifles. Koja whimpered his pain.

"You are clever," she said thoughtfully as she started to peel the pelt from his back. "Did you never notice the sled?"

Koja clawed at his thoughts, looking for sense. Sofiya had sometimes trailed a sled behind her to carry food to the widows' home. He remembered now that it had also been heavy when she had returned. What horrors had she hidden beneath those woolen blankets?

Koja tested his bonds. He tried to rattle his drugged mind from its stupor.

"It is always the same trap," she said gently. "You longed for conversation. The bear craved jokes. The gray wolf missed music. The boar just wanted someone to tell her troubles to. The trap is loneliness, and none of us escapes it. Not even me."

"I am a magic fox . . . ," he rasped.

"Your coat is sad and patchy. I will use it for a lining. I will keep it close to my heart."

Koja reached for the words that had always served him, the wit that had been his tether and his guide. His clever tongue would not oblige. He moaned as his life bled into the snowbank to water the fallen tree. Then, hopeless and dying, Koja did what he had never done before. He cried out, and high in the branches of her birch tree, the nightingale heard.

Lula came flying, and when she saw what Sofiya had done, she set upon her, pecking at her eyes. Sofiya screamed and slashed at the little bird with her knife. But Lula's beak was sharp. She did not relent. In the wood, even songbirds must be survivors.

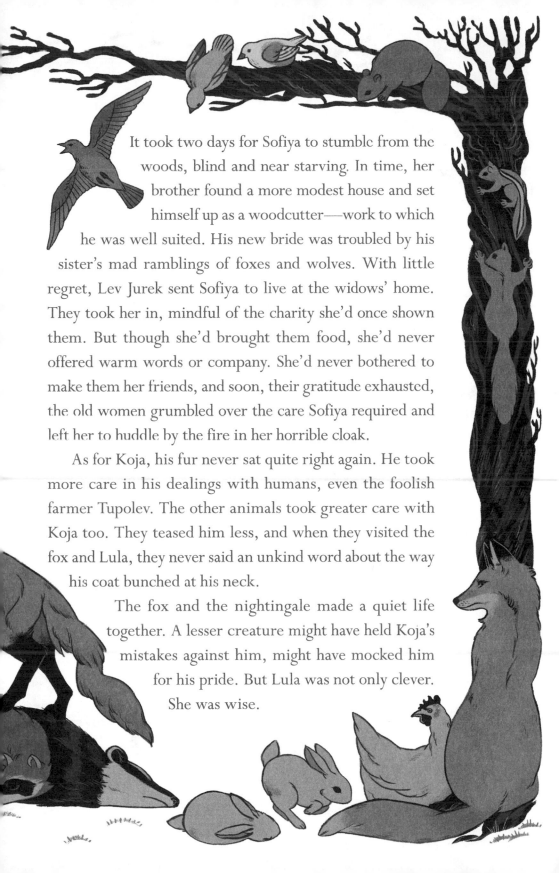

It took two days for Sofiya to stumble from the woods, blind and near starving. In time, her brother found a more modest house and set himself up as a woodcutter—work to which he was well suited. His new bride was troubled by his sister's mad ramblings of foxes and wolves. With little regret, Lev Jurek sent Sofiya to live at the widows' home. They took her in, mindful of the charity she'd once shown them. But though she'd brought them food, she'd never offered warm words or company. She'd never bothered to make them her friends, and soon, their gratitude exhausted, the old women grumbled over the care Sofiya required and left her to huddle by the fire in her horrible cloak.

As for Koja, his fur never sat quite right again. He took more care in his dealings with humans, even the foolish farmer Tupolev. The other animals took greater care with Koja too. They teased him less, and when they visited the fox and Lula, they never said an unkind word about the way his coat bunched at his neck.

The fox and the nightingale made a quiet life together. A lesser creature might have held Koja's mistakes against him, might have mocked him for his pride. But Lula was not only clever. She was wise.

THE WITCH OF DUVA

THERE WAS A TIME WHEN THE woods near Duva ate girls.

It's been many years since any child was taken. But still, on nights like these, when the wind comes cold from Tsibeya, mothers hold their daughters tight and warn them not to stray too far from home. "Be back before dark," they whisper. "The trees are hungry tonight."

In those black days, on the edge of these very woods, there lived a girl named Nadya and her brother, Havel, the children of Maxim Grushov, a carpenter and woodcutter. Maxim was a good man, well-liked in the village. He made roofs that did not leak or bend, sturdy chairs, toys when they were called for, and his clever hands could fashion edges so smooth and fasten joints so neatly you might never find the seam. He traveled all over the countryside seeking work, to towns as far as Ryevost. He went by foot and by hay cart when the weather was kind, and in the winter, he hitched his two black horses to a sledge, kissed his children, and set out in the snow. Always he returned home to them, carrying bags of grain or a new bolt of wool, his pockets stuffed with candy for Nadya and her brother.

But when the famine came, people had no coin and nothing to trade for a prettily carved table or a wooden duck. They used their furniture for kindling and prayed

they would make it through to spring. Maxim was forced to sell his horses, and then the sledge they'd once pulled over the snow-blanketed roads.

As Maxim's luck faded, so did his wife. Soon she was more ghost than woman, drifting silently from room to room. Nadya tried to get her mother to eat what little food they had, giving up portions of turnip and potato, bundling her mother's frail body in shawls and seating her on the porch in the hope that the fresh air might return some appetite to her. The only thing she seemed to crave were little cakes made by the widow Karina Stoyanova, scented with orange blossom and thick with icing. Where Karina got the sugar, no one knew—though the old women had their theories, most of which involved a rich and lonely tradesman from the river cities. The thaw came, then the summer, another failed harvest. Eventually, even Karina's supplies dwindled, and when the little cakes were gone, Nadya's mother would touch neither food nor drink, not even the smallest sip of tea.

Nadya's mother died on the first real day of winter, when the last bit of autumn fled from the air, and any hope of a mild year went with it. But the poor woman's death passed largely unremarked upon, because two days before she finally breathed her last ghostly sigh, another girl went missing.

Her name was Lara Deniken, a shy girl with a nervous

laugh, the type to stand at the edges of village dances watching the fun. All they found of her was a single leather shoe, its heel thick with crusted blood. She was the second girl lost in as many months, after Shura Yeshevsky went out to hang the wash on the line and never came back in, leaving nothing but a pile of clothespins and sodden sheets lying in the mud.

Real fear came upon the town. In the past, girls had vanished every few years. True, there were rumors of girls being taken from other villages from time to time, but those children hardly seemed real. Now, as the famine deepened and the people of Duva went without, it was as if whatever waited in the woods had grown greedier and more desperate, too.

Lara. Shura. All those who had gone before: Betya. Ludmilla. Raiza. Nikolena. Other names now forgotten. In those days, they were whispered like an incantation. Parents sent up prayers to their Saints, girls walked in pairs, people watched their neighbors with wary eyes. On the edge of the woods, the townspeople built crooked altars—careful stacks of painted icons, burnt-down prayer candles, little piles of flowers and beads.

Men grumbled about bears and wolves. They organized hunting parties, talked about burning sections of the forest. Poor bumbling Uri Pankin was nearly stoned to death when he was found in possession of one of the missing girls' dolls, and only his mother's weeping and her insistence that she had found the sorry thing on the Vestopol Road saved him.

Some wondered if the girls might have just walked into the wood, lured by their hunger. There were smells that wafted off the trees when the wind blew a certain way, impossible scents of lamb dumplings or sour-cherry babka. Nadya had almost given in to them herself, sitting on the porch beside her mother, trying to get her to take another spoonful of broth. She would smell roasting pumpkin, walnuts, brown sugar, and find her feet carrying her down the stairs toward the waiting shadows, where the trees shuffled and sighed as if ready to part for her.

Stupid Nadya, you think. *Stupid girls. I would never be so foolish.* But you've never known real hunger. The crops have been good these last years and people forget what the lean times are like. They forget the way mothers smothered infants in their cribs to stop their hungry howls, or how the trapper Leonid Gemka was found gnawing on the muscle of his slain brother's calf when their hut was iced in for two long months.

Sitting on the porch of Baba Olya's house, the old women peered into the forest and muttered, "Khitka." The word raised the hairs on Nadya's arms, but she was no longer a child, so she laughed with her brother at such silly talk. The khitkii were spiteful forest spirits, bloodthirsty and vengeful.

But in stories, they were known to hunger after newborns, not full-grown girls near old enough to marry.

"Who can say what shapes an appetite?" Baba Olya said with a dismissive wave of her gnarled hand. "Maybe this one is jealous. Or angry."

"Maybe it just likes the taste of our girls," said Anton Kozar, limping by on his one good leg and waggling his tongue obscenely. The old women squawked like geese and Baba Olya hurled a rock at him. War veteran or no, the man was disgusting.

When Nadya's father heard the old women muttering that Duva was cursed and demanding that the priest say blessings in the town square, he simply shook his head.

"It's just an animal," he insisted. "A wolf mad with hunger."

Maxim knew every path and corner of the forest, so he and his friends took up their rifles and headed back into the woods, full of grim determination. But again they found nothing, and the old women grumbled louder. What animal left no tracks, no trail, no trace of a body?

Suspicion crept through the town. That lecherous Anton Kozar had returned from the northern front much changed, had he not? Peli Yerokin had always been a violent boy. And Bela Pankin was a most peculiar woman, living out on that

83

farm with her strange son, Uri. A khitka could take any form. Perhaps she had not "found" that missing girl's doll at all.

Standing at the lip of her mother's grave, Nadya noted Anton's seeping stump and lewd grin, wiry Peli Yerokin with his tangled hair and balled fists, Bela Pankin's worried frown, and the sympathetic smile of the widow Karina Stoyanova, the way her lovely black eyes stayed on Nadya's father as the coffin he'd carved with such care was lowered into the hard ground.

The khitka might take any form, but the shape it favored most was that of a beautiful woman.

Soon Karina seemed to be everywhere, bringing Nadya's father food and gifts of kvas, whispering in his ear that someone was needed to take care of him and his children. Havel would be gone for the draft soon, off to train in Poliznaya and begin his military service, but Nadya would still need minding.

"After all," said Karina in her warm honey voice, "you do not want her to disgrace you."

Later that same night, Nadya went to her father as he sat drinking kvas by the fire. Maxim was whittling. When he had nothing to do, he sometimes made dolls for Nadya, though she'd long since outgrown them. His sharp knife moved in restless sweeps, leaving curls of soft wood on the floor. He'd been too long at home. The summer and fall that he might have spent seeking out work had been lost to his wife's illness, and the winter snows would soon close the roads. As his family went hungry, his wooden dolls gathered on the mantel, like a silent, useless choir. He cursed when he cut into his thumb, and only then did he notice Nadya standing nervously by his chair.

"Papa," Nadya said, "please do not marry Karina."

She hoped that he would deny that he had been contemplating such a thing. Instead, he sucked his wounded thumb and said, "Why not? Don't you like Karina?"

"No," said Nadya honestly. "And she doesn't like me."

Maxim laughed and ran his rough knuckles over her cheek. "Sweet Nadya, who could not love you?"

"Papa—"

"Karina is a good woman," Maxim said. His knuckles brushed her cheek again. "It would be better if . . ." Abruptly, he dropped his hand and turned his face back to the fire. His eyes were distant, and when he spoke, his voice was cold and strange, as if rising from the bottom of a well. "Karina is a good woman," he repeated. His fingers gripped the arms of his chair. "Now leave me be."

She has him already, thought Nadya. *He is under her spell.*

The night before Havel left for the south, a dance was held in the barn by the Pankin farm. In better years, it might have

85

been a raucous night, the tables piled high with plates of nuts and apples, pots of honey, and jars of peppery kvas. The men still drank and the fiddle played, but even pine boughs and the high shine of Baba Olya's treasured samovar could not hide the fact that now the tables were empty. And though people stomped and clapped their hands, they could not chase away the gloom that seemed to hang over the room.

Genetchka Lukin was chosen Dros Koroleva, Queen of the Thaw, and made to dance with all who asked her, in the hope that it would bring about a short winter, but only Havel looked truly happy. He was off to the army, to carry a gun and eat hot meals from the king's pocket. He might die or come back wounded as so many had before him, but on this night, his face glowed with the relief of leaving Duva behind.

Nadya danced once with her brother, once with Victor Yeronoff, then took a seat with the widows and wives and children. Her eyes fell on Karina, standing close to her father. Her limbs were white birch branches; her eyes were ice over black water. Maxim looked unsteady on his feet.

Khitka. The word drifted down to Nadya from the barn's shadowed eaves as she watched Karina weave her arm through Maxim's like the pale stalk of a climbing vine. Nadya pushed her foolish thoughts away and turned to watch Genetchka Lukin dance, her long golden hair braided with bright red ribbons. Nadya was ashamed to feel a pang of envy. Silly, she told herself, watching Genetchka struggle through a dance with Anton Kozar. He simply stood and swayed, one arm keeping balance on his crutch, the other clutching tightly to poor Genetchka's waist. Silly, but she felt it just the same.

"Go with Havel," said a voice at her shoulder.

Nadya nearly jumped. She hadn't noticed Karina standing beside her. She looked up at the slender woman, her dark hair lying in coils around her white neck.

Nadya turned her gaze back to the dance. "I can't and you know it. I'm not old enough." It would be two more years before she was called to the draft.

"So lie."

"This is my home," Nadya whispered furiously, embarrassed by the tears that rose behind her eyes. "You can't just send me away." *My father won't let you*, she added silently. But somehow, she did not have the courage to speak the words aloud.

Karina leaned in close to Nadya. When she smiled, her lips split wet and red around what seemed like far too many teeth.

"Havel could at least work and hunt," she whispered. "You're just another mouth." She reached out and tugged one of Nadya's curls, hard. Nadya knew that if her father happened to look over he would just see a beautiful woman, grinning and talking to his daughter, perhaps encouraging her to dance.

"I will warn you just this once," hissed Karina Stoyanova. "Go."

The next day Genetchka Lukin's mother discovered that her daughter's bed had not been slept in. The Queen of the Thaw had never made it home from the dance. At the edge of the wood, a red ribbon fluttered from the branches of a narrow birch, a few golden hairs trailing from the knot, as if it had been torn from her head.

Nadya stood silent as Genetchka's mother fell to her knees and began to wail, calling out to her Saints and pressing the red ribbon to her lips as she wept. Across the road, Nadya saw Karina watching, her eyes black, her lips turned down like peeling bark, her long, slender fingers like raw spokes of branches, stripped bare by a hard wind.

When Havel said his good-byes, he drew Nadya close. "Be safe," he whispered in her ear.

"How?" Nadya replied, but Havel had no answer.

A week later, Maxim Grushov and Karina Stoyanova were wed in the little whitewashed chapel at the center of town. There was no food for a wedding feast, and there were no flowers for the bride's hair, but she wore her

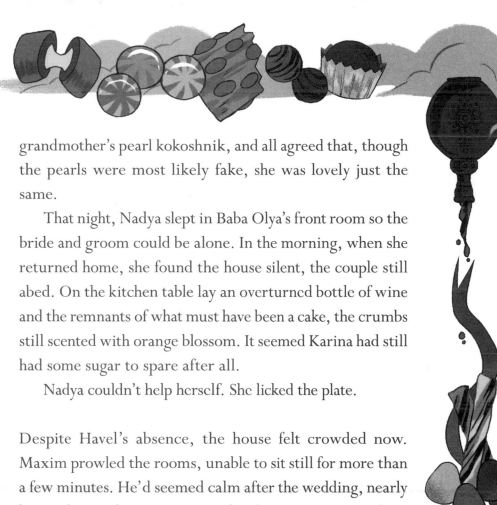

grandmother's pearl kokoshnik, and all agreed that, though the pearls were most likely fake, she was lovely just the same.

That night, Nadya slept in Baba Olya's front room so the bride and groom could be alone. In the morning, when she returned home, she found the house silent, the couple still abed. On the kitchen table lay an overturned bottle of wine and the remnants of what must have been a cake, the crumbs still scented with orange blossom. It seemed Karina had still had some sugar to spare after all.

Nadya couldn't help herself. She licked the plate.

Despite Havel's absence, the house felt crowded now. Maxim prowled the rooms, unable to sit still for more than a few minutes. He'd seemed calm after the wedding, nearly happy, but with every passing day, he grew more restless. He drank and cursed his lack of work, his lost sledge, his empty stomach. He snapped at Nadya and turned away when she came too near, as if he could barely stand the sight of her.

On the rare occasions Maxim showed Nadya any affection, Karina would appear, hovering in the doorway, her black eyes greedy, a rag twisting in her narrow hands. She would order Nadya into the kitchen and burden her with some ridiculous chore, commanding her to stay out of her father's way.

At meals, Karina watched Nadya eat as if her every bite of watered-down broth was an offense, as if every scrape of Nadya's spoon hollowed out Karina's belly a little more, widening the hole inside her.

Little more than a week had passed before Karina took hold of Nadya's arm and nodded toward the woods. "Go check the traps," she said.

"It's almost dark," Nadya protested.

"Don't be foolish. There's plenty of light. Now go and make yourself useful and don't come back without a rabbit for our supper."

"Where's my father?" Nadya demanded.

"He is with Anton Kozar, playing cards and drinking, and trying to forget that he was cursed with a useless daughter." Karina gave Nadya a hard push out the door. "Go, or I'll tell him that I caught you with Victor Yeronoff."

Nadya longed to march to Anton Kozar's shabby rooms, knock the glass from her father's hands, tell him that she wanted her home back from this dangerous dark-eyed stranger. And if she'd been sure that her father would take her side, she might have done just that.

Instead, Nadya walked into the woods.

When the first two snares were empty, she ignored her pounding heart and the lengthening shadows and forced herself to walk on, following the white stones that Havel had used to mark the path. In the third trap she found a brown hare, trembling with fright. She ignored the panicked whistle from its lungs as she snapped its neck with a single determined twist and felt its warm body go limp. As she walked home with her prize, she let herself imagine her father's pleasure at the evening meal. He would tell her she was brave and foolish to go into the wood alone, and when she told him that his new wife had insisted, he would send Karina from their home forever.

But when she stepped inside the house, Karina was waiting, her face pale with fury. She seized Nadya, tore the rabbit from her hands, and shoved her into her room. Nadya heard the bolt slide home. For a long while, she pounded at the door, shouting to be let free. But who was there to hear her?

Finally, weak with hunger and frustration, she let her tears come. She curled on her bed, shaken by sobs, kept awake by the hollow growling of her gut. She missed Havel. She missed her mother. All she'd had to eat was a piece of turnip at breakfast, and she knew that if Karina hadn't taken the hare from her, she would have torn it open and eaten it raw.

Later, she heard the door to the house bang open, heard her father's unsteady footsteps coming down the

hall, the tentative scratch of his fingers at her door. Before she could answer she heard Karina's voice, crooning, crooning. Silence, the rustle of fabric, a thump followed by a groan, then the steady thud of bodies against the wall. Nadya clutched her pillow to her ears, trying to drown out their pants and moans, sure that Karina knew she could hear and that this was some kind of punishment. She buried her head beneath the covers but could not escape that shaming, frantic rhythm, keeping time to the echo of Karina's voice that night at the dance: *I will warn you just this once. Go. Go. Go.*

The next day, Nadya's father did not rise until after noon. When he entered the kitchen and Nadya handed him his tea, he flinched away from her, eyes skittering across the floor. Karina stood at the basin, face pinched, mixing up a batch of lye.

"I'm going to Anton's," Maxim said.

Nadya wanted to beg him not to leave her, but even in her own head, the plea sounded foolish. In the next moment, he was gone.

This time, when Karina took hold of her and said, "Go check the traps," Nadya did not argue.

She had braved the woods once and she would do it again. This time, she would clean and cook the rabbit herself and

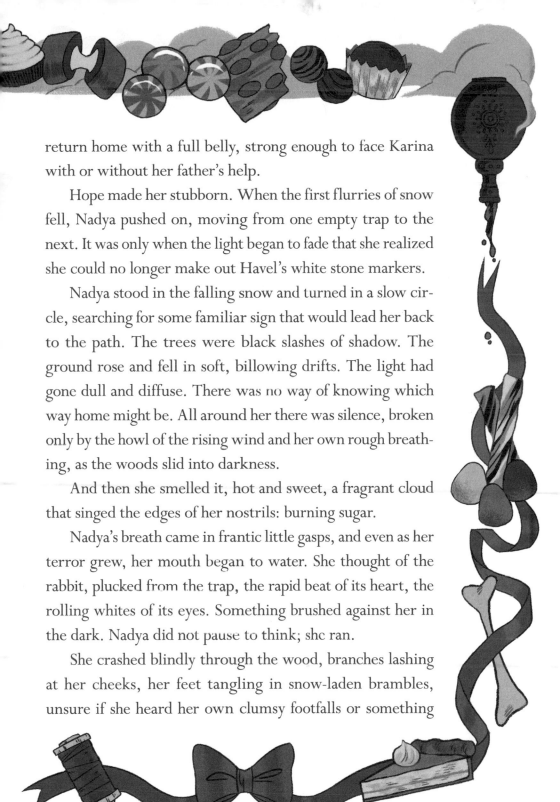

return home with a full belly, strong enough to face Karina with or without her father's help.

Hope made her stubborn. When the first flurries of snow fell, Nadya pushed on, moving from one empty trap to the next. It was only when the light began to fade that she realized she could no longer make out Havel's white stone markers.

Nadya stood in the falling snow and turned in a slow circle, searching for some familiar sign that would lead her back to the path. The trees were black slashes of shadow. The ground rose and fell in soft, billowing drifts. The light had gone dull and diffuse. There was no way of knowing which way home might be. All around her there was silence, broken only by the howl of the rising wind and her own rough breathing, as the woods slid into darkness.

And then she smelled it, hot and sweet, a fragrant cloud that singed the edges of her nostrils: burning sugar.

Nadya's breath came in frantic little gasps, and even as her terror grew, her mouth began to water. She thought of the rabbit, plucked from the trap, the rapid beat of its heart, the rolling whites of its eyes. Something brushed against her in the dark. Nadya did not pause to think; she ran.

She crashed blindly through the wood, branches lashing at her cheeks, her feet tangling in snow-laden brambles, unsure if she heard her own clumsy footfalls or something

slavering behind her, something with crowded teeth and long white fingers that clutched at the hem of her coat.

When she glimpsed the glow of light filtering through the trees ahead, for one delirious moment she thought she'd somehow made it home. But as she burst into the clearing, she saw that the hut silhouetted before her was all wrong. It was lean and crooked, with lights that glowed in every window. No one in her village would ever waste candles that way.

The hut seemed to shift, almost as if it were turning to welcome her. She hesitated, took a step back. A twig snapped behind her. She bolted for the hut's painted door.

Nadya rattled the handle, sending the lantern above swaying.

"Help me!" she cried. And the door swung open. She slipped inside, slamming it behind her. Was that a thump she heard? The frustrated scrabble of paws? It was hard to tell over the hoarse sobs wheezing from her chest. She stood with her forehead pressed to the door, waiting for her heart to stop hammering, and only then, when she could take a full breath, did she turn.

The room was warm and golden, like the inside of a currant bun, thick with the smells of browning meat and fresh-baked bread. Every surface gleamed like new, cheerfully painted with leaves and flowers, animals and tiny people, the

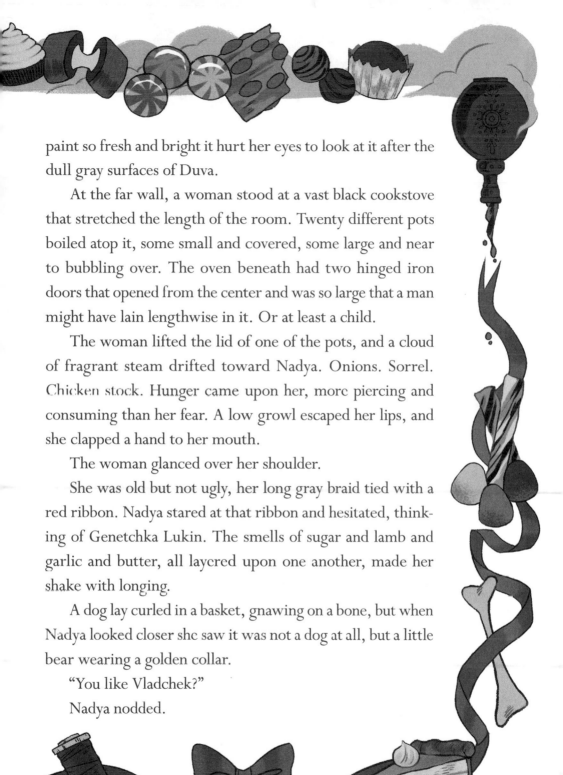

paint so fresh and bright it hurt her eyes to look at it after the dull gray surfaces of Duva.

At the far wall, a woman stood at a vast black cookstove that stretched the length of the room. Twenty different pots boiled atop it, some small and covered, some large and near to bubbling over. The oven beneath had two hinged iron doors that opened from the center and was so large that a man might have lain lengthwise in it. Or at least a child.

The woman lifted the lid of one of the pots, and a cloud of fragrant steam drifted toward Nadya. Onions. Sorrel. Chicken stock. Hunger came upon her, more piercing and consuming than her fear. A low growl escaped her lips, and she clapped a hand to her mouth.

The woman glanced over her shoulder.

She was old but not ugly, her long gray braid tied with a red ribbon. Nadya stared at that ribbon and hesitated, thinking of Genetchka Lukin. The smells of sugar and lamb and garlic and butter, all layered upon one another, made her shake with longing.

A dog lay curled in a basket, gnawing on a bone, but when Nadya looked closer she saw it was not a dog at all, but a little bear wearing a golden collar.

"You like Vladchek?"

Nadya nodded.

The woman set a heaping plate of stew down on the table. "Sit," said the woman as she returned to the stove. "Eat."

Nadya removed her coat and hung it by the door. She pulled her damp mittens from her hands and sat down carefully at the table. She lifted her spoon, but still she hesitated. She knew from stories that you must not eat at a witch's table.

But in the end, she could not resist. She ate the stew, every hot and savory bite of it, then flaky rolls, plums in syrup, egg pudding, and a rum cake thick with raisins and brown sugar. Nadya ate and ate while the woman tended to the pots on the stove, sometimes humming a little as she worked.

She's fattening me up, thought Nadya, her eyelids growing heavy. *She'll wait for me to fall asleep, then stuff me in the oven and cook me up to make more stew.* But Nadya found she didn't care. The woman set a blanket by the stove, next to Vladchek's basket, and Nadya fell off to sleep, glad that at least she would die with a full belly.

But when she woke the next morning, she was still in one piece and the table was set with a hot bowl of porridge, stacks of rye toast slathered with butter, and plates of shiny little herring swimming in oil.

The old woman introduced herself as Magda, then sat silent, sucking on a sugared plum, watching Nadya eat her breakfast.

Nadya ate till her stomach ached while outside the snow continued to fall. When she was done, she set her empty bowl down on the floor, where Vladchek licked it clean. Only then did Magda spit the plum pit into her palm and say, "What is it you want?"

"I want to go home," Nadya replied.

"So go."

Nadya looked outside to where the snow was still falling. "I can't."

"Well then," said Magda. "Come help me stir the pot."

For the rest of the day, Nadya darned socks, scrubbed pans, chopped herbs, and strained syrups. She stood at the stove for long hours, her hair curling from the heat and steam, stirring many little pots, and wondering all the while what might become of her. That night they ate stuffed cabbage leaves, crispy roast goose, little dishes of apricot custard.

The next day, Nadya breakfasted on butter-soaked blini stuffed with cherries and cream. When she finished, the witch asked her, "What is it you want?"

"I want to go home," said Nadya, glancing at the snow still falling outside. "But I can't."

"Well then," said Magda. "Come help me stir the pot."

This was how it went, day after day, as the snow fell and

filled the clearing, rising up around the hut in great white waves.

On the morning the snow finally stopped, the witch fed Nadya potato pie and sausages and asked her, "What is it you want?"

"I want to go home," said Nadya.

"Well then," said Magda. "You'd better start shoveling."

So Nadya took up the shovel and cleared a path around the hut, accompanied by Vladchek snuffling in the snow beside her and an eyeless crow that Magda fed on rye crumbs, and that sometimes perched upon the witch's shoulder. In the afternoon, Nadya ate a slab of black bread spread with soft cheese and a dish of baked apples. Magda gave her a mug of hot tea laced with sugar, and back out she went.

When she finally reached the edge of the clearing, she wondered just where she was supposed to go. The frost had come. The woods were a frozen mass of snow and tangled branches. What might be waiting for her in there? And even if she could make it through the deep snow and find her way back to Duva, what then? A tentative embrace from her weak-willed father? Far worse from his hungry-eyed wife? No path could lead her back to the home she had known. The thought opened a bleak crack inside of her, a fissure where the cold seeped through. For a terrifying moment,

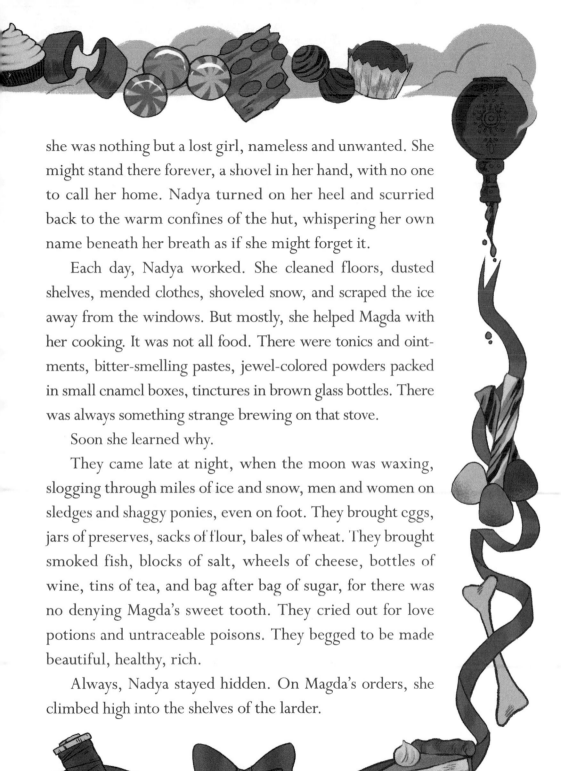

she was nothing but a lost girl, nameless and unwanted. She might stand there forever, a shovel in her hand, with no one to call her home. Nadya turned on her heel and scurried back to the warm confines of the hut, whispering her own name beneath her breath as if she might forget it.

Each day, Nadya worked. She cleaned floors, dusted shelves, mended clothes, shoveled snow, and scraped the ice away from the windows. But mostly, she helped Magda with her cooking. It was not all food. There were tonics and ointments, bitter-smelling pastes, jewel-colored powders packed in small enamel boxes, tinctures in brown glass bottles. There was always something strange brewing on that stove.

Soon she learned why.

They came late at night, when the moon was waxing, slogging through miles of ice and snow, men and women on sledges and shaggy ponies, even on foot. They brought eggs, jars of preserves, sacks of flour, bales of wheat. They brought smoked fish, blocks of salt, wheels of cheese, bottles of wine, tins of tea, and bag after bag of sugar, for there was no denying Magda's sweet tooth. They cried out for love potions and untraceable poisons. They begged to be made beautiful, healthy, rich.

Always, Nadya stayed hidden. On Magda's orders, she climbed high into the shelves of the larder.

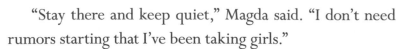

"Stay there and keep quiet," Magda said. "I don't need rumors starting that I've been taking girls."

So Nadya sat with Vladchek, nibbling on a spice cookie or sucking on a hunk of black licorice, watching Magda work. She might have announced herself to these strangers at any time, pleaded to be taken home or given shelter, shouted that she'd been trapped by a witch. Instead, she stayed silent, sugar melting on her tongue, watching as they came to this old woman, how they turned to her with desperation, with resentment, but always with respect.

Magda gave them drops for the eyes, tonics for the scalp. She ran her hands over their wrinkles, tapped a man's chest till he hacked up black bile. Nadya was never sure how much was real and how much was show until the night the wax-skinned woman came.

She was gaunt, as they all were, her face a skull of hard-carved hollows. Magda asked the question she asked anyone who came to her door: "What is it you want?"

The woman collapsed in her arms, weeping, as Magda murmured soothing words, patted her hand, dried her tears. They conferred in voices too low for Nadya to decipher, and before the woman left, she took a tiny pouch from her pocket and shook the contents into Magda's palm. Nadya

craned her neck to get a better look, but Magda's hand clamped shut too quickly.

The next day, Magda sent Nadya out of the house to shovel snow. When she returned at lunchtime, she was shooed back out with a cup of codfish stew. Dusk came, and as Nadya finished sprinkling salt along the edges of the path, the scent of gingerbread drifted to her across the clearing, rich and spicy, filling her nose until she felt nearly drunk.

All through dinner, she waited for Magda to open the oven, but when the meal was finished, the old woman set a piece of yesterday's lemon cake before her. Nadya shrugged. As she reached for the cream, she heard a soft sound, a gurgle. She looked at Vladchek, but the bear was fast asleep, snoring softly.

And then she heard it again, a gurgle followed by a plaintive coo. From inside the oven.

Nadya pushed back from the table, nearly knocking her chair over, and stared at Magda, horrified, but the witch did not flinch.

A knock sounded at the door.

"Go into the larder, Nadya."

For a moment, Nadya hovered between the table and the door, caught like a fly that might still free itself from the web. Then she backed into the larder, pausing only to grab hold of

Vladchek's collar and drag him with her onto the top shelf, comforted by his drowsy snuffling and the warm feel of his fur beneath her hands.

Magda opened the door. The wax-faced woman stood waiting at the threshold, almost as if she were afraid to move. Magda wrapped her hands in towels and pulled open the oven's iron doors. A squalling cry filled the room. The woman grabbed at the doorposts as her knees buckled, then pressed her hands to her mouth, her chest heaving, tears streaming over her sallow cheeks. Magda swaddled the gingerbaby in a red kerchief and handed it, squirming and mewling, into the woman's trembling, outstretched arms.

"Milaya," the woman crooned. *Sweet girl.* She turned her back on Magda and disappeared into the night, not bothering to close the door behind her.

The next day, Nadya left her breakfast untouched, placing her cold bowl of porridge on the floor for Vladchek. He turned up his nose at it until Magda put it back on the stove to warm.

Before Magda could ask her question, Nadya said, "That wasn't a real child. Why did she take it?"

"It was real enough."

"What will happen to it? What will happen to her?" Nadya asked, a wild edge to her voice.

"Eventually it will be nothing but crumbs," said Magda.

"And then what? Will you just make her another?"

"The mother will be dead long before that. She has the same fever that took her infant."

"Then cure her!" Nadya shouted, smacking the table with her unused spoon.

"She didn't ask to be cured. She asked for a child."

Nadya put on her mittens and stomped out into the yard. She did not go inside for lunch. She meant to skip dinner too, to show what she thought of Magda and her terrible magic. But by the time night came her stomach was growling, and when Magda put down a plate of sliced duck with hunter's sauce, Nadya picked up her fork and knife.

"I want to go home," she muttered to her plate.

"So go," said Magda.

Winter dragged on with frost and cold, but the lamps always burned golden in the little hut. Nadya's cheeks grew rosy and her clothes grew snug. She learned how to mix up Magda's tonics without looking at the recipes and how to bake an almond cake in the shape of a crown. She learned which herbs were valuable and which were dangerous, and which herbs were valuable because they were dangerous.

Nadya knew there was much that Magda didn't teach her. She told herself she was glad of it, that she wanted

nothing to do with Magda's abominations. But sometimes she felt her curiosity clawing at her like a different kind of hunger.

And then, one morning, she woke to the tapping of the blind crow's beak on the sill and the drip, drip, drip of melted snow from the eaves. Bright sun shone through the windows. The thaw had come.

That morning, Magda laid out sweet rolls with prune jam, a plate of boiled eggs, and bitter greens. Nadya ate and ate, afraid to reach the end of her meal, but eventually she could not take another bite.

"What is it you want?" asked Magda.

This time Nadya hesitated, afraid. "If I go, couldn't I just—"

"You cannot come and go from this place like you're fetching water from a well. I will not have you bring a monster to my door."

Nadya shivered. *A monster.* So she'd been right about Karina.

"What is it you want?" asked Magda again.

Nadya thought of Genetchka dancing, of nervous Lara, of Betya and Ludmilla, of the others she had never known.

"I want my father to be free of Karina. I want Duva to be safe. I want to go home."

Gently, Magda reached out and touched Nadya's left hand—first the ring finger, then the pinkie. Nadya thought of the wax-faced woman, of the little bag she'd emptied into the witch's palm.

"Think on it," said Magda.

The next morning when Magda went to lay out the breakfast, she found the cleaver Nadya had placed there.

For two days, the cleaver lay untouched on the table, as they measured and sifted and mixed, making batch after batch of batter. On the second afternoon, when the hardest of the work was done, Magda turned to Nadya.

"You know that you are welcome to remain here with me," said the witch.

Nadya stretched out her hand.

Magda sighed. The cleaver flashed once in the afternoon sun, the edge gleaming the dull gray of Grisha steel, then fell with a sound like a gunshot.

At the sight of her fingers lying forlorn on the table, Nadya fainted.

Magda healed the stumps of Nadya's fingers, bound her hand, let her rest. And while she slept, Magda took the two fingers and ground them down to a wet red meal that she mixed into the batter.

When Nadya revived, they worked side by side, shaping

the gingergirl on a damp plank as big as a door, then shoved her into the blazing oven.

All night the gingergirl baked, filling the hut with a marvelous smell. Nadya knew she was smelling her own bones and blood, but still her mouth watered. She dozed. Near dawn, the oven doors creaked open and the gingergirl crawled out. She crossed the room, opened the window, and lay down on the counter to let herself cool.

In the morning, Nadya and Magda attended the gingergirl, dusted her with sugar, gave her frosted lips and thick ropes of icing for hair.

Finally, they dressed her in Nadya's clothes and boots and set her on the path toward Duva.

They ate a small meal of herring and soft eggs to keep up their strength. Then Magda sat Nadya down at the table and took a small jar from one of the cabinets. She opened the window and the eyeless black crow came to rest on the table, picking at the crumbs the gingergirl had left behind.

Magda tipped the contents of the jar into her palm and held them out to Nadya. "Open your mouth," she said.

In Magda's hand, floating in a pool of shiny fluid, lay a pair of bright blue eyes. Hatchling's eyes.

"Do not swallow," said Magda sternly, "and do not retch."

Nadya closed her eyes and forced her lips to part. She tried not to gag as the crow's eyes slid onto her tongue.

"Open your eyes," commanded Magda.

Nadya obeyed, and when she did, the whole room had shifted. She saw herself sitting in a chair, eyes still closed, Magda beside her. She tried to raise her hands, but found that her wings rose instead. She hopped on her little crow feet and released a startled squawk of surprise.

Magda shooed her to the window and Nadya, elated from the feeling of her wings and the wind spreading beneath them, did not see the sadness in the old woman's gaze.

Nadya rose high into the air in a great wheeling arc, dipping her wings, learning the feel of them, slicing through the long shadows of the dwindling afternoon. She saw the woods spread beneath her, the clearing, and Magda's hut. She saw the jagged peaks of the Petrazoi in the distance, and gliding lower, she saw the gingergirl's path through the woods. She swooped and darted between the trees, unafraid of the forest for the first time since she could remember.

She circled over Duva, saw the main street, the cemetery, two new altars laid out. Two more girls gone during the long winter while she grew fat at the witch's table. They would be

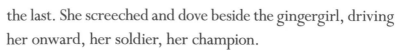

the last. She screeched and dove beside the gingergirl, driving her onward, her soldier, her champion.

Nadya watched from a clothesline as the gingergirl crossed the clearing to her father's house. Inside, she could hear raised voices arguing. Did he know what Karina had done? Had he begun to suspect what she truly was?

The gingergirl knocked and the voices quieted. When the door swung open, her father squinted into the dusk. Nadya was shocked at the toll the winter had taken on him. His broad shoulders looked hunched and narrow, and, even from a distance, she could see the way the skin hung loose on his frame. She waited for him to cry out in horror at the monster that stood before him.

"Nadya?" Maxim gasped. "Nadya!" He pulled the gingergirl into his arms with a rough cry.

Karina appeared behind him in the door, face pale, eyes wide. Nadya felt a twinge of disappointment. Somehow she'd imagined that Karina would take one look at the gingergirl and crumble to dust, or that the sight of Nadya alive and well on her doorstep would force her to blurt out some ugly confession.

Maxim drew the gingergirl inside and Nadya fluttered down to the windowsill to peer through the glass.

The house looked more cramped and gray than ever after

the warmth of Magda's hut. She saw that the collection of wooden dolls on the mantel had grown.

Nadya's father caressed the gingergirl's burnished brown arm, peppering her with questions, but the gingergirl stayed silent, huddling by the fire. Nadya wasn't even sure that she *could* speak.

Maxim did not seem to notice her silence. He babbled on, laughing, crying, shaking his head in wonder. Karina hovered behind him, watching as she always had. There was fear in her eyes, but something else, too, something troubling that looked almost like gratitude.

Then Karina stepped forward, touched the gingergirl's soft cheek, her frosted hair. Nadya waited, sure Karina would be singed, that she would let out a shriek as the flesh of her hand peeled away like bark, revealing not bones but branches and the monstrous form of the khitka beneath her pretty skin.

Instead, Karina bowed her head and murmured what might have been a prayer. She took her coat from the hook.

"I am going to Baba Olya's."

"Yes, yes," Maxim said distractedly, unable to pull his gaze from his daughter.

She's running away, Nadya realized in horror. And the gingergirl was making no move to stop her.

Karina wrapped her head in a scarf, pulled on her gloves,

and slipped out the door, shutting it behind her without a backward glance.

Nadya hopped and squawked from the window ledge.

I will follow her, she thought. *I will peck out her eyes.*

Karina bent down, picked up a pebble from the path, and hurled it at Nadya.

Nadya released an indignant caw.

But when Karina spoke, her voice was gentle. "Fly away now, little bird," she said. "Some things are better left unseen." Then she disappeared into the dusk.

Nadya fluttered her wings, unsure of what to do. She peered back through the window.

Her father had pulled the gingergirl into his lap and was stroking her white hair.

"Nadya," he said again and again. "Nadya." He nuzzled the brown flesh of her shoulder, pressed his lips to her skin.

Outside, Nadya's small heart beat against her hollow bones.

"Forgive me," Maxim murmured, the tears on his cheeks dissolving the soft curve of icing at her neck.

Nadya shivered. Her wings stuttered a futile, desperate tattoo on the glass. But her father's hand slipped beneath the hem of her skirts, and the gingergirl did not move.

It isn't me, Nadya told herself. *Not really. It isn't me.*

She thought of her father's restlessness, of his lost horses, his treasured sledge. Before that . . . before that, girls had gone missing from other towns, one here, one there. Stories, rumors, faraway crimes. But then the famine had come, the long winter, and Maxim had been trapped, forced to hunt closer to home.

"I've tried to stop," he said as he pulled his daughter close. "Believe me," he begged. "Say you believe me."

The gingergirl stayed silent.

Maxim opened his wet mouth to kiss her again, and the sound he made was something between a groan and a sigh as his teeth sank into the sweetness of her shoulder.

The sigh turned to a sob as he bit down.

Nadya watched her father consume the gingergirl, bite by bite, limb by limb. He wept as he ate, but he did not stop, and by the time he was finished, the fire was cold in the grate. When he was done, he lay stretched out on the floor, his belly distended, his fingers sticky, his beard crusted with crumbs. Only then did the crow turn away.

They found Nadya's father there the next morning, his insides ruptured and stinking of rot. He had spent the night on his knees, vomiting blood and sugar. Karina had not been home to help him. When they took up the bloodstained

floorboards, they found a stash of objects, among them a child's prayer book, a bracelet of glass beads, the rest of the vivid red ribbons Genetchka had worn in her hair the night of the dance, and Lara Deniken's white apron, embroidered with her clumsy stitches, the strings stained with blood. From the mantel, the little wooden dolls looked on.

Nadya flew back to the witch's hut, returned to her body by Magda's soft words and Vladchek licking her limp hand. She spent long days in silence, working beside Magda, only picking at her food.

It was not her father she thought of, but Karina. Karina who had found ways to visit their home when Nadya's mother took ill, who had filled the rooms when Havel left, keeping Nadya close. Karina who had driven Nadya into the woods, so that there would be nothing left for her father to use but a ghost. Karina who had given herself to a monster, in the hope of saving just one girl.

Nadya scrubbed and cooked and cleared the garden, and thought of Karina alone with Maxim over the long winter,

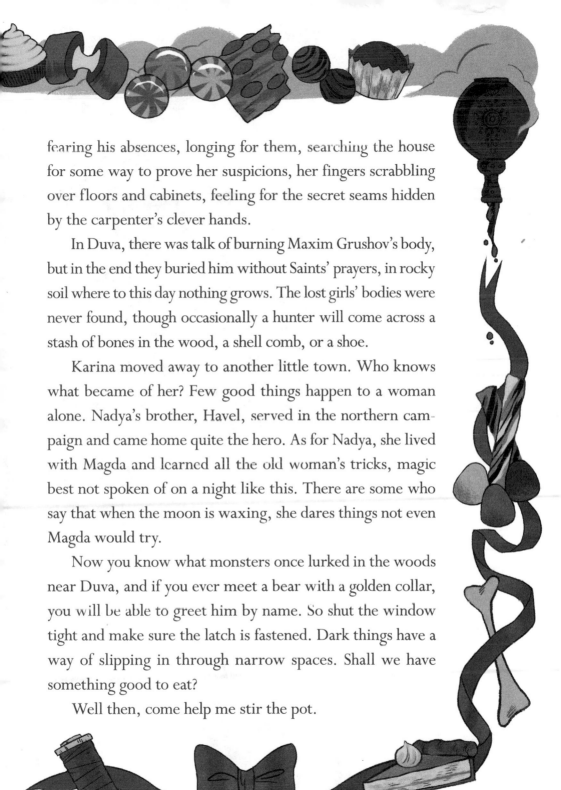

fearing his absences, longing for them, searching the house for some way to prove her suspicions, her fingers scrabbling over floors and cabinets, feeling for the secret seams hidden by the carpenter's clever hands.

In Duva, there was talk of burning Maxim Grushov's body, but in the end they buried him without Saints' prayers, in rocky soil where to this day nothing grows. The lost girls' bodies were never found, though occasionally a hunter will come across a stash of bones in the wood, a shell comb, or a shoe.

Karina moved away to another little town. Who knows what became of her? Few good things happen to a woman alone. Nadya's brother, Havel, served in the northern campaign and came home quite the hero. As for Nadya, she lived with Magda and learned all the old woman's tricks, magic best not spoken of on a night like this. There are some who say that when the moon is waxing, she dares things not even Magda would try.

Now you know what monsters once lurked in the woods near Duva, and if you ever meet a bear with a golden collar, you will be able to greet him by name. So shut the window tight and make sure the latch is fastened. Dark things have a way of slipping in through narrow spaces. Shall we have something good to eat?

Well then, come help me stir the pot.

LITTLE KNIFE

IT IS DANGEROUS TO TRAVEL THE

northern road with a troubled heart. Just south of Arkesk is a break in the trees, a place where no bird sings and the shadows hang from the branches with strange weight. On this lonely mile, travelers stay close to their companions, they sing loud songs and beat the drum, for if you are lost to your own thoughts, you may find yourself stepping off the path and into the dark woods. And if you continue, ignoring the shouts of your companions, your feet may carry you to the silent streets and abandoned houses of Velisyana, the cursed city.

Weeds and wildflowers crowd the cobblestones. The shops are empty, and the doors have rotted on their hinges, leaving only gaping mouths. The town square is overgrown with brambles and the church roof has long since given way; amid the shattered pews, the great dome lies on its side, collecting rainwater, its gold leaf stripped away by time or some enterprising thief.

You may recognize this quiet as you stand in what was once Suitors' Square, staring up at the grand facade of a crumbling palace and the little window high above the street, its casement carved with lilies. This is the sound of a heart gone silent. Velisyana is a corpse.

In days past, the town was known for two things: the quality of its flour—used by every kitchen for nearly a

hundred miles—and the beauty of Yeva Luchova, the old duke's daughter.

The duke was not a particular favorite of the king, but he'd grown rich anyway. He'd installed dams and dikes to contain the river so that it no longer flooded his lands, and he'd built the great mill where Velisyana's flour was ground, commissioning a giant waterwheel with sturdy steel spokes, perfect in its balance.

There is some debate over what Yeva Luchova actually looked like, whether her hair was burnished gold or lustrous black, whether her eyes were blue as sapphires or green as new grass. It is not the particulars of her beauty but the power of it that concerns us, and we need only know that Yeva was lovely from the moment of her birth.

She was so beautiful, in fact, that the midwife attending her mother snatched up the wailing infant and locked herself in a linen closet, begging for just another moment to gaze upon Yeva's face and refusing to relinquish the baby until the duke called for an axe to break down the door. The duke had the midwife whipped, but that didn't stop several of Yeva's nursemaids from trying to steal the child away. Finally, her father hired a blind old woman to care for his daughter, and there was peace in his home. Of course, that peace did not last, for Yeva only grew more beautiful as she aged.

No one could make sense of it, for neither the duke nor

his wife were much to look at. There were rumors that Yeva's mother had found her way into the camp of a Suli traveler, and more jealous sorts liked to whisper that a handsome demon had crept in with the moonlight and tricked his way into her mother's bed. Most of the townspeople laughed away these stories, for no one could know Yeva's kindness and think that she was anything but a good and righteous girl. And yet, when Yeva walked down the street, the wind lifting her hair, her lovely feet barely seeming to touch the cobblestones, it was hard not to wonder. Every year on Yeva's birthday, under the guise of placing flowers in her braids, the blind nursemaid would check Yeva's scalp, feeling with trembling fingers for the bumps of new horns.

As Yeva's beauty grew, so did her father's pride. When she turned twelve, he had a portrait artist come all the way from Os Alta to paint her surrounded by lilies, and had her image stamped on every bag of flour from his mill. So women in their kitchens came to wear their hair like Yeva, and men from all over Ravka traveled to Velisyana to see if such a creature could be real.

Of course, the artist fell in love with Yeva too. He put dropwort in her milk and got all the way to Arkesk with her before he was apprehended. The duke found his daughter sleeping soundly in the back of the pony cart, wedged between canvases and jars of pigments. Yeva was quite unharmed and

had little memory of the event, though she forever had an aversion to portrait galleries, and the smell of oil paint would always make her drowsy.

By the time Yeva was fifteen, it was no longer safe for her to leave the house. She tried cutting her hair and covering her face in ashes, but this only made her more intriguing to the men who spied her on her daily walk, for when they saw her, their imaginations ran wild. When Yeva stopped to remove a stone from her shoe and unwittingly gave the crowd a glimpse of her perfect ankle, a riot broke out, and her father decided she must be confined to the palace.

She spent her days reading and sewing, walking back and forth through the halls for exercise, always in a veil so as not to distract the servants. Every day, when the clock on the bell tower chimed the noon hour, she appeared at her window to wave at the people gathered in the square below, and to let her suitors come forward to declare their love and beg for her hand. They would sing songs or perform tricks or stage duels to prove their daring—though the duels sometimes got out of hand, and after the second death, the retired army colonel who acted as constable had to put a stop to them.

"Papa," Yeva said to the duke, desperate to stand beneath an open sky again. "Why must I be the one to hide?"

The duke patted her hand. "Enjoy this power, Yeva. For one day you will grow old and no one will notice when you walk down the street."

Yeva did not think her father had answered her question, but she kissed his cheek and returned to her sewing.

On the morning of her sixteenth birthday, Nestor Levkin appeared at the door with his son. He was one of the wealthiest men of the town, second only to the duke, and had come to barter for a union between Yeva and his boy. But as soon as he stepped into the parlor and saw Yeva sitting by the fire, he declared that he would be the one to marry her.

Father and son took to arguing and then went at each other with their fists. The retired colonel was called upon to settle the dispute, but at his first real glimpse of Yeva, he drew his sword and challenged both of her other suitors. Yeva's father sent her to her room and called for guards to pull the men apart. In time, free from the spell of Yeva's beauty, the men returned to their senses. They drank tea together and lowered their heads in shame at their behavior.

"You cannot let this go on," said the colonel. "Every day the crowd in the square grows. You must choose a husband for Yeva and be done with this madness before the town is torn apart."

Now, the duke might have put an end to all of this by simply asking his daughter what she desired. But he enjoyed the attention Yeva received, and it certainly sold a lot of flour. So he devised a plan that suited his greed and his love for spectacle.

It happened that the duke had many acres of forest that

he wished to clear in order to plant more wheat. At noon
the next day, he stepped out on the balcony that overlooked
Suitors' Square and waved to the men below. The crowd
sighed in disappointment when they saw the duke instead
of Yeva, but their ears perked up when they heard what he
had to say.

"It is time for my daughter to marry." A cheer went up
from the crowd. "But only a worthy man may have her. Yeva
is delicate and must be kept warm. Each of you will go into
my woods and bring a pile of lumber to the fallow field at
the southernmost edge of the forest. At sunrise tomorrow,
whoever has the tallest pile will win Yeva as his bride."

The suitors did not stop to contemplate the strangeness
of this task, but bolted off to fetch their axes.

As the duke shut the balcony doors, Yeva said, "Papa,
forgive me, but what way is this to choose a husband?
Tomorrow, I will certainly have a lot of firewood, but will I
have a good man?"

The duke patted her hand. "Darling Yeva," he said. "Do
you think I am so foolish or so cruel? Did you not see the
prince standing in the square this past week, waiting patiently
each day for a glimpse of you? He has gold enough to hire a
thousand men to wield their axes for him. He will win this
contest easily, and you will live in the capital and wear only
silk for the rest of your days. What do you think of that?"

Yeva doubted that her father had answered her question, but she kissed his cheek and told him that he was very wise indeed.

What neither Yeva nor her father knew was that deep in the shadows of the clock tower, Semyon the Ragged was listening. Semyon was a Tidemaker, and though he was powerful, he was poor. This was in the days before the Second Army, when Grisha were welcome in few places and greeted with suspicion everywhere. Semyon made his living traveling from town to town, diverting rivers when there were droughts, keeping rains at bay when the winter storms came too soon, or finding the right places to sink wells. It was simple to Semyon. "Water only wants direction," he would say on the rare occasion he was asked. "It wants to be told what to do."

He was usually paid in barley or trade, and as soon as he was done with a task the villagers would ask him to move on. It was no kind of life. Semyon longed for a home and a wife. He wanted new boots and a fine coat so that when he walked down the street people would look on him with respect. And as soon as he saw Yeva Luchova, he wanted her too.

Semyon made his way through town to the edge of the southern wood, where the suitors were already hacking away at the trees and building their piles of timber. He had no axe and no money to buy one. He was clever and even desperate

enough to steal, but he'd seen the prince loitering beneath Yeva's window, and he thought he understood the duke's plan well enough. His heart sank as he watched teams of men building the prince's pile while the prince himself looked on, golden haired and smiling, twirling an ivory-handled axe with an edge that glinted the strange dark gray of Grisha steel.

Semyon went down to the river to the sorry camp he had made, where he kept his bundle of rags and his few belongings. He sat on the banks and listened to the steady thump and splash of the waterwheel beside the great mill. Around people, Semyon was tongue-tied and sullen, but on the sloping riverbank, amid the soft rustle of reeds, he spoke freely, unburdening his heart to the water, confiding all his secret aspirations. The river laughed at his jokes, listened and murmured assent, roared in shared anger and indignation when he'd been wronged.

But as the sun set and the axes fell silent in the distance, Semyon knew the men would go home with the last of the daylight. The contest was as good as over.

"What am I to do?" he said to the river. "Tomorrow Yeva will have a prince for a husband and I will still have nothing. Always you have done my bidding, but what good are you to me now?"

To his surprise, the river burbled a high, sweet sound,

almost like a woman singing. It splashed left, then right, breaking up against the rocks, frothing and foaming, as if troubled by a storm. Semyon stumbled backward, his boots sinking in the mud as the water rose.

"River, what do you do?" he cried.

The river swelled in a great, curling wave and rushed toward him, breaching its banks. Semyon covered his head with his arms, sure he would be drowned, but just as the water was about to strike him, the river split and raced around his shaking body.

Through the woods the river tumbled, tearing ancient trees from the soil, stripping away branches. The river cut a path through the forest under the cover of night, all the way to the fallow field at the edge of the southern wood. There it swirled and eddied, and tree upon tree, branch upon branch, a structure began to take form. All night the river worked, and when the townspeople arrived in the morning, they found Semyon standing beside a massive tower of timber that dwarfed the sad little pile of kindling assembled by the prince's men.

The prince hurled his ivory-handled axe away in anger, and the duke was most distressed. He could not break a promise made so publicly, but he could not bear the thought of his daughter married to such an unnatural creature as Semyon. He forced himself to smile and thump Semyon on

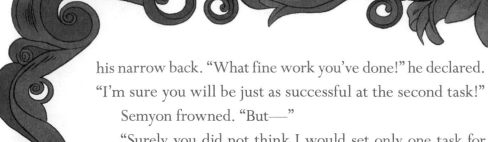

his narrow back. "What fine work you've done!" he declared. "I'm sure you will be just as successful at the second task!"

Semyon frowned. "But—"

"Surely you did not think I would set only one task for Yeva's hand? I'm certain you can agree, my daughter is worth more than that!"

All the townspeople and the eager suitors concurred—especially the prince, whose pride was still smarting. Semyon did not want anyone to think he priced Yeva so low. He swallowed his protest and nodded.

"Very good! Then listen closely. A girl like Yeva must be able to behold her own lovely face. High in the Petrazoi lives Baba Anezka, the maker of mirrors. Whoever returns with a piece of her handiwork will have my daughter as his bride."

The suitors scattered in all directions while the prince called orders to his men.

When her father had returned to the palace and Yeva heard what he had done, she said, "Papa, forgive me, but what way is this to find a husband? Soon I will have a fine mirror, but will I have a good man?"

"Darling Yeva," said the duke. "When will you learn to trust in your father's wisdom? The prince has Ravka's fastest horses, and only he can afford such a mirror. He will win this contest easily, and then you will wear a jeweled crown and eat cherries in winter. What do you think of that?"

Yeva wondered if her father had simply misheard her question, but she kissed his cheek and told him she was very fond of cherries indeed.

Semyon went down to the river and put his head in his hands. "What am I to do?" he said miserably. "I have no horse, nor have I money to trade with the mountain witch. You helped me before, but what good are you now, river?"

Then Semyon gasped as the river once more breached its banks and grabbed hold of his ankle. It dragged him into its depths as he sputtered and gasped.

"River," cried Semyon, "what do you do?"

The river burbled its reply, dunking him deep, then buoying him to the surface and carrying him safely along. It bore him south through lakes and creeks and rapids, west through tributaries and streams, mile after mile, until finally they came to the north-facing slopes of the Petrazoi, and Semyon understood the river's intent.

"Faster, river, faster!" he commanded as it carried him up the mountainside, and soon enough, he arrived soaked but triumphant at the entrance to the witch's cave.

"You have been a loyal friend, and so I think I must name you," Semyon said to the river as he tried to wring the water from his ragged coat. "I will call you Little Knife because of the way you flash silver in the sunlight and because you are my fierce defender."

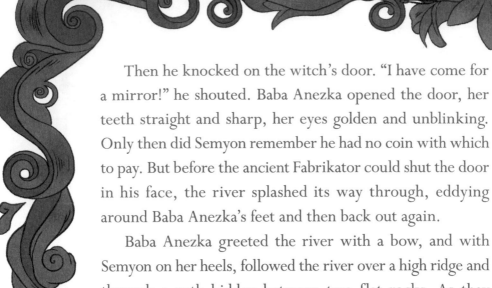

Then he knocked on the witch's door. "I have come for a mirror!" he shouted. Baba Anezka opened the door, her teeth straight and sharp, her eyes golden and unblinking. Only then did Semyon remember he had no coin with which to pay. But before the ancient Fabrikator could shut the door in his face, the river splashed its way through, eddying around Baba Anezka's feet and then back out again.

Baba Anezka greeted the river with a bow, and with Semyon on her heels, followed the river over a high ridge and through a path hidden between two flat rocks. As they squeezed through, they found themselves at the edge of a shallow valley, its floor all gray gravel, barren and unwelcoming as the rest of the Petrazoi. But at its center lay a pool, nearly perfect in its roundness, its surface smooth as highly polished glass, reflecting the sky so purely that it looked as if one could step into it and fall straight through the clouds.

The witch smiled, showing all her sharp teeth. "Now *this* is a mirror," she said, "and seems a fair trade."

They returned to the cave, and when Baba Anezka handed Semyon one of her finest mirrors, he laughed in his joy.

"That gift is for the river," she said.

"It belongs to Little Knife, and Little Knife does as I ask. Besides, what could a river want with a mirror?"

"That is a question for the river," replied Baba Anezka.

But Semyon ignored her. He called out for Little Knife, and once more the river grabbed his ankle and they went rushing

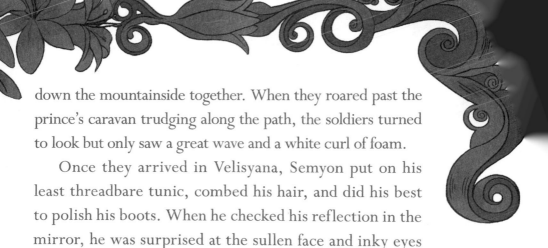

down the mountainside together. When they roared past the prince's caravan trudging along the path, the soldiers turned to look but only saw a great wave and a white curl of foam.

Once they arrived in Velisyana, Semyon put on his least threadbare tunic, combed his hair, and did his best to polish his boots. When he checked his reflection in the mirror, he was surprised at the sullen face and inky eyes that stared back at him. He'd always thought himself quite handsome, and the river had never told him differently.

"There is something wrong with this mirror, Little Knife," he said. "But this is what the duke demanded, and so Yeva shall have it for her wall."

When the duke looked out his window and saw Semyon striding across Suitors' Square with a mirror in his hands, he reeled back in shock.

"See what you have done with your foolish tasks?" said the retired colonel, who was awaiting the contest's outcome with the duke. "You should have given me Yeva's hand when you had the chance. Now she will be married to that outcast, and no one will want to sit at your table. You must find a way to be rid of him."

But the duke was not so sure. A prince would make a fine son-in-law, but Semyon must have great power to accomplish such extraordinary tasks, and the duke wondered if he might make use of such magic.

He sent the colonel away, and when Semyon knocked on

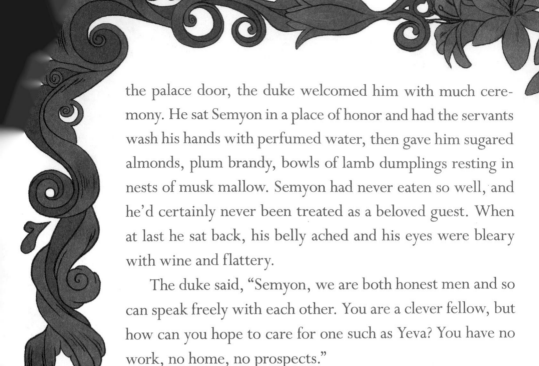

the palace door, the duke welcomed him with much cere-mony. He sat Semyon in a place of honor and had the servants wash his hands with perfumed water, then gave him sugared almonds, plum brandy, bowls of lamb dumplings resting in nests of musk mallow. Semyon had never eaten so well, and he'd certainly never been treated as a beloved guest. When at last he sat back, his belly ached and his eyes were bleary with wine and flattery.

The duke said, "Semyon, we are both honest men and so can speak freely with each other. You are a clever fellow, but how can you hope to care for one such as Yeva? You have no work, no home, no prospects."

"I have love," said Semyon, nearly toppling his glass, "and Little Knife."

The duke didn't know what knives had to do with any-thing, but he said, "One cannot live on love or cutlery, and Yeva has had an easy life. She knows nothing of struggle or hardship. Would you be the one to teach her suffering?"

"No!" cried Semyon. "Never!"

"Then we must make a plan, you and I. Tomorrow I will set a final task, and if you accomplish it, then you will have Yeva's hand and all the riches you could ever want."

Semyon thought the duke might try to cheat him once more, but he liked the sound of this bargain and resolved to be on his guard.

"Very well," he said, and offered the duke his hand.

The duke shook it, hiding his distaste, then said, "Come to the square tomorrow morning and listen closely."

Word of the new task spread, and the next day the square was packed with even more suitors, including the prince, who stood with his tired horses, his boots glittering with tiny shards of the mirror he had smashed in his frustration.

"There is an ancient coin forged by a great sorcerer and buried somewhere beneath Ravka," the duke declared. "Each time you spend it, it returns to you twofold, so your pockets will always be full. Bring back this coin so that Yeva will never want for anything, and you will have her as your bride."

The crowd raced off in all directions to gather shovels and pickaxes.

When the duke stepped back from the balcony, Yeva said, "Papa, forgive me, but what way is this to find a husband? Soon I will be very rich, but will I have a good man?"

This time, the duke looked on his daughter with pity. "When the coffers are empty and their bellies growl, even good men turn bad. Whoever may win this contest, the magic coin will be ours. We will dance in marble halls and drink from cups of frozen amber, and if you do not like your husband, we will drown him in a sea of gold, then send a silver ship to find you a new one. What do you think of that?"

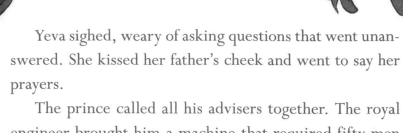

Yeva sighed, weary of asking questions that went unanswered. She kissed her father's cheek and went to say her prayers.

The prince called all his advisers together. The royal engineer brought him a machine that required fifty men to turn the crank. Once it was spinning, it could drill for miles beneath the earth. But the engineer did not know how to stop it, and the machine and the fifty men were never heard from again. The minister of the interior claimed he could train an army of moles if he only had more time, and the king's spymaster swore that he had heard stories of a magic spoon that could dig through solid rock.

Meanwhile, Semyon returned to the river. "Little Knife," he called. "I need you. If I do not find the coin, then another man will have Yeva and I will have nothing."

The river splashed, its surface rippling in consternation. It sloshed against its banks, returning again and again to break upon the dam that bound the millpond. It took many minutes, but soon Semyon understood: the river was divided, too weak to dig beneath the ground.

He snatched up the ivory-handled axe he had taken from the woods when the prince had cast it away, and hacked at the dam with all his might. The clang of Grisha steel against stone echoed through the forest, until finally, with a creaking sigh, the dam burst. The river roiled and frothed in its newfound strength, whole once more.

"Now slice through the ground and fetch me the coin, Little Knife, or what good are you to me?"

The river dove through the earth, moving with strength and purpose, leaving caverns and caves and tunnels in its wake. It crossed the length of Ravka, from border to border and back, as the rock tore at its current and the soil drank from its sides. The deeper the river plunged, the weaker it became, but on it went, and when it was at its most frail, little more than a breath of fog in a clump of earth, it felt the coin, small and hard. Whatever face the metal bore had been long worn away by time.

The river clutched the coin and hurtled to the surface, gathering its strength, growing dense with mud and rainwater, swelling as it reclaimed each rivulet and tiny stream. It erupted through the millpond, a gout of mist that glittered with rainbows, bouncing the coin this way and that.

Semyon bounded into the water to seize it, but the river swirled around him, making worried murmurs. Semyon paused, and he wondered, *What if I bring the coin to the duke and he sets yet another task? What if he takes it and murders me where I sit?*

"I am no fool," said Semyon to the river. "Keep the coin in the shallows until I return."

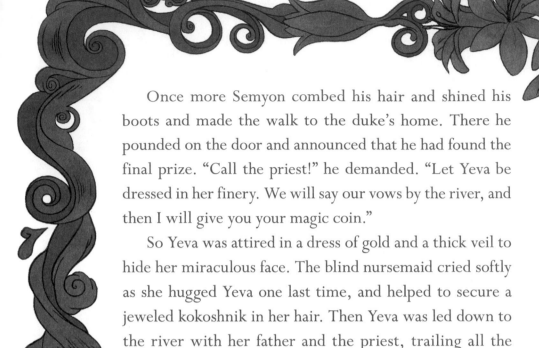

Once more Semyon combed his hair and shined his boots and made the walk to the duke's home. There he pounded on the door and announced that he had found the final prize. "Call the priest!" he demanded. "Let Yeva be dressed in her finery. We will say our vows by the river, and then I will give you your magic coin."

So Yeva was attired in a dress of gold and a thick veil to hide her miraculous face. The blind nursemaid cried softly as she hugged Yeva one last time, and helped to secure a jeweled kokoshnik in her hair. Then Yeva was led down to the river with her father and the priest, trailing all the townspeople and the grumbling prince behind them.

They found Semyon by the shattered dam, the river spilling its banks.

"What has happened here?" asked the duke.

Semyon still wore his threadbare rags, but now he spoke with pride. "I have your coin," he said. "Give me my bride."

The duke held out his hand in expectation.

"Show them, Little Knife," said Semyon to the seething waters.

Yeva frowned. "What is little about the river?" she asked. But no one heard her question.

The coin shot from the river's depths to skip and dance on its surface.

"It's true!" exclaimed the duke. "By all the Saints, he's found it!"

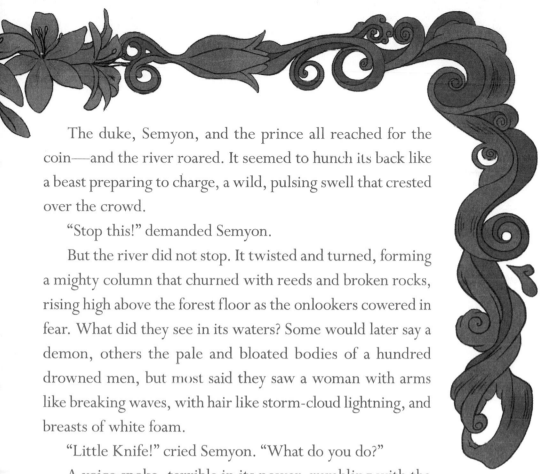

The duke, Semyon, and the prince all reached for the coin—and the river roared. It seemed to hunch its back like a beast preparing to charge, a wild, pulsing swell that crested over the crowd.

"Stop this!" demanded Semyon.

But the river did not stop. It twisted and turned, forming a mighty column that churned with reeds and broken rocks, rising high above the forest floor as the onlookers cowered in fear. What did they see in its waters? Some would later say a demon, others the pale and bloated bodies of a hundred drowned men, but most said they saw a woman with arms like breaking waves, with hair like storm-cloud lightning, and breasts of white foam.

"Little Knife!" cried Semyon. "What do you do?"

A voice spoke, terrible in its power, rumbling with the sound of rain-choked waterfalls, of tempests and floods. "I am no blunt knife to cut your sorry bread," it said. "I feed the fields and drown the harvest. I am bounty and destruction."

The people fell to their knees and wept. The duke clutched the priest's hand.

"Then who are you?" begged Semyon. "What are you?"

"Your tongue is not fit for my true name," the river boomed. "I was once a spirit of the Isenvee, the great North Sea, and I roamed these lands freely, tumbling down through Fjerda, to the rocky coast and back again. Then, by unhappy accident, my spirit was trapped here, bound by this dam, free to run but doomed to return, forced to keep that cursed wheel spinning, in endless service to this miserable hamlet. Now the dam is no more. Your greed and the prince's axe have seen to that."

It was Yeva who found the courage to speak, for the question to ask seemed simple. "What do you want, river?"

"It was I who built the tower of trees," said the river. "And I who earned the mirror from Baba Anezka. It was I who found the magic coin. And now I say to you, Yeva Luchova: Will you remain here with the father who tried to sell you, or the prince who hoped to buy you, or the man too weak to solve his riddles for himself? Or will you come with me and be bride to nothing but the shore?"

Yeva looked at Semyon, at the prince, at her father standing beside the priest. Then she tore the veil from her face— her eyes were bright, her cheeks were flushed and glowing. The people cried out and shielded their gazes, for in that moment she was too lovely to look at. She was terrifying in her beauty, bright like a devouring star.

Yeva leapt from the banks and the river caught her up in its waters, keeping her afloat as her jeweled kokoshnik sank and her silken gown billowed around her. She hovered there on the surface, a flower caught in the current. Then, as the duke stood stunned and quaking in his wet boots, the river

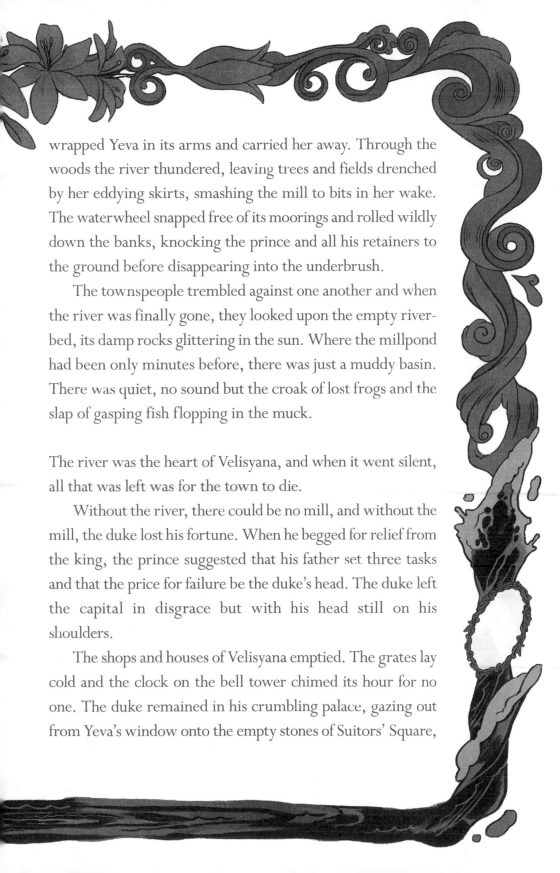

wrapped Yeva in its arms and carried her away. Through the woods the river thundered, leaving trees and fields drenched by her eddying skirts, smashing the mill to bits in her wake. The waterwheel snapped free of its moorings and rolled wildly down the banks, knocking the prince and all his retainers to the ground before disappearing into the underbrush.

The townspeople trembled against one another and when the river was finally gone, they looked upon the empty river-bed, its damp rocks glittering in the sun. Where the millpond had been only minutes before, there was just a muddy basin. There was quiet, no sound but the croak of lost frogs and the slap of gasping fish flopping in the muck.

The river was the heart of Velisyana, and when it went silent, all that was left was for the town to die.

Without the river, there could be no mill, and without the mill, the duke lost his fortune. When he begged for relief from the king, the prince suggested that his father set three tasks and that the price for failure be the duke's head. The duke left the capital in disgrace but with his head still on his shoulders.

The shops and houses of Velisyana emptied. The grates lay cold and the clock on the bell tower chimed its hour for no one. The duke remained in his crumbling palace, gazing out from Yeva's window onto the empty stones of Suitors' Square,

and cursing Semyon. If you keep very still, you may see him there, surrounded by stone lilies, awaiting the water's return.

But you will not glimpse lovely Yeva. The river carried her all the way to the seashore, and there she stayed. She said her prayers in a tiny chapel where the waves ran right up to the door, and each day she sat by the ocean's edge and watched the tides come and go. She lived in happy solitude, and grew old, and never worried when her beauty faded, for in her reflection she always saw a free woman.

As for poor Semyon, he was driven out of town, blamed for the tragedy that had befallen it. His misery was short, however. Not long after he left Velisyana, he withered to a husk and died. He would not let any drop of water pass his lips, certain it would betray him.

Now, if you have been foolish enough to wander from the path, it is up to you to make your way back to the road. Follow the voices of your worried companions and perhaps this time your feet will lead you past the rusting skeleton of a waterwheel resting in a meadow where it has no right to be.

If you are lucky, you will find your friends again. They will pat you on the back and soothe you with their laughter. But as you leave that dark gap in the trees behind, remember that to use a thing is not to own it. And should you ever take a bride, listen closely to her questions. In them you may hear her true name like the thunder of a lost river, like the sighing of the sea.

THE SOLDIER PRINCE

IN THE END, THE CLOCKSMITH WAS

to blame. But Mr. and Mrs. Zelverhaus should not have let him into the house. This is the problem with even lesser demons. They come to your doorstep in velvet coats and polished shoes. They tip their hats and smile and demonstrate good table manners. They never show you their tails.

The clocksmith was called Droessen, though there were rumors he was not Kerch, but Ravkan—an exiled nobleman's son, or possibly a disgraced Fabrikator, banished from his homeland for reasons unknown. His shop was on Wijnstraat, where the canal crooked like a finger beckoning you closer, and he was known the world over for his fantastical timepieces, for the little bronze birds that sang different songs at every hour, and for the tiny wooden men and women who played out amusing scenes at midnight, then again at noon.

He'd risen to fame when he'd built a clockwork fortune-teller that, when a certain lever was pulled, would move its polished wooden hand over your palm and predict your future. A merchant brought his daughter to the shop before her wedding. The fortune-teller had clicked and clanked, opened its wooden jaws, and said, "You will find great love and more gold than you could wish for." He bought the clever automaton for his beloved child as a wedding gift, and everyone who attended the celebration agreed they'd never seen a bride and groom more in love. But the ship his daughter boarded to begin her honeymoon was so heavily weighted with goods and coin that it sank at the first breath of a storm and all were lost to the uncaring sea. When the news reached the merchant, he remembered the automaton's clever words and, drunk on misery and brandy, smashed the thing to bits with his own fists. His servants found him lying amid the wreckage the next day, still weeping, shirt stained, knuckles bloody. But the sad tale drew new customers to the clock-smith's door in search of the marvelous and uncanny.

In his shop, they found many wonders: tawny golden lions who hunted mechanical gazelles across a velvet veldt; a garden of enamel flowers pollinated by jeweled humming-birds that whirred and buzzed on wires so thin they truly seemed to be flying; a rotating calendar clock—kept on the highest shelf away from curious young eyes—populated by human automata who committed different ghastly murders every month. On the first of January, a duel was fought on an icy field, puffs of smoke emerging from the combatants' pistols with tinny pops. In February, a man climbed atop his wife to strangle her as her lover cowered beneath the rumpled bed. And so on.

Despite his accomplishments, Droessen was still a young man, and he became a coveted party guest among the merchant families who served as his customers. He dressed well, conversed pleasantly, and always brought charming gifts to his hosts. It was true that when he entered a room, the people there would find themselves shifting uneasily on their feet, rubbing their arms at the sudden chill, wondering if a door somewhere needed closing. Yet, somehow, it only made him more interesting. Without that sense of the unwholesome, Droessen might have been a pathetic character, a grown man fiddling with what were little more than elaborate toys. Instead, there was much talk of his smart velvet coat and his nimble white fingers. Mamas clutched their handkerchiefs and daughters blushed when he was near.

Every winter, the Zelverhauses, a wealthy family of tea merchants, hosted the clocksmith at their country home for the parties and entertainments given during the week of Nachtspel. The house itself was a model of merchant restraint, all dark wood, stolid brick, and hard lines. But it was perfectly situated by a lake that froze early for skating, and it was effusive in its comforts, with fireplaces alight in each room to keep the house always snug and merry, and every floor polished to the warm syrup shine of a glazed cake.

From the very first year Droessen visited the house by the lake, troubling rumors followed. During his first stay, the Zelverhauses' neighbors, the De Kloets, wore mourning through Nachtspel and into the new year after Elise De Kloet gave birth to a baby composed entirely of dandelion fluff. When a careless maid opened a window, it blew away at the first gust. The next year, one of the Zelverhaus cousins had a bloom of little gray mushrooms break out over her forehead, and a boy visiting from Lij claimed he'd woken to find a single wing jutting from between his shoulder blades, but that it had burned to ash when he'd passed through a sunbeam in the hall.

Were these strange occurrences linked to the clocksmith? No one could be certain, but they whispered about it.

"That young man Droessen is a charming fellow, but most unusual, and peculiarities seem to follow him," a woman once said to Althea Zelverhaus.

"Most unusual," Althea agreed, but she knew that Droessen accepted few invitations, and that this woman with her fussy lace collar could only hope Droessen might someday make an appearance at one of her salons. So Althea smiled, repeated, "Most unusual indeed," and left it at that.

It all seemed harmless at the time.

Droessen was not just unusual in his talents or his habits, but also in his greed. He had spent his life tinkering in corners, bowing and scraping to the merchants who graced his door, and he had learned early that talent was not enough. When he realized customers preferred to buy from handsome faces, he had his hair cut into a fashionable style and made himself a set of even white teeth so fine that they sometimes fooled even him. When he saw the respect his patrons gave military men, he'd worn a painful brace to correct his stoop and had the shoulders of his jackets padded so that he could affect a soldier's upright bearing. Because he'd discerned that popularity was dependent upon demand, he made sure to refuse two out of every three invitations.

But he grew tired of eating cold dinners in his darkened shop, the doors locked and lights turned off to create the illusion that he was somewhere having fun. He wanted a grand house instead of a dank rented room. He wanted money for his inventions. He never wanted to have to say *yes sir, no sir, right away sir* again. So he would have to marry well, but whom could he make his bride? The young women of marriageable age who came to his shop with their fathers and flirted with him at parties saw him as a bit of danger. They would never take a mere tradesman seriously as a prospect. No, he needed a girl, still malleable, one that he could make admire him.

Clara Zelverhaus was not yet twelve then, lovely enough, rich enough, and of just the dreamy disposition he required.

He would learn her wants and wishes. He would deliver them to her, and in time, she would come to love him for it. Or so he thought. Droessen knew the properties of every kind of wood and paint and lacquer; he could finesse the gears of a clock until they spun with silent precision. And yet, though he could smile readily, charm easily, and play the part of a gentleman, he had never truly understood people or the workings of their steady-running but inconstant hearts.

The house by the lake bustled with excitement whenever the clocksmith arrived, and the children were always first to greet him when he emerged from his coach. They would trail after the house servants who unloaded his luggage, the trunks and chests invariably filled with splendid objects—dolls in the costumes of the Komedie Brute, music boxes, rows of cannons, even a grand castle to defend.

Though young Frederik liked to stage long battles, he would eventually grow bored—no matter how finely made the tiny armaments and troops—and put on his coat to go find mischief in the snow. Clara was different. To Droessen's dismay, she ignored the elaborate clockworks and mechanicals he brought her, and spared only a small smile for the exquisite replica of a Ravkan palace with its carved wooden arches and domes plated in real gold. But she could play for hour upon hour with the dolls he made, vanishing into the house and emerging only when the dinner bell had been rung more than once, and her mother had been forced to shout up the stairs and down every corridor for Clara to cease her make-believe and come be fed.

So over many long nights in his workshop, Droessen made for her an elegant, pale-eyed nutcracker with a bright blue coat and shiny black boots, a wicked little bayonet tucked into one blocky fist.

"You must tell him all your secrets," said Droessen as he placed the doll in Clara's arms, "and he will keep them safe for you."

She promised that she would.

Clara's mother and father assumed that as she grew older, Clara would leave such childish things behind and begin to care more for dresses and the prospect of a husband and a family, as her friends did. But as the years passed, Clara stayed the same strange, dreamy girl who might let a sentence trail off because some secret, unspoken thought had caught her, who would endure language lessons and cotillions with distracted grace, then smile and drift off to some dim corner where whatever invisible world her mind had conjured might unfurl without distraction.

When Clara turned sixteen, her parents threw her a grand party. She ate sweets, teased her brother, and danced beautifully with every eligible merchant's son in attendance.

Althea Zelverhaus heaved a happy sigh of relief and went to bed without a worry for the first time in months. But that night, when she woke from her sleep, she had the sudden need to check on her children. Frederik, seventeen and happy to be home from school, snored loudly in his room. Clara's bed was empty.

Althea found Clara curled on her side by the hearth in the dining room, one of her favorite dolls in her arms. She saw that her daughter had put on her slippers and coat and that both were wet with snow.

"Clara," her mother whispered, rocking her shoulder gently to rouse her from sleep. "Why did you go outside?"

Clara blinked drowsily at her mother and smiled a sweet, vague smile. "He loves the snow," she said, then clutched her doll closer and fell back into slumber.

Althea looked down at her daughter in her nightgown and damp coat, the ugly little face of the wooden doll in her arms. It was Althea's least favorite of Droessen's creations, a nutcracker with a grotesque smile and garish blue coat. Standing there, she had the sudden thought that inviting the clocksmith into her home years ago had been a terrible mistake. Her fingers itched to snatch the doll from Clara and toss the wretched thing into the fire.

She reached for the nutcracker, then yanked her hand back. For a moment—it could not be and yet she was sure of it—it seemed the toy soldier had turned his square head to look at her. And there had been sorrow in his eyes. *Nonsense*, she told herself, cradling her hand to her chest. *You are becoming as fanciful as Clara.*

Even so, she stepped away, certain that if she dared touch the nutcracker, dared throw it into the flames, the thing would cry out. Or worse, it might not burn at all.

She put a blanket over her daughter and returned to her own bed, and when she woke the next morning, she'd all but forgotten her foolish notions of the night before. Nachtspel was beginning and her guests would soon arrive. She rose and rang for tea, seeking fortification for the arduous day ahead. But when she went downstairs to see to the menus, she checked to make sure that Clara was sorting chestnuts with the cook, and paused once by the cabinet in the dining room where they displayed Droessen's gifts. Not for any reason really. Certainly not to make sure that the nutcracker was safely locked away behind the glass.

Clara knew her mother worried. She worried too. When she was seated at dinner or at some party with a friend or even occasionally at her lessons, she would think, *This is*

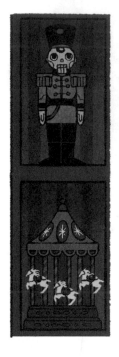

pleasant. This is enough. But then she'd arrive back home and she'd find herself in the dining room in front of the cabinet. She'd reach once more for the nutcracker and take him to her bedroom or up to the attic, where she would lie on her side amid the dust motes and whisper to him until he whispered back.

It always took some time and felt a bit awkward at the start. It had been easier when she was a child, but she was self-conscious now in a way she hadn't been then. Clara felt foolish moving the nutcracker's arms, making his jaws open and close to answer her questions. She couldn't help but see herself as others would: a young woman, nearly grown, lying on a dusty attic floor, talking to a doll. But she persisted, reminding him of the adventures they'd had, though they had changed a bit over the years.

You are a soldier. You fought bravely on the front and returned to me, your darling.

You killed a monster for me once, a rat with seven heads, on the last evening of Nachtspel.

You are a prince I woke from a curse with a kiss. I loved you when no other would, and you chose me for your queen.

She would place a walnut between his hard teeth—then *crack,* the noise so loud in the still attic.

Are you my soldier? she would ask, again and again. *Are you my prince?*

Are you my darling?

Are you mine?

And at last, sometimes after mere moments, sometimes after what seemed like forever, his jaws would move and he would speak.

Are you my soldier?

"I am."

Are you my prince?

"I am."

As he spoke, his limbs would grow, his chest would broaden, his skin would turn supple.

Are you my darling?

"I am."

Are you mine?

"Sweet Clara," the nutcracker would say, tall and handsome and perfect now, the grotesque rictus of his face softened into tender human lines. "Of course I am."

He would offer her his hand and with a *whoosh,* they would fly through the attic window, out into the cold. She would find herself atop a great white horse, clutching her beloved's waist, whooping with joy as they sailed through the night, past the clouds, and into the lands beyond.

She did not know what to call the place he brought her

to. Fairyland? The Land of Dreaming? When she was a child, it had looked different. They'd ridden a spun-sugar boat on a sweet water stream. She'd walked on marzipan cobblestones past gingerbread villages and castles made of marmalade. Children had danced for them and greeted the nutcracker as their prince. They'd sat on gumdrop cushions and his mother had called Clara a hero.

Now much of that was gone, replaced by deep green forests and shining rivers. The air was warm and silken like the places she'd read about—summer lands where the sun shone all year and balmy breezes were thick with the scent of orange blossoms. The white horse carried them to new places every time: a valley where wild ponies with manes of mist ranged; a quicksilver lake as big as a sea, where they met with dashing pirates who had gems for teeth; a palace of dogwood walls and larkspur towers that rose from a grove where clouds of butterflies hovered, wings chiming like bells. The queen there had pale green skin perpetually dotted with dew and her crown rose like antlers, directly from her forehead, in twists of bone that gleamed like mother-of-pearl. When she touched her lips to Clara's mouth, Clara felt two delicate wings sprout from her back. She spent the day flying, swooping and dropping like a hummingbird, pausing only to drink honey wine and let the queen twine helle-bore into her hair.

And yet it was not enough. Did her prince love her? Could he? Why did he return her to her home at the end of every magical journey? It wasn't fair to show her that such a world could exist and then take it from her so cruelly. If he loved her as she loved him, surely she would be allowed to stay. At every visit, she hoped his mother would greet her as a daughter rather than a guest, that she would open a new door on a wedding bower.

Instead the dinner gong would sound or she'd hear Frederik stomping up the stairs or her moth-er's voice calling, and she would find herself sailing back through the starry sky to the cold, empty attic, her joints stiff from lying on the slats of the floor, the hard body of the nutcracker beside her, shrunken and ugly, the leavings of walnuts between his wooden jaws.

She would place him back in the cabinet and return to her parents. She would try to smile at the drab world around her, though her cheeks were still warm with sunshine, though her tongue was still sweet with the taste of honey wine.

As for the nutcracker, he was sure of nothing, and sometimes it frightened him. His memories were a blur. He knew there had been a battle, many battles, and that he'd fought bravely. Hadn't he been made for it? He had been born with a bayonet in hand.

He'd fought for her. But where was she now? Where was Clara? She of the star eyes and soft hands. They'd faced the Rat King together. She'd wrapped him in her kerchief. He'd bled into its white lace folds.

Clara. Why could he remember her name and not his own?

He'd fought bravely. At least he thought he had.

The details were hard to recall—the screams, the blood, the squealing of the rats with their thick pink tails and teeth like yellow knives, gums red with blood from the bites they'd taken. How those teeth had glistened in the golden light! Had it been sunrise or sunset? He remembered the smell of pines.

He squinted now, from his place in the barracks, through the wide plate-glass window. But the view confused him too. He could see a long table set for a feast, candied fruit, pine boughs laid upon the mantel. But everything was far too large, as if seen through a distorting lens.

He counted the brass buttons on his fine blue coat. Whose uniform did he wear? Which country was his home? Who had polished the dust of the battlefield from his boots?

Had there been a battle? Had he fought or only dreamed of fighting? Other memories seemed clearer. He was a prince, her prince. She'd told him so. He'd wanted nothing more than to show her all the wonders of his home, to explore its endless horizons. And yet, why did he feel no gladness when he returned to the palace where he supposed he had been raised? Why was everything as new to him as it seemed to be to her?

Nothing felt certain. He was sure the streets they'd walked had been narrow before, bordered by houses with frosted roofs instead of wide boulevards that swept past mansions tiled in gold. Gifts of nougat and sweet cream had pleased Clara before, but now he gave her jewels and gowns because he knew she would prefer them. How he came by this knowledge, he could not fathom.

He watched the people at the table—giants it seemed, and yet there was Clara, who he'd held in his

arms. Sometimes her eyes strayed to him and he tried to cry out to her, but he had no voice, no way to move his limbs. He must have been injured.

He watched her eat her supper and speak to . . . it took him a moment to remember—Frederik, her brother, a commander in the war, bold and sometimes reckless, but the nutcracker had executed every order given. There was another familiar face at the table, a man with long hair and pale blue eyes who studied Clara as if she were a piece of machinery to be taken apart and put back together. *I know him*, thought the nutcracker. *Droessen. I know his name.* But he could not think how. This man did not look like a soldier, though he had the bearing of one.

A memory clawed up through the nutcracker's thoughts. He was lying on his back, staring at shelves packed with clocks and slumped marionettes. He smelled paint and oil, the fresh shavings of wood. Droessen loomed over him, huge and cold-eyed with terrible focus. *I was wounded*, thought the nutcracker. Droessen must be a surgeon then. But that wasn't quite right.

The meal ended. The guests drank little glasses of garnet-colored liquid. Clara sipped at hers, cheeks flushed. They played games before the fire, and someone shouted, "It's snowing!"

They raced to gather around the great window, but the

nutcracker could not see well enough to tell what interested them so. There was talk and laughter and then they were all racing out of the dining room to . . . he did not know. He did not know what lay beyond this room. It might be a palace or a prison or a pine grove. He knew only that they were gone.

Servants came and banked the fire, doused the candles. He'd fought bravely, and yet somehow, he always ended up here, alone in the dark.

Clara did not come that night.

The nutcracker awoke to shrill squeaking and found the Rat King at his bedside. He sat up hurriedly and reached for his saber, realizing as he grasped at his sword belt that his weapon was gone, and at the same time, that he could move again.

"Peace, Captain," the Rat King said. "I have not come to fight, only to talk." His voice was high and reedy, and his whiskers twitched—yet the monster still managed to look grave when he spoke.

This creature had the nutcracker's blood on his filthy paws, and would have murdered Clara too. But if he came to speak under conditions of a truce, the nutcracker supposed he must honor that. He dipped his chin the barest amount.

The Rat King adjusted his felt cloak and looked around. "Do you have anything to drink? If only they'd stuck you in a liquor cabinet, eh?"

Cabinet. The nutcracker frowned at the word. He'd been resting in the barracks, had he not? And yet as he looked around, he saw that what had simply seemed the vague shapes of beds and other soldiers were strange items indeed. Girls with glass eyes and stiffly curled hair were propped against the wall. Rows of soldiers with bayonets at their shoulders marched in frozen lockstep.

"I don't know," he replied at last.

The Rat King perched on the gilded lip of an enormous music box. But was it enormous? Or were they small?

"When was the last time you ate?" he asked.

The nutcracker hesitated. Had it been with Clara? In the Land of Snow? The Court of Flowers? "I can't recall."

The Rat King sighed. "You should eat something."

"I do eat." Surely he did?

"Something other than walnuts." The Rat King scratched behind his ear with his little pink claws, then removed the crown from his gray head and placed it gently in his lap. "Do you know I started life as a sugar mouse?"

The nutcracker's confusion must have shown, for the Rat King continued, "I realize that's hard to believe, but I was just a confection. Not even for eating, just for looking at, a

160

charming little marvel, a testament to my maker's skill. It seemed a shame that I should go untasted. My first thought was, *I wish someone would eat me.* But that was enough."

"Enough for what?"

"To get free of the cabinet. Wanting is why people get up in the morning. It gives them something to dream of at night. The more I wanted, the more I became like them, the more real I became."

"I am perfectly real," protested the nutcracker.

The Rat King looked at him sadly. Sitting there, without his crown in the dim light, his whiskers drooping slightly, he looked less like a dreadful monster than a sweet-faced mouse.

A memory came to the nutcracker. "You had seven heads—"

The Rat King nodded. "Clara imagined me fearsome, and so fearsome I became. But a rat can't live with seven heads always talking and arguing. It took us hours to make the simplest decisions, so when the others were asleep, I cut them from me one by one. There was an awful amount of blood." He shifted slightly in his seat. "Who are you when she isn't here, Captain?"

"I am . . ." He wavered. "I am a soldier."

"Are you? What is your rank? Lieutenant?"

"Lieutenant, of course," answered the nutcracker.

"Or is it captain?" the Rat King inquired.

Are you my soldier? Are you my prince?

"I—"

"Surely you must know your rank."

Are you my darling?

"Who are you when no one picks you up to hold you?" asked the Rat King. "When no one is looking at you, or whispering to you, who are you then? Tell me your name, soldier."

Are you mine? The nutcracker opened his mouth to answer, but he could not recall. He was Clara's prince, her protector. He had a name. Of course he had a name. Only the shock of battle had driven it from his mind.

He'd fought bravely.

He'd taken Clara to meet his mother.

He'd ridden a horse through a gleaming field of stars.

He was heir to nothing. He was prince of a marzipan palace.

He slept on spun sugar. He slept on gold.

"You walk and talk and laugh when Clara dreams with you," said the Rat King. "But those are her desires. They cannot sustain you. My life began with wanting something

162

for myself. I wished to be eaten, then I wished to eat. A piece of cake. A bit of bacon. A sip of wine. I wanted these things from their table. That was when I moved my legs and blinked my eyes. I wanted to see beyond the cabinet door. That was when I found my way into the walls. There I met my rat brothers. They are not charming or pretty, but they live even when no one is looking. I have made a life in the walls with them, unwatched and undesired. I know who I am without anyone there to tell me."

"But why did you attack us?" said the nutcracker. The blood. The screaming. "I know that was real."

"As real as anything. When Clara was a child, she dreamed of heroes, and heroes require a foe. But the desire to conquer was the will she gave me, not my own. It is simple hunger that keeps me alive now: crumbs from the cupboard, cheese in the larder, a chance to venture outside to the woodpile, see the wide sky, feel the cold bite of the snow."

Snow. Another memory emerged—not the place of dreaming that Clara so longed for, but a new place beyond the cabinet. She had taken him outside one night. He had felt *cold*. He had seen clouds moving over the starlit sky. He had taken the air into his lungs,

felt them expand, exhaled, seen the puff of his breath in the chill night. He remembered trees clustered against the horizon, a road, the desperate desire to see what lay beyond it.

"That's it, Captain," said the Rat King as he slowly rose and placed the crown back atop his head. "It helps to live in the shelter of the walls where there are no human eyes to look upon me. It helps to be a rat who no one wants to look at. Your desire must be stronger if you wish to get free of the cabinet, if you wish to be real. She loves you, though, and that will make it harder."

Clara loved him. And he loved her. Didn't he?

The Rat King nudged open the cabinet door. "One last thing," he said as he skittered onto the ledge. "Beware of Droessen. You were meant to be a gift to Clara, a means of enchanting her and nothing more."

"He loves her too, then?"

"Who knows what the clocksmith loves? Best not to ask. I think the answer would please no one."

The Rat King vanished, his pink tail slithering behind him.

Clara tried to stay away. She managed it for a night, the wine and the guests a happy distraction. But the next day, she snuck from the skating out on the lake and ran to the cabinet, clutching the nutcracker beneath her coat and racing up the stairs to the quiet of the attic.

Are you my soldier? she whispered as the cold winter light made bright squares on the dusty floor.

Are you my prince? She tucked a walnut between his jaws.

Are you my darling?

Are you mine?

It did not take long this time. The nutcracker's body stretched and his head split to reveal her handsome prince's face.

"I am," he said. He smiled as he always did, touched his gentle hand to her face, but then trouble came into his eyes.

He pressed his fingertips to his mouth, licked his lips, and frowned as if the taste of walnuts did not agree with him.

"Where will we go today, my prince?" Clara asked.

But he did not take her hand. He sat up, ran his fingers through the beam of sunlight from the window, and then rose to peer out through the glass.

"Outside," he said. "I'd like to see where that road goes."

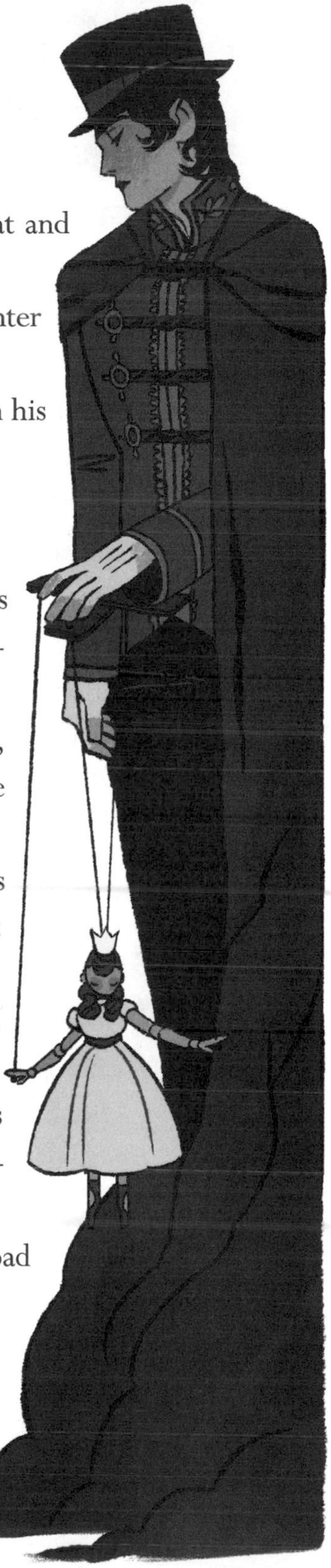

165

The request was so ordinary and yet so unexpected, Clara couldn't quite make sense of it for a moment. "That isn't possible."

"It's what I want." He said the words as if he'd made some great discovery, a new invention, a magic spell. His smile was radiant. "Dear Clara, it's what I want."

"But it cannot be," she replied, unsure of how to explain.

His cheer vanished and she saw fear in his eyes. "I cannot return to the cabinet."

Now she understood. *At last. At last.*

She took his hands. "You need never return to the cabinet. Only take me with you to your home and I will forsake this place. We can stay forever in the land of dreams."

He hesitated. "That is what you want."

"Yes," said Clara, tilting her head up. "It is what I have always wanted." The fervor of it filled her. Sweat broke out over her neck. *Kiss me,* she willed him. In all the stories a kiss was required. *Take me from this place.*

She could not wait. Clara stood on tiptoe and pressed her lips to his. She tasted walnut and something else, maybe lacquer. But he did not take her hand, did not draw her closer. She felt no wind on her face nor horse galloping beneath her. When she opened her eyes, she was still in the same dull, dusty attic.

The nutcracker brushed his knuckles against her cheek. "I want to go outside," he said.

Now Clara scowled and stamped her foot as if she were the child she'd been when Droessen had first placed the nutcracker in her arms instead of a girl of seventeen. *I want.* She was not sure why those words enraged her so. Perhaps it was because the nutcracker had never spoken them to her before.

"I told you," she said more sharply than she intended. "It cannot be. You don't belong here."

"I will take you outside," said Frederik.

Clara flinched at the sound of her brother's voice. He stood at the top of the attic stairs, gazing at the nutcracker with fascinated eyes.

"Get out!" she cried. He was not supposed to be here. He was not supposed to share this. She rushed at him, frantic with fear and shame, and tried to strike him, to push him back toward the stairs.

But Frederik simply held her wrists, keeping her at bay. He was a year older and far stronger. He

shook his head, his eyes never leaving the nutcracker. "Stop it, Clara."

"I remember you," said the nutcracker, watching him. He came to attention and saluted. "My commander."

Frederik gave Clara a warning look and let her hands drop. With a bemused grin, he returned the nutcracker's salute.

"Yes," said Frederik, walking toward him. "Your commander. I sent you to die a hundred times."

The nutcracker frowned. "I remember."

"How changed you are," Frederik murmured.

Confusion crossed the nutcracker's face. "Am I?"

Frederik nodded. "I'll take you downstairs," he said softly, as if coaxing a kitten with a bit of food. "I'll take you outside."

"Where does the road go?" asked the nutcracker.

"To Ketterdam. A magical place. I'll tell you all about it."

"Frederik," said Clara angrily. "You cannot do this."

"We'll say he's my friend from school. We'll say he's just enlisted."

She shook her head. "We can't."

"Mama will be so pleased to have a dashing young man

168

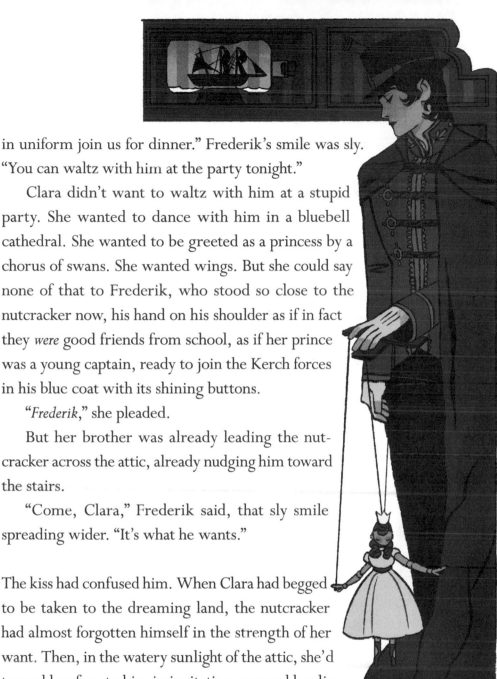

in uniform join us for dinner." Frederik's smile was sly. "You can waltz with him at the party tonight."

Clara didn't want to waltz with him at a stupid party. She wanted to dance with him in a bluebell cathedral. She wanted to be greeted as a princess by a chorus of swans. She wanted wings. But she could say none of that to Frederik, who stood so close to the nutcracker now, his hand on his shoulder as if in fact they *were* good friends from school, as if her prince was a young captain, ready to join the Kerch forces in his blue coat with its shining buttons.

"*Frederik*," she pleaded.

But her brother was already leading the nutcracker across the attic, already nudging him toward the stairs.

"Come, Clara," Frederik said, that sly smile spreading wider. "It's what he wants."

The kiss had confused him. When Clara had begged to be taken to the dreaming land, the nutcracker had almost forgotten himself in the strength of her want. Then, in the watery sunlight of the attic, she'd turned her face to him in invitation, pressed her lips

to his, and he'd felt desire—hers or his? It had been impossible to untangle, but he must have wanted her, because suddenly he could feel the cold from the window again, drawing him outward to the gravel drive, the woods, the snow. Then Frederik was there with his blazing eyes and claiming gaze, the power of his longing bright as a flame, dangerous. The nutcracker felt his resolve soften, turn waxen and easily molded. He thought if he looked at the place where Frederik had touched his shoulder, he might see the deep depressions of Frederik's fingers still there, the emphatic divot of his thumb. The nutcracker's thoughts of the road and what might lie beyond faded.

Down the stairs they went. The house was already filling with guests for the last evening of Nachtspel. How luminous they all were, how sharp in their lines, how needful their eyes as they looked at him in his false uniform and saw a lost son, a lover, a friend, a threat. He managed to greet Clara and Frederik's parents, execute the appropriate bow.

Frederik called him Josef, and so he was Josef. Clara said she'd met him one afternoon at a sledding party and it was so. Where was he from? Zierfoort. Who was his commanding officer?

"Father," complained Frederik with a wink at the nutcracker, "do not vex Josef with so many questions. I

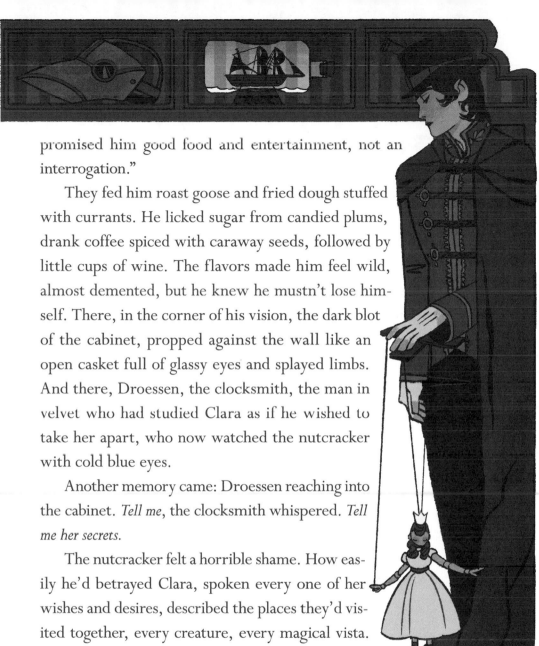

promised him good food and entertainment, not an interrogation."

They fed him roast goose and fried dough stuffed with currants. He licked sugar from candied plums, drank coffee spiced with caraway seeds, followed by little cups of wine. The flavors made him feel wild, almost demented, but he knew he mustn't lose himself. There, in the corner of his vision, the dark blot of the cabinet, propped against the wall like an open casket full of glassy eyes and splayed limbs. And there, Droessen, the clocksmith, the man in velvet who had studied Clara as if he wished to take her apart, who now watched the nutcracker with cold blue eyes.

Another memory came: Droessen reaching into the cabinet. *Tell me*, the clocksmith whispered. *Tell me her secrets.*

The nutcracker felt a horrible shame. How easily he'd betrayed Clara, spoken every one of her wishes and desires, described the places they'd visited together, every creature, every magical vista. No torture had been necessary. He'd simply talked. He had not been made to be a soldier but a spy.

He could make no amends for that

now. He knew he must hold to the shape of himself, to the desire for the outside just a few steps, just a door or an open window away. *Ketterdam*—he must remember. But the world began to blur—the scent of perfume, perspiration, Frederik's arm around his shoulder, Clara's feverish eyes as they danced. How he knew the steps he could not say, but they spun and spun and she whispered to him, "Take me from this place."

He kissed her beneath the stairs. He kissed Frederik in the darkened hall.

"Do you love her?" Frederik asked. "Could you love me too?"

He loved them both. He loved no one. In the dark shadows beyond the circle of light cast by the flames of the fire, the nutcracker caught the shine of black eyes, the glint of a tiny crown, and knew it must be the Rat King. *My life began with wanting something for myself.*

The nutcracker thought of the bend in the road and what might lie beyond it.

One by one the guests departed in their carriages or headed upstairs to fall into their beds.

"He can sleep in my room," said Frederik.

"Yes," said the nutcracker.

"I will come to meet you," murmured Clara.

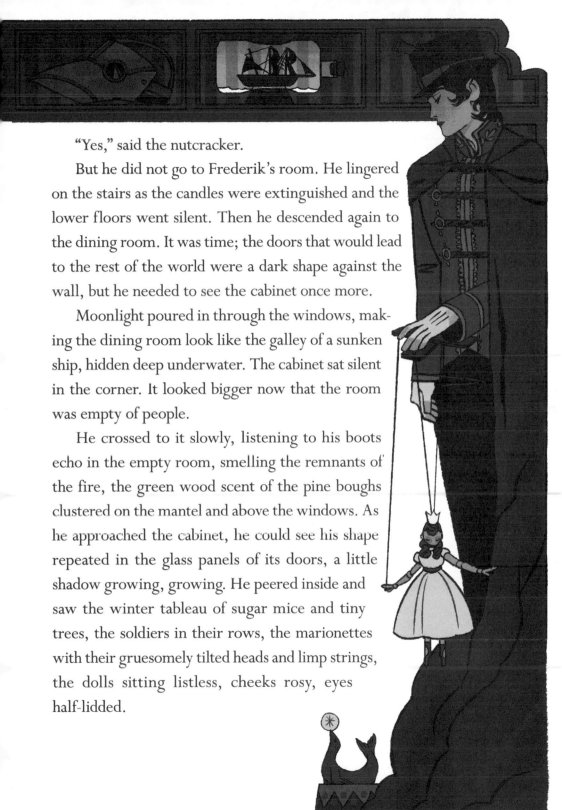

"Yes," said the nutcracker.

But he did not go to Frederik's room. He lingered on the stairs as the candles were extinguished and the lower floors went silent. Then he descended again to the dining room. It was time; the doors that would lead to the rest of the world were a dark shape against the wall, but he needed to see the cabinet once more.

Moonlight poured in through the windows, making the dining room look like the galley of a sunken ship, hidden deep underwater. The cabinet sat silent in the corner. It looked bigger now that the room was empty of people.

He crossed to it slowly, listening to his boots echo in the empty room, smelling the remnants of the fire, the green wood scent of the pine boughs clustered on the mantel and above the windows. As he approached the cabinet, he could see his shape repeated in the glass panels of its doors, a little shadow growing, growing. He peered inside and saw the winter tableau of sugar mice and tiny trees, the soldiers in their rows, the marionettes with their gruesomely tilted heads and limp strings, the dolls sitting listless, cheeks rosy, eyes half-lidded.

"I know you," he whispered, and touched his fingers to the glass. The perfect little fairies dangling from wires with their filigree wings and their gossamer skirts, wide-hipped Mother Ginger, and the Queen of the Grove with her green skin and silvery antlers.

"I made them all." The nutcracker whirled to find Droessen watching him from the center of the room. His voice was smooth as buttercream. "Every hinge, every daub of paint. I fashioned the world of her dreaming from the details you told me. And yet it is the toys she loves and not me." He walked so silently, as if he might be made of feathers or smoke. "Do you admire my handiwork?"

The nutcracker knew he should nod and say that he did, yes, he did, for this was the clocksmith the Rat King had warned him about, the one who had wanted Clara, or her wealth, or her family, or something else entirely for himself. But the nutcracker found it hard to speak.

"I confess," said the clocksmith, "I am proud. I love to have my creations looked upon, see children smile. I eat the wonder in their eyes. But it seems not even I knew the marvels I might achieve."

He was close now, and he smelled of tobacco and linseed oil. He smelled familiar.

"I should go," the nutcracker said, relieved to find he could still speak at all.

Droessen laughed softly. "Where could you possibly have to go?"

"To Zierfoort. To my regiment."

"You are no soldier."

I am, thought the nutcracker. *No*, he scolded himself. *You are pretending to be a soldier. It is not the same thing.*

The clocksmith laughed again. "You have no idea what you are."

Josef. That was his name, wasn't it? Or had it been another guest at the party?

"Who are you?" asked the nutcracker, wishing he could back away, but there was nothing behind him except the glass cabinet. "What are you?"

"A humble tradesman."

"Why did you make me betray Clara?"

Now a smile split Droessen's face, and none of the kind ladies and handsome gentlemen who had welcomed the clocksmith into their parlors would have recognized this wolf, his many teeth. "You owe no loyalty to Clara. *I* made you in my workshop," he

175

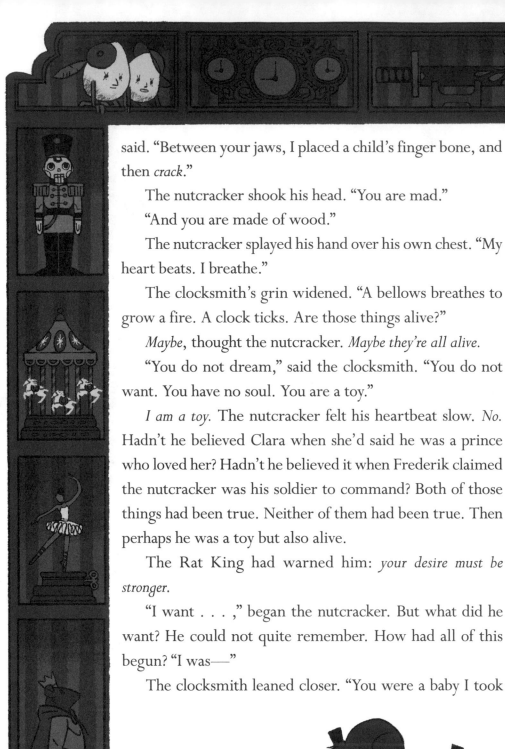

said. "Between your jaws, I placed a child's finger bone, and then *crack*."

The nutcracker shook his head. "You are mad."

"And you are made of wood."

The nutcracker splayed his hand over his own chest. "My heart beats. I breathe."

The clocksmith's grin widened. "A bellows breathes to grow a fire. A clock ticks. Are those things alive?"

Maybe, thought the nutcracker. *Maybe they're all alive.*

"You do not dream," said the clocksmith. "You do not want. You have no soul. You are a toy."

I am a toy. The nutcracker felt his heartbeat slow. *No.* Hadn't he believed Clara when she'd said he was a prince who loved her? Hadn't he believed it when Frederik claimed the nutcracker was his soldier to command? Both of those things had been true. Neither of them had been true. Then perhaps he was a toy but also alive.

The Rat King had warned him: *your desire must be stronger.*

"I want . . . ," began the nutcracker. But what did he want? He could not quite remember. How had all of this begun? "I was—"

The clocksmith leaned closer. "You were a baby I took

from a foundling home. I fed you on sawdust until you were more wood than boy."

"No," said the nutcracker, but he felt his belly fill with wood chips, his throat choke with dust.

"You were a child I stole from a sick ward. Where you had tendons, I wound string. Where you had bones, I fixed wood and metal. You screamed and screamed until I took your vocal cords and made your throat a hollow I might fill with silence or any words I liked."

The nutcracker crumpled to the ground. He could not cry out for help. His head was empty. His chest was empty. His mouth was bitter with the taste of walnuts.

Now Droessen leaned over the poor broken toy. He seemed too large, too tall, too far away, and the nutcracker knew that his own body was shrinking.

"You were an idea in my head," said the clocksmith. "You were nothing, and to nothing you will return when I think of you no more."

The nutcracker looked into Droessen's pale blue eyes and he recognized the color. *He painted my eyes to look like his.* The nutcracker felt the idea of himself

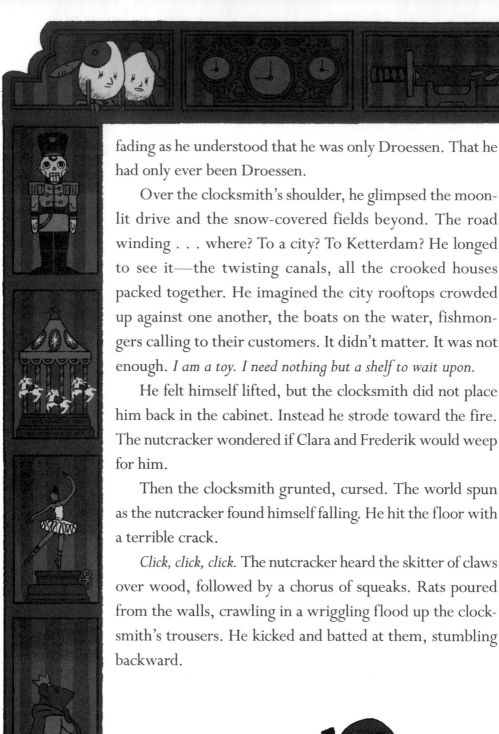

fading as he understood that he was only Droessen. That he had only ever been Droessen.

Over the clocksmith's shoulder, he glimpsed the moonlit drive and the snow-covered fields beyond. The road winding . . . where? To a city? To Ketterdam? He longed to see it—the twisting canals, all the crooked houses packed together. He imagined the city rooftops crowded up against one another, the boats on the water, fishmongers calling to their customers. It didn't matter. It was not enough. *I am a toy. I need nothing but a shelf to wait upon.*

He felt himself lifted, but the clocksmith did not place him back in the cabinet. Instead he strode toward the fire. The nutcracker wondered if Clara and Frederik would weep for him.

Then the clocksmith grunted, cursed. The world spun as the nutcracker found himself falling. He hit the floor with a terrible crack.

Click, click, click. The nutcracker heard the skitter of claws over wood, followed by a chorus of squeaks. Rats poured from the walls, crawling in a wriggling flood up the clocksmith's trousers. He kicked and batted at them, stumbling backward.

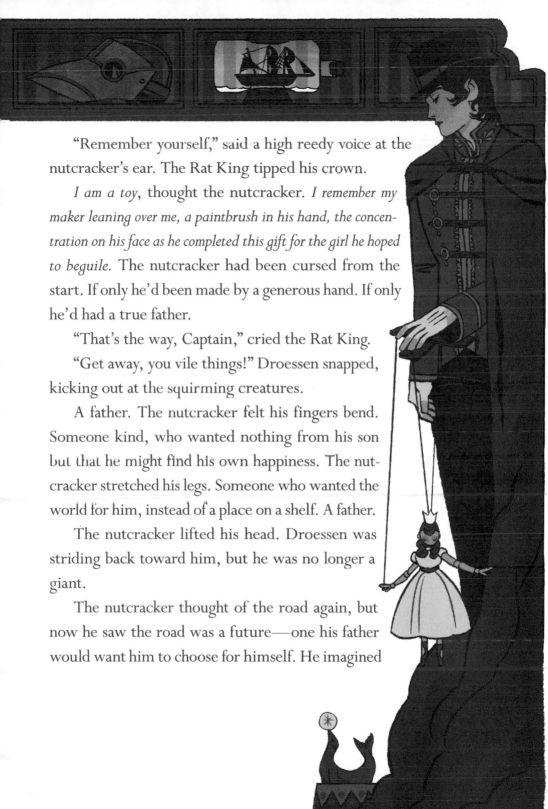

"Remember yourself," said a high reedy voice at the nutcracker's ear. The Rat King tipped his crown.

I am a toy, thought the nutcracker. *I remember my maker leaning over me, a paintbrush in his hand, the concentration on his face as he completed this gift for the girl he hoped to beguile.* The nutcracker had been cursed from the start. If only he'd been made by a generous hand. If only he'd had a true father.

"That's the way, Captain," cried the Rat King.

"Get away, you vile things!" Droessen snapped, kicking out at the squirming creatures.

A father. The nutcracker felt his fingers bend. Someone kind, who wanted nothing from his son but that he might find his own happiness. The nutcracker stretched his legs. Someone who wanted the world for him, instead of a place on a shelf. A father.

The nutcracker lifted his head. Droessen was striding back toward him, but he was no longer a giant.

The nutcracker thought of the road again, but now he saw the road was a future—one his father would want him to choose for himself. He imagined

the snow in his hair, the ground beneath his boots, the limitless horizon, a world full of chance and mishap and changing weather—gray clouds, hail, thunder, the unexpected. A new sound echoed in his rising chest, a round *thump, thump, thump*.

There would be woods along that road, animals in them, a river floating with ice, pleasure boats tethered with their sails trussed for the winter. He would grow hungry on that road. He would require food. He would eat cabbage rolls and gingerbread and drink cold cider. His stomach rumbled.

"I should have burned you as kindling the day I made you in my shop," the clocksmith said. But it was too late. The nutcracker rose and met his gaze, eye to eye.

"You couldn't," said the nutcracker. "You loved me too much." It was not true. But Clara had made him a prince through the power of her desire; he could desire too.

Droessen laughed. "It seems you have a gift for fancy."

"You are my father," said the nutcracker.

"I am your *maker*," snarled the clocksmith.

"You breathed life into me with all the love in your heart."

The clocksmith shook his head, took a step backward as

the nutcracker advanced. "I crafted you with skill. Determination."

"You gave me your eyes that I might see."

"No."

"You gave me to Clara that she might wake me like a prince in a fairy tale, to Frederik so I might learn the ways of war."

"You were my messenger!" gasped the clocksmith. "My spy and nothing more!" But his voice sounded strange and small. He stumbled as if he could not quite make his legs work.

"You dreamed a son," said the nutcracker, his need driving him on. "No clumsy clockwork, but a boy who might learn, a boy with a will and wishes of his own."

Droessen gave a strangled cry and toppled to the floor in a wooden clatter, his limbs stiff, his mouth twisting, his teeth bared.

"You wanted only that I might live," said the young man as he knelt to look at the crumpled doll lying in a heap on the floor. "You would have sacrificed your own life to make it so."

He picked up Droessen, cradled him gently in the

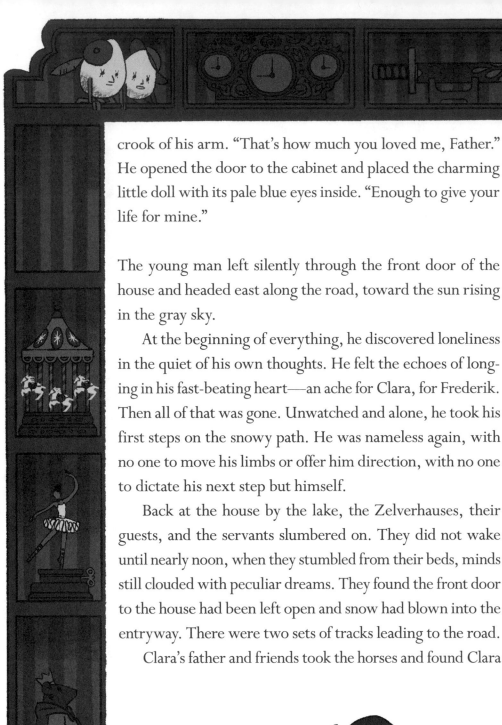

crook of his arm. "That's how much you loved me, Father." He opened the door to the cabinet and placed the charming little doll with its pale blue eyes inside. "Enough to give your life for mine."

The young man left silently through the front door of the house and headed east along the road, toward the sun rising in the gray sky.

At the beginning of everything, he discovered loneliness in the quiet of his own thoughts. He felt the echoes of longing in his fast-beating heart—an ache for Clara, for Frederik. Then all of that was gone. Unwatched and alone, he took his first steps on the snowy path. He was nameless again, with no one to move his limbs or offer him direction, with no one to dictate his next step but himself.

Back at the house by the lake, the Zelverhauses, their guests, and the servants slumbered on. They did not wake until nearly noon, when they stumbled from their beds, minds still clouded with peculiar dreams. They found the front door to the house had been left open and snow had blown into the entryway. There were two sets of tracks leading to the road.

Clara's father and friends took the horses and found Clara

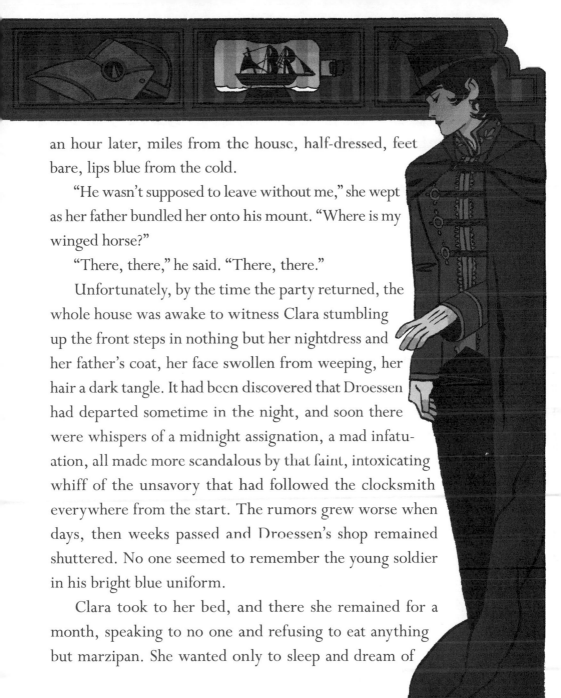

an hour later, miles from the house, half-dressed, feet bare, lips blue from the cold.

"He wasn't supposed to leave without me," she wept as her father bundled her onto his mount. "Where is my winged horse?"

"There, there," he said. "There, there."

Unfortunately, by the time the party returned, the whole house was awake to witness Clara stumbling up the front steps in nothing but her nightdress and her father's coat, her face swollen from weeping, her hair a dark tangle. It had been discovered that Droessen had departed sometime in the night, and soon there were whispers of a midnight assignation, a mad infatuation, all made more scandalous by that faint, intoxicating whiff of the unsavory that had followed the clocksmith everywhere from the start. The rumors grew worse when days, then weeks passed and Droessen's shop remained shuttered. No one seemed to remember the young soldier in his bright blue uniform.

Clara took to her bed, and there she remained for a month, speaking to no one and refusing to eat anything but marzipan. She wanted only to sleep and dream of

183

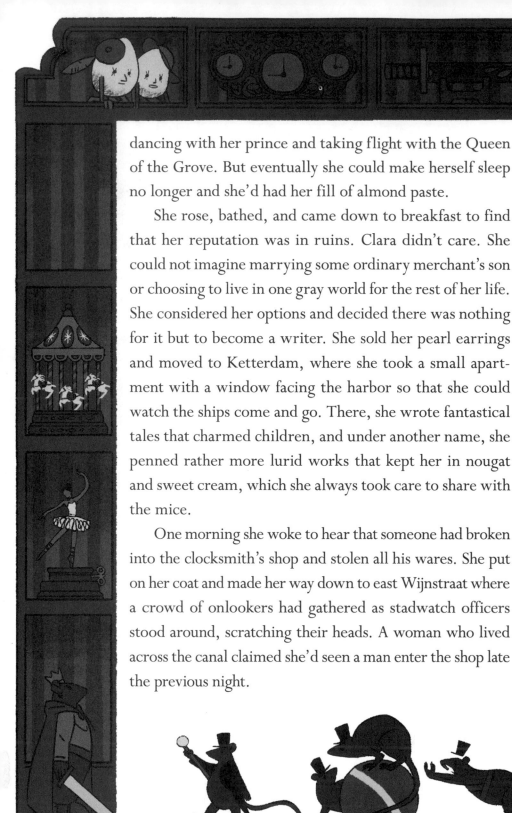

dancing with her prince and taking flight with the Queen of the Grove. But eventually she could make herself sleep no longer and she'd had her fill of almond paste.

She rose, bathed, and came down to breakfast to find that her reputation was in ruins. Clara didn't care. She could not imagine marrying some ordinary merchant's son or choosing to live in one gray world for the rest of her life. She considered her options and decided there was nothing for it but to become a writer. She sold her pearl earrings and moved to Ketterdam, where she took a small apartment with a window facing the harbor so that she could watch the ships come and go. There, she wrote fantastical tales that charmed children, and under another name, she penned rather more lurid works that kept her in nougat and sweet cream, which she always took care to share with the mice.

One morning she woke to hear that someone had broken into the clocksmith's shop and stolen all his wares. She put on her coat and made her way down to east Wijnstraat where a crowd of onlookers had gathered as stadwatch officers stood around, scratching their heads. A woman who lived across the canal claimed she'd seen a man enter the shop late the previous night.

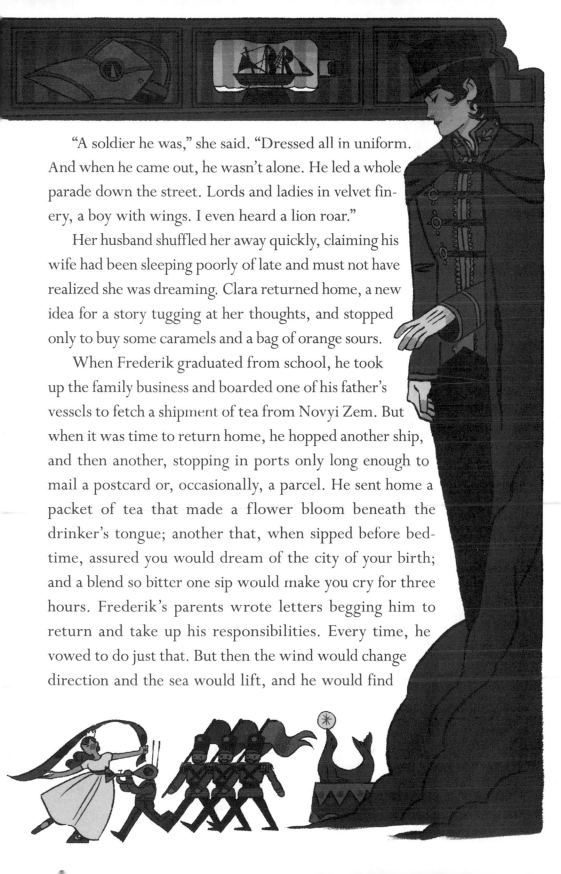

"A soldier he was," she said. "Dressed all in uniform. And when he came out, he wasn't alone. He led a whole parade down the street. Lords and ladies in velvet finery, a boy with wings. I even heard a lion roar."

Her husband shuffled her away quickly, claiming his wife had been sleeping poorly of late and must not have realized she was dreaming. Clara returned home, a new idea for a story tugging at her thoughts, and stopped only to buy some caramels and a bag of orange sours.

When Frederik graduated from school, he took up the family business and boarded one of his father's vessels to fetch a shipment of tea from Novyi Zem. But when it was time to return home, he hopped another ship, and then another, stopping in ports only long enough to mail a postcard or, occasionally, a parcel. He sent home a packet of tea that made a flower bloom beneath the drinker's tongue; another that, when sipped before bedtime, assured you would dream of the city of your birth; and a blend so bitter one sip would make you cry for three hours. Frederik's parents wrote letters begging him to return and take up his responsibilities. Every time, he vowed to do just that. But then the wind would change direction and the sea would lift, and he would find

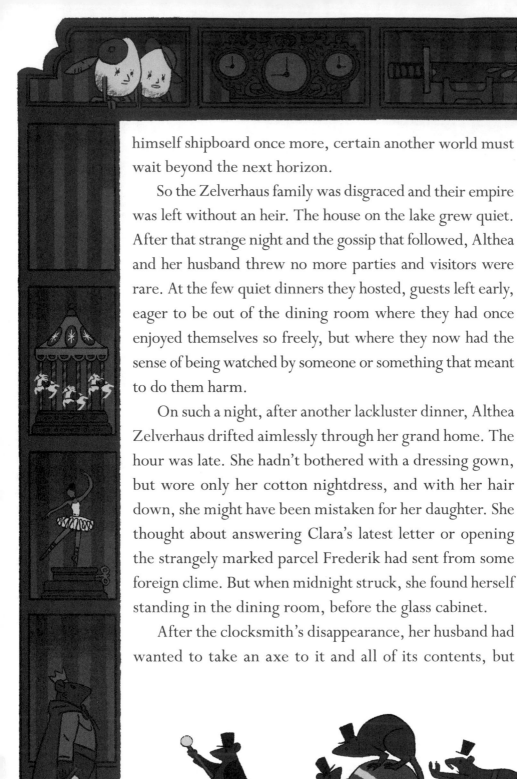

himself shipboard once more, certain another world must wait beyond the next horizon.

So the Zelverhaus family was disgraced and their empire was left without an heir. The house on the lake grew quiet. After that strange night and the gossip that followed, Althea and her husband threw no more parties and visitors were rare. At the few quiet dinners they hosted, guests left early, eager to be out of the dining room where they had once enjoyed themselves so freely, but where they now had the sense of being watched by someone or something that meant to do them harm.

On such a night, after another lackluster dinner, Althea Zelverhaus drifted aimlessly through her grand home. The hour was late. She hadn't bothered with a dressing gown, but wore only her cotton nightdress, and with her hair down, she might have been mistaken for her daughter. She thought about answering Clara's latest letter or opening the strangely marked parcel Frederik had sent from some foreign clime. But when midnight struck, she found herself standing in the dining room, before the glass cabinet.

After the clocksmith's disappearance, her husband had wanted to take an axe to it and all of its contents, but

Althea had claimed it would only lend credence to the rumors, and the cabinet had remained in its corner, gathering dust.

Something was missing from its shelves, she felt sure of it, but she couldn't say what.

Althea opened the cabinet door. She reached past the sugar mice and fairies to the small, ugly doll she had never noticed before. There was something familiar in the jut of his chin, the smart cut of his velvet coat. She ran her finger down one tiny lapel. Now that she looked closer, his angry little face held a certain charm.

Are you my soldier? she crooned in the quiet of the moonlight. *Are you my prince?* She opened her mouth to laugh at herself, but the sound never came. She clutched the doll closer.

Are you my darling? she whispered as she began to climb the stairs.

The clock chimed softly. Somewhere in the house she could hear her husband snoring.

Are you mine?

WHEN WATER SANG FIRE

YOU WISH TO STRIKE A BARGAIN,
and so you come north, until the land ends, and you can go
no farther. You stand on the rocky coast and face the water,
see the waves break upon two great islands, their coastlines
black and jagged. Maybe you pay a local to help you find a
boat and a safe place to launch it. You wrap yourself in seal-
skins to keep the cold and wet away, chew whale fat to keep
your mouth moist beneath the hard winter sun. Somehow
you cross that long stretch of stone-colored sea and find the
strength to scale the angry cliff face, breath tight in your
chest, fingers nearly numb in your gloves.

Then, tired and trembling, you traverse the island and
find the single crescent of gray sand beach. You make your
way to a circle of rocks, to a little tide pool, your wish burning like a sun in your mortal heart. You come as so many have
before—lonely, troubled, sick with avarice. A thousand desperate wishes have been spoken on these shores, and in the
end they are all the same: *Make me someone new.*

But before you speak, before you trade some small part
of your soul for the hunger writ so clear on your face, there
is a story you should know.

Kneeling there, you hear the ice moan. The wind scrapes
away at you, a razor on the strop. Even so. Be still and listen.
Think of it as part of the bargain.

There was a time when the northern seas were neither so black nor so cold, when pines covered these islands and deer grazed in the meadows, when the land could be farmed up to Elling and beyond.

In those days, the sildroher did not cower beneath the waves, afraid of sailors who might spy their smooth limbs and silver tails. They built vast palaces that sprawled along the seabed, sang songs to draw storms and keep their waters safe, and each year, a lucky few carved legs from their tails and went to walk boldly among the men of the shore, to learn their ways and steal their secrets. It was almost a game to them. For three months, they made themselves sick on human food, let their skin freckle and burn beneath the sun. They walked on grass, on cool tile, the slats of boards polished to the slick feel of silk beneath their new toes. They kissed warm human lips.

But look at them now. No better than selkies with their wet, pleading eyes, darting from wave to rock as if waiting to be clubbed. Now their laws are different. They know the land is a place of danger. Yet still they long for a taste of mortal life. This is the problem with making a thing forbidden. It does nothing but build an ache in the heart.

The old city of the sildroher was a rugged outcropping of rock, covered in the dark green sway of seagrass, so no diver or sailor tossed beneath the waves would ever know what wonders lay beneath him. It ran for mile after mile, rising and falling with the ocean floor, and the sea folk darted through its coral caverns and shell-laden hollows in the thousands. The dwelling place of its kings and queens was distinguishable only by its six spires that rose like grasping fingers around a craggy plain. Those bony spires were layered with the scales of trench-dwelling creatures so that, in the daytime hours, they glowed with blue light like a captured moon, and at night their chambers and catacombs gleamed phosphorescent in the heavy dark.

Beneath the rock and cockleshells, hidden below the center of the city, was the nautilus hall, shaped like a great horn curled in on itself and so large you could fit an armada of ships inside its curved walls. It had been enchanted long ago, a gift from a prince to his father before he took the throne himself, and it was the heart of sildroher power. Its base flowed with seawater and the level might be raised or lowered while the rest of the hall remained dry, so that the sea folk could practice their harmonies in both elements—water or air, as the spell required.

Song was not just a frivolity then, something meant to entertain or lure sailors to their doom. The sildroher used it to summon storms and protect their homes, to keep warships

and fishing boats from their seas. They used *it* to make their shelters and tell their histories. They had *no* word for *witch*. Magic flowed through all of them, a song no mortal could hear, that only the water folk could reproduce. In some it seemed to rush in and out like the tide, leaving little in its wake. But in others, in girls like Ulla, the current caught on some dark thing in their hearts and eddied there, forming deep pools of power.

Maybe the trouble began with Ulla's birth and the rumors that surrounded it. Or in her lonely childhood, when she was shunned for her sallow skin and strange eyes. Or maybe it began not with one girl but with two, on the first day Ulla sang with Signy, in the echoing cavern of the concert hall.

They were still just girls, neither yet thirteen, and though they had been educated in the same places, attended the same tidal celebrations and hunts for sturgeon, they were not friends. Ulla knew Signy because of her hair— vibrant red that flashed like a warning and gave her away wherever she went. And of course Signy knew Ulla with her black hair and her gray-tinged skin. Ulla, who had sung a song to scrape barnacles from her nursery when she was just an infant; who, without a single lesson, had hummed a tune to set the reedy skirts of her kelp dolls dancing. Ulla, who wielded more power in a single simple melody than singers twice her age.

But Ulla's classmates did not care about the surety of her pitch, or the novelty of the songs she composed. These things only made them jealous and caused them to whisper more about her murky parentage, the possibility that her father was not her father at all, that her mother had returned from a summer ashore with some human boy's child in her belly. It was not supposed to be possible. Humans were lesser beings and could not breed with the sildroher. And yet, the children heard their parents whisper and gossip and so they did the same. They claimed Ulla had been born with legs, that her mother had used blood magic to fashion her a tail, and taken a knife to the skin of Ulla's throat to give her daughter gills.

Ulla told herself it wasn't true, that it could not be, that her father's lineage was clear in the pattern of her silver scales. But she could not deny that she looked like neither of her parents, or that occasionally, when her mother braided Ulla's hair and set pearl combs above her ears, there was an expression on her face that might have been fear, or worse, disgust.

Ulla sometimes dreamed of a life in distant waters, of finding other sea folk somewhere who would want her, who would not care what she looked like or who had sired her.

But mostly she dreamed of becoming a court singer—venerated, valued. She imagined herself arrayed in gems and cusk bones, a general with a choir as her army, commanding storms and building new cities for the king and queen. Court singers were appointed by the king and nearly always carried noble blood. But that did not stop Ulla from hoping or from clinging to that dream when she was left alone in the nautilus hall as the other students drew into pairings for duets or formed groups for ensembles, when yet again she was forced to sing with the choirmaster, his face soft with pity.

All of that changed the first time she sang with Signy.

On that day, the concert hall had been nearly emptied, the rocks at its base exposed to the dry air as the sea outside flowed on. The students lay upon the smooth stones, faces bored, a sinuous pile of curled tails and pretty cheeks resting on damp forearms. Signy was at the periphery of the group, leaning into their slippery bulk. All morning she had cast Ulla sour glances, her pink conch mouth turned down at the corners, and it was only when the choirmaster began pairing them off for duets that Ulla understood why: Lis, Signy's usual partner, had not come to class. Their numbers were even and Signy would be forced to sing with Ulla.

That day the class was practicing simple storm magic with little success. Each pair made their attempt, and some managed to summon a few puffs of cloud or a mist that might generously be called a sprinkle. At one point, a rumble of thunder began, but it was only the growling of young Kettil's stomach.

When at last it was time for Ulla and Signy to perform, they slid onto the spit of rock that served as a stage, Signy keeping her distance as her classmates tittered at her misfortune.

Ulla thought for a moment of an easy melody, something that would end this humiliation quickly. Then she shoved the thought away. She hated Signy for being so afraid to be paired with her even briefly, hated her classmates for their stifled giggles and sly eyes, but mostly Ulla wished that she could kill the thing inside herself that still longed for their approval. She cast Signy a cold glance and said, "Follow me. If you can."

Ulla began a spell she'd been practicing on her own, a staccato tune, full of sudden syncopation. She leapt nimbly from note to note, plucking the melody from the secret song she could hear so clearly, happy to leave Signy behind to struggle with her sweet, wobbly voice.

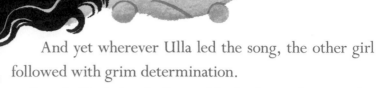

And yet wherever Ulla led the song, the other girl followed with grim determination.

Gray-bellied clouds formed high above them in the ceiling.

Ulla glanced at Signy, and the first rain began to fall.

There are different kinds of magic. Some call for rare herbs or complicated incantations. Some demand blood. Other magic is more mysterious still, the kind that fits one voice to another, one being to another, when moments before they were as good as strangers.

The song rose louder. Thunder rolled and shook the nautilus hall. The wind howled and tore at the hair of the students on the rocks.

"No lightning!" cried the choirmaster over the din, waving his arms and thumping his massive orange tail.

The song slowed. The other students mewled and thrashed. But Ulla and Signy didn't care. When the last note had faded, instead of turning to their classmates, hoping for praise, they turned to each other. The song had built a shield around them, the shelter of something shared that belonged to no one else.

The next day Lis returned to class and Ulla steeled herself, prepared to be stuck with the choirmaster once more. But when he told them to pair up for duets, Signy pressed her hand into Ulla's.

For the briefest moment, Ulla despised Signy, as we can only hate those who rescue us from loneliness. It was unbearable that this girl had such power, and that Ulla hadn't the will to refuse her kindness. But when Signy looked at Ulla and grinned—shyly, a star emerging at twilight—all of that bitterness dissolved, gone like words drawn on the ocean floor, and Ulla felt nothing but love. That moment tied her to Signy forever.

From then on, that was the way of things—Signy and Ulla together, and poor Lis, forced to sing with the choirmaster, her mouth set in a crimped frown that seemed to pull all her notes a little flat.

Trouble roused that day as two girls tangled together like rockweed, but then closed its eyes, pretending to sleep, leaving Ulla and Signy to their games and whispered confidences, letting them murmur their secrets and muddle their dreams as the years passed, waiting for winter and the prince's birthday party.

Roffe was the youngest of six princes, fathoms away from the throne, and perhaps because he was a threat to no one, his parents and his brothers coddled him. The royal sons had their own tutors, but Roffe's distaste for scholarship or responsibility of any kind was well known and remarked upon with a kind of fond indulgence among the nobility. On his seventeenth birthday, sildroher from the surrounding waters came to offer gifts, and all who had any sort of talent for song were called to the rocky plain between the palace spires to perform. The royal family sat curled against a milky sea-glass hollow, wedged into the spine of the tallest spire—the king and queen with their crowns of shark teeth, and all the handsome brothers with their pale gold hair, dressed in whalebone armor.

Each singer or ensemble came forward to perform, some old, some young, all famous for the magic they could sing. Hjalmar, the great master who had served as court singer under two kings, brought a cascade of sunlight from the surface to warm the crowd. Sigrid of the Eastern Current sang a huge pile of emeralds that rose all the way to the royal balcony. The twins, Agda and Linnea, called a pod of bowhead whales to block out the sun and then filled the seas around the partygoers with the bright, dreaming bodies of moon jellyfish.

When it was time, at last, for Ulla and Signy to perform, they drifted to the center of the plain, fingers entwined.

Neither of their families was rich, but the

girls had arrayed themselves as best they could for the occasion. In their hair they wore wreaths of salt lilies and small pearl combs they'd borrowed from their mothers. They had adorned their bodies with slivers of abalone shell, so that their torsos glittered and their tails flashed like treasure. Ulla looked well enough, still gray, still sullen, but Signy looked like a sun rising, her red hair splayed in a blazing corona. Ulla did not yet know how to name that color. She had never seen flame.

Ulla gazed at the crowd above her, around her. She could feel their curiosity like a questing tentacle, hear her name like a warbling, hateful melody.

Is that the girl? She's positively gray.

Looks nothing like her mother or her father.

Well, she belongs to someone, unlucky soul.

Signy trembled too. She had chosen Ulla that day in the nautilus hall, drunk on the power they'd created together, and they had built a secret world for themselves where it did not matter that Signy was poor, or that she was pretty but not pretty enough to rise above her station. Here, before the sildroher and the royal family, the shelter of that world seemed very far away.

But Ulla and Signy were not the same frightened girls who had once cast each other bitter glances in class. Hands clasped tight, they lifted their chins.

The song began sweetly. Ulla's tail twitched, keeping the tempo, and she saw the king and queen nodding their heads in time high above. She knew they were already thinking of the feast to come. They were just polite enough not to show their boredom—unlike their handsome sons.

Though Ulla had composed the spell, it had been Signy's idea, a daydream she had described to Ulla with giddy, fluttering hands, one they had embellished in lazy hours, warming themselves in the shallows.

Ulla let the song rise, and a series of slender, pearly arches began to form on the craggy plain. The floating crowd murmured its approval, thinking this was all the girls had to offer, two promising students who had, for some reason, been allowed to perform with the masters. The melody moved in simple escalating then descending scales, creating symmetry for the sparkling paths that spread below them, and soon the new paths and colonnades formed the shape of a great flower with six perfect petals that radiated from the plain's center.

A smattering of applause rose.

The song changed. It was not quite pleasant now, and the princes winced at the dissonance. The crowd looked away, embarrassed, a few of them smirking. Signy gripped Ulla's fingers so hard their knuckles rubbed together, but Ulla had warned her their audience wouldn't understand, and instead of stopping, they sang louder. The king cringed. The queen turned narrow blue eyes on the choirmaster. His face was serene. He knew what Ulla intended.

She'd written the song to a new scale, one with a different number of intervals, and though the sound was discord to the others' ignorant ears, Ulla knew better. She could hear the shape of a different harmony. She and Signy held close to the notes—not letting them resolve to something more commonplace—and as they did, their voices vibrated through the water and over the plain. A riot of color exploded between the paths laid beneath them. Pale pink anemones and bright red sea fans, thick purple stalks of kelp, and florid spines of coral.

The crowd cried out in wonder as the gardens grew. Ulla felt her pulse race, her blood crackle as if lightning flowed through her veins, as if the song she'd built had always existed, and had simply been waiting for her to find it. Storm magic was easy. Even raising buildings or crafting gems was simple enough with the right notes. But to create living things? The song could not just call them into being. It had to teach

them to understand their own needs, to take sustenance and survive.

That was how the royal gardens came to be. Ulla and Signy were its architects. Two nothing girls who until that moment might as well have been invisible.

When the performance ended, it was young Prince Roffe who clapped the loudest and dispensed with the formal patterns of the dance that would have kept him swimming in circles for hours before he reached Ulla and Signy, lowly as they were. He cut straight through the crowd, and Ulla watched Signy's face turn to the prince's as if caught by an undertow.

Roffe's eyes went to glittering Signy first. "Tell me how it's done," he begged her. "Those creatures and plants, will they live on? Or is it all just show?"

But now that the song was gone, it was as if Signy had forgotten her voice.

The prince tried again. "The plants—"

"They'll live," replied Ulla.

"The sound was so ugly."

"Was it?" Ulla asked, a hard carapace glinting from beneath all her gems. "Or was it just something you hadn't heard before?"

Signy was horrified. Then, as now, one did not contradict a prince, even if he required it.

But Prince Roffe looked only thoughtful. "It was not entirely unpleasant."

"It wasn't unpleasant at all," said Ulla, unsure of why her tongue had turned so sharp. This boy was royalty, his notice might mean a route to becoming a court singer. She should flatter him, indulge him. Instead she continued, "Your ears just didn't know what to make of it."

He looked at Ulla then, really looked at her. His family had always possessed extraordinary eyes, blue deeper than any sea. Roffe turned those eyes on Ulla and took in her flat black gaze, the white wreath of lilies sitting at an awkward angle in her black hair. Was it the directness of his stare that made Ulla bold? She was used to everyone but Signy looking away from her, even her mother sometimes.

"Magic doesn't require beauty," she said. "Easy magic is pretty. Great magic asks that you trouble the waters. It requires a disruption, something new."

"Something rare," added Roffe with a glimmering smile.

"Yes," she agreed grudgingly.

"And what trouble might you make above the surface?" Roffe asked.

Ulla and Signy went very still, as if bespelled by those simple words, an offer glinting like a lure, and maybe just as perilous. Every summer the royal sons traveled to the shore, to the great city at Söndermane. Only the most favored sons and daughters of the nobility were permitted to accompany them.

Now it was Ulla who could not quite seem to speak, and it was Signy who answered, a new lilt in her voice, as if she had finally found herself again, and something else besides.

"We might make quite a lot of trouble on shore," she said, the whole of her shimmering like pearl and amber. "But beyond that, who knows?"

The prince's smile gleamed.

"Well then," he said. "We must find out."

They became a new constellation: Ulla like a black flame, Signy burning red, and golden Roffe, always laughing, a yellow sun. In some ways, Roffe was not so different from them. Being the sixth son, he was barely a prince, and his chief duty was staying out of the way. He wasn't expected to study hard or to worry overmuch about statecraft or the ways of war. It made him lazy. When he was hungry, people brought him food. When he grew

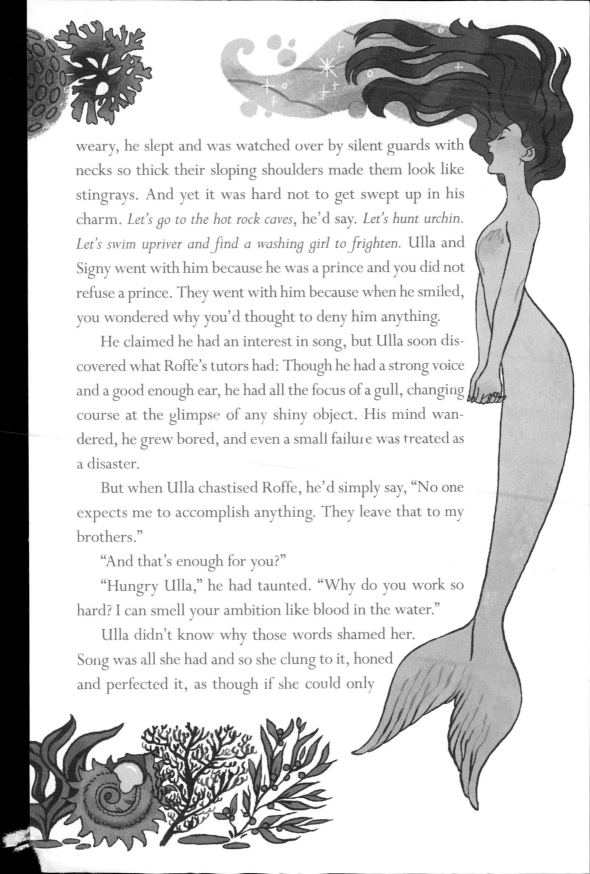

weary, he slept and was watched over by silent guards with necks so thick their sloping shoulders made them look like stingrays. And yet it was hard not to get swept up in his charm. *Let's go to the hot rock caves*, he'd say. *Let's hunt urchin. Let's swim upriver and find a washing girl to frighten.* Ulla and Signy went with him because he was a prince and you did not refuse a prince. They went with him because when he smiled, you wondered why you'd thought to deny him anything.

He claimed he had an interest in song, but Ulla soon discovered what Roffe's tutors had: Though he had a strong voice and a good enough ear, he had all the focus of a gull, changing course at the glimpse of any shiny object. His mind wandered, he grew bored, and even a small failure was treated as a disaster.

But when Ulla chastised Roffe, he'd simply say, "No one expects me to accomplish anything. They leave that to my brothers."

"And that's enough for you?"

"Hungry Ulla," he had taunted. "Why do you work so hard? I can smell your ambition like blood in the water."

Ulla didn't know why those words shamed her. Song was all she had and so she clung to it, honed and perfected it, as though if she could only

sharpen her skill to a fine enough point, she might carve a true place for herself in the world.

"What would you know about ambition?" she scoffed.

But the prince had only winked. "I know that you should keep it like a secret, not shout it like a curse."

Maybe the lesson should have stung, but Ulla liked Roffe best when he let her glimpse the cunning beneath his charming mask.

The sildroher who had once sneered at Ulla and Signy continued to sneer, to wonder what Roffe was playing at, to taunt that the girls were mere diversions. But now they were forced to hide their disdain. Roffe's favor had transformed Ulla and Signy, granting them protection no song ever could. Their classmates' envy hung around them in poisoned clouds, and Ulla watched Signy drink that poison like it was wine. It made her movements slow, her skin sleek, her hair silky. She bloomed in the hunger of their regard. And then, at long last, Roffe asked Ulla and Signy to be his guests on shore.

"Can you imagine!" Signy cried, seizing Ulla's hands, spinning her, the water churning around them as they circled faster and faster.

Yes, thought Ulla, the wonders of the shore unspooling in her mind, the chance to be someone

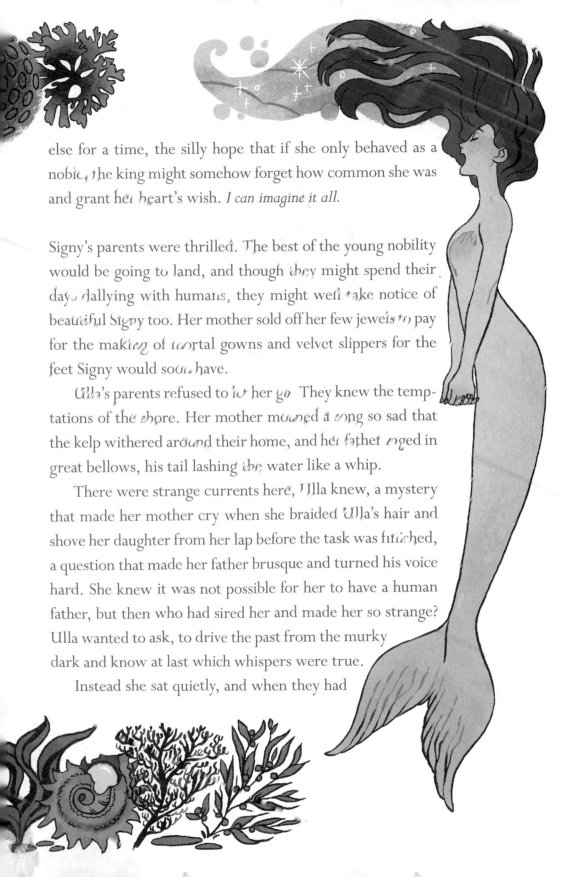

else for a time, the silly hope that if she only behaved as a noble, the king might somehow forget how common she was and grant her heart's wish. *I can imagine it all.*

Signy's parents were thrilled. The best of the young nobility would be going to land, and though they might spend their days dallying with humans, they might well take notice of beautiful Signy too. Her mother sold off her few jewels to pay for the making of mortal gowns and velvet slippers for the feet Signy would soon have.

Ulla's parents refused to let her go. They knew the temptations of the shore. Her mother moaned a song so sad that the kelp withered around their home, and her father raged in great bellows, his tail lashing the water like a whip.

There were strange currents here, Ulla knew, a mystery that made her mother cry when she braided Ulla's hair and shove her daughter from her lap before the task was finished, a question that made her father brusque and turned his voice hard. She knew it was not possible for her to have a human father, but then who had sired her and made her so strange? Ulla wanted to ask, to drive the past from the murky dark and know at last which whispers were true.

Instead she sat quietly, and when they had

done with their wailing and warnings, she said, "You cannot stop me."

They could not. But they could refuse her gowns and human coin.

"Walk naked amid the men of the shore and see what joy it brings you," decreed her father.

"Perhaps I will," Ulla replied with more courage than she felt. Maybe she would find answers onshore, or a human lover, or nothing at all, but she would go.

That night she swam to the wreck of the *Djenaller*, a ship brought low only months before, a warning to the men of the land to keep from these waters. She pulled scraps of cloth and pearl from the skeletons in its cabins, and over those ragged leavings she sang a song of making. She barely knew what mortal gowns should look like, but she drew seed pearl and lost silk together and made three dresses that pleased her, then sealed them dry in an enchanted trunk.

"You cannot wear such dresses," said Signy. "They will draw too much notice." Ulla shrugged and pretended that she didn't care. She could not tell Signy that her mother and father had refused to let her accompany the party, nor could she bear to tell her why. "Besides, three gowns will hardly get you through three months on land!"

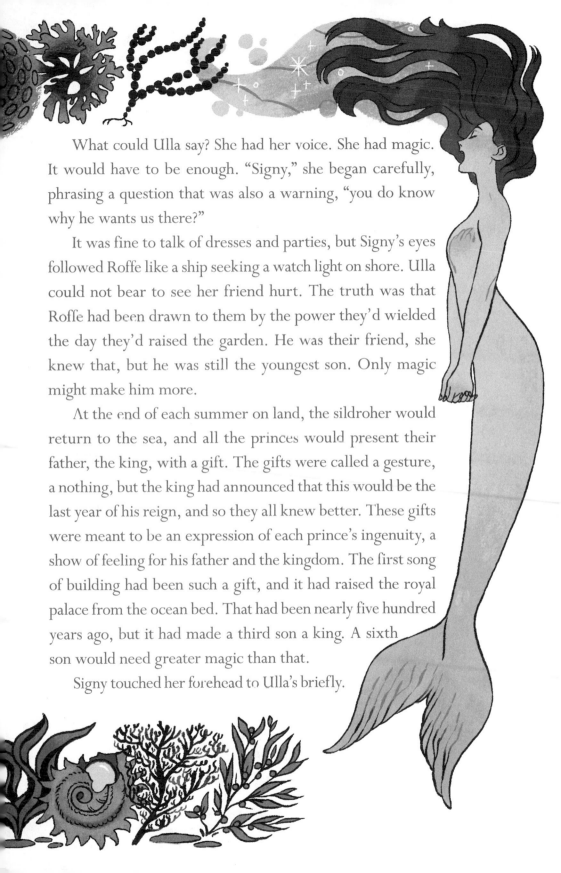

What could Ulla say? She had her voice. She had magic. It would have to be enough. "Signy," she began carefully, phrasing a question that was also a warning, "you do know why he wants us there?"

It was fine to talk of dresses and parties, but Signy's eyes followed Roffe like a ship seeking a watch light on shore. Ulla could not bear to see her friend hurt. The truth was that Roffe had been drawn to them by the power they'd wielded the day they'd raised the garden. He was their friend, she knew that, but he was still the youngest son. Only magic might make him more.

At the end of each summer on land, the sildroher would return to the sea, and all the princes would present their father, the king, with a gift. The gifts were called a gesture, a nothing, but the king had announced that this would be the last year of his reign, and so they all knew better. These gifts were meant to be an expression of each prince's ingenuity, a show of feeling for his father and the kingdom. The first song of building had been such a gift, and it had raised the royal palace from the ocean bed. That had been nearly five hundred years ago, but it had made a third son a king. A sixth son would need greater magic than that.

Signy touched her forehead to Ulla's briefly.

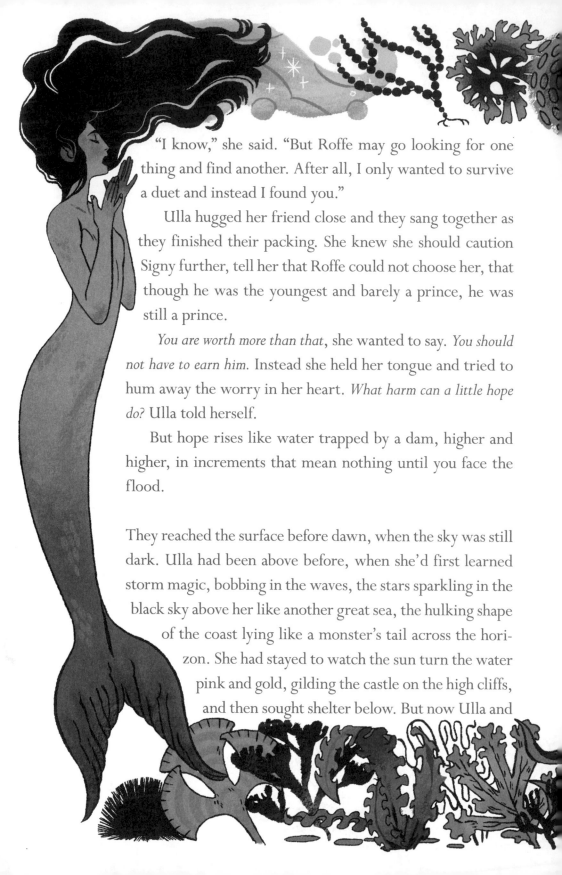

"I know," she said. "But Roffe may go looking for one thing and find another. After all, I only wanted to survive a duet and instead I found you."

Ulla hugged her friend close and they sang together as they finished their packing. She knew she should caution Signy further, tell her that Roffe could not choose her, that though he was the youngest and barely a prince, he was still a prince.

You are worth more than that, she wanted to say. *You should not have to earn him.* Instead she held her tongue and tried to hum away the worry in her heart. *What harm can a little hope do?* Ulla told herself.

But hope rises like water trapped by a dam, higher and higher, in increments that mean nothing until you face the flood.

They reached the surface before dawn, when the sky was still dark. Ulla had been above before, when she'd first learned storm magic, bobbing in the waves, the stars sparkling in the black sky above her like another great sea, the hulking shape of the coast lying like a monster's tail across the horizon. She had stayed to watch the sun turn the water pink and gold, gilding the castle on the high cliffs, and then sought shelter below. But now Ulla and

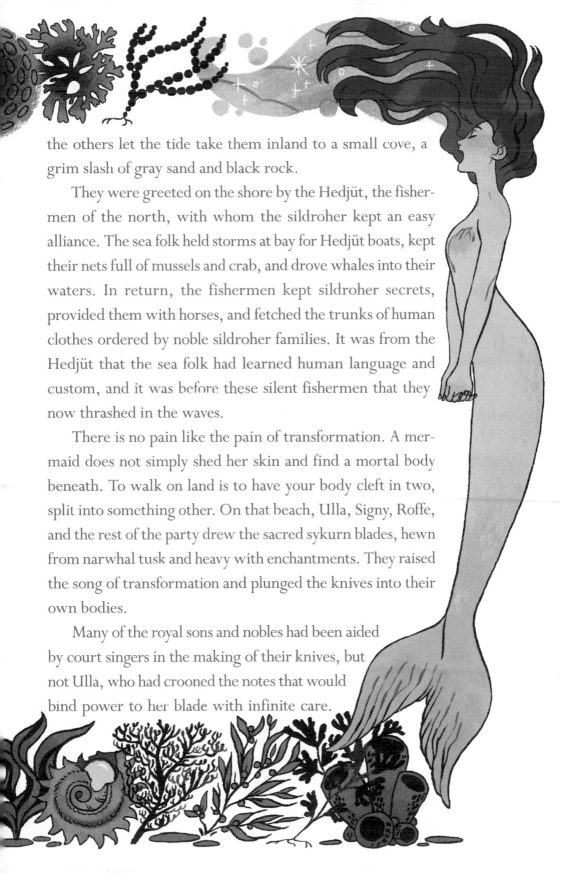

the others let the tide take them inland to a small cove, a
grim slash of gray sand and black rock.

They were greeted on the shore by the Hedjüt, the fishermen of the north, with whom the sildroher kept an easy
alliance. The sea folk held storms at bay for Hedjüt boats, kept
their nets full of mussels and crab, and drove whales into their
waters. In return, the fishermen kept sildroher secrets,
provided them with horses, and fetched the trunks of human
clothes ordered by noble sildroher families. It was from the
Hedjüt that the sea folk had learned human language and
custom, and it was before these silent fishermen that they
now thrashed in the waves.

There is no pain like the pain of transformation. A mer-
maid does not simply shed her skin and find a mortal body
beneath. To walk on land is to have your body cleft in two,
split into something other. On that beach, Ulla, Signy, Roffe,
and the rest of the party drew the sacred sykurn blades, hewn
from narwhal tusk and heavy with enchantments. They raised
the song of transformation and plunged the knives into their
own bodies.

Many of the royal sons and nobles had been aided
by court singers in the making of their knives, but
not Ulla, who had crooned the notes that would
bind power to her blade with infinite care.

Still, no matter how well-crafted the knife, the song was the greater challenge. It was the deepest magic, music of rending and healing, the only song all royalty were trained in from birth. It was not complicated but required great will, and Ulla worried that Signy would not have the strength for it. But with eyes locked on Roffe, Signy raised her voice and made the cut. Only then did Ulla add her own voice to the song and drive her blade into her tail.

The terror was worse than the pain, the surety that something had gone wrong and that she would be torn apart from head to fin. Blood spilled around her in torrents, staining the sea-foam pink before the tide brought another wave of salt to clean her wounds. And still she sang on, holding the notes steady, knowing that if she did not, she would never heal completely but simply lie there bleeding, a mess of scales and half-formed limbs.

The pain eased. The last notes were sung. Ulla marveled at the strange curve of her hips, the dark thatch of hair between her legs, the odd, awkward knobs of her knees. And feet! Sad little flippers with their crenellated toes. She could hardly believe such things would support her, let alone propel her forward.

The Hedjüt fishermen averted their eyes and

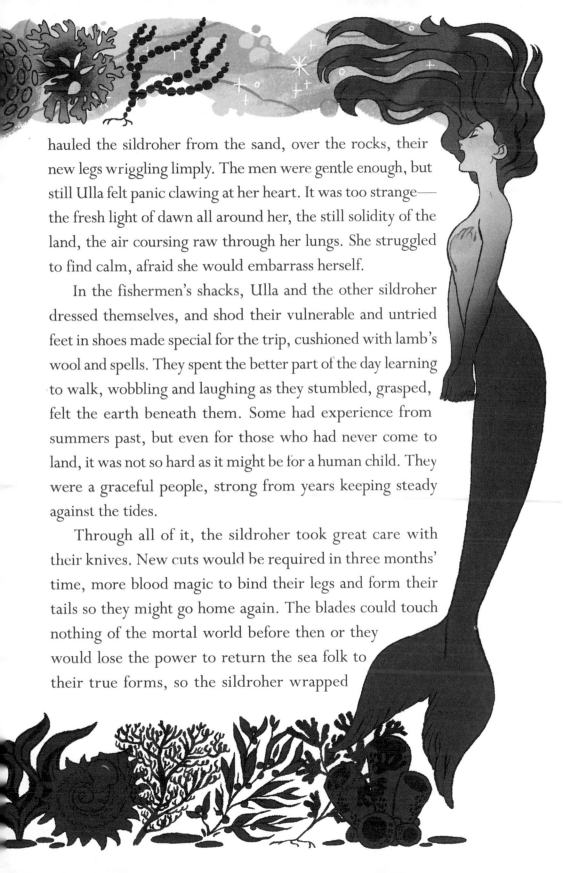

hauled the sildroher from the sand, over the rocks, their new legs wriggling limply. The men were gentle enough, but still Ulla felt panic clawing at her heart. It was too strange— the fresh light of dawn all around her, the still solidity of the land, the air coursing raw through her lungs. She struggled to find calm, afraid she would embarrass herself.

In the fishermen's shacks, Ulla and the other sildroher dressed themselves, and shod their vulnerable and untried feet in shoes made special for the trip, cushioned with lamb's wool and spells. They spent the better part of the day learning to walk, wobbling and laughing as they stumbled, grasped, felt the earth beneath them. Some had experience from summers past, but even for those who had never come to land, it was not so hard as it might be for a human child. They were a graceful people, strong from years keeping steady against the tides.

Through all of it, the sildroher took great care with their knives. New cuts would be required in three months' time, more blood magic to bind their legs and form their tails so they might go home again. The blades could touch nothing of the mortal world before then or they would lose the power to return the sea folk to their true forms, so the sildroher wrapped

the sykurn knives in the skin and scales they had shed and stored them safely in their trunks.

Ulla saw that Signy and Roffe were looking at her strangely, but there was little time to think on it, for the coaches had arrived, wrought in silver and gold, their doors bright with lacquer and emblazoned with the symbol of the sildroher royal family—though that emblem would mean nothing to the men of the shore. The horses, vast beasts of dappled gray with black eyes like seals, stamped their massive hooves as Signy and Ulla gasped and Roffe doubled over with laughter. None of these wonders were new to him.

Soon they were thundering down the great road that ran along the edge of the coast to the city of Söndermane. They had all seen the city from afar, perched on the tip of the white cliffs they called the Severed Moon, the towers of the church where the great iron bells, enchanted by sildroher magic, were said to compel even the worst sinners to prayer. But Ulla could barely think for all the sensations racing through her—the seat beneath her newly formed thighs, the brush of her skirts against her legs, the jouncing of the carriage. With every jolt the sildroher whooped or clutched their sides, wild with the strangeness of it all.

Through the chaos and commerce of the lower

town they rattled, over punishing cobblestones, then past the gates to the great palace. How it glittered, white and silver and surrounded by towering pines, as if hewn from pearl and possessed of its own magic. Its spires were so slender it seemed a breath might topple them, and each balcony, railing, and casement was worked in gauzy stonework so light it looked less like masonry and more like airy tongues of frost. Over all of it loomed the legendary Prophetic's Tower, where scholars from every country came to study and debate their findings with the king's chief advisers and seers. Ulla found it hard to believe mortal hands could have made such a place.

"Many human nobles spend the warm days here," said Roffe, nodding toward another cluster of carriages. "They think we're from an estate far to the south."

When the footman opened their door, Kalle, the eldest of Roffe's brothers, was waiting, mouth full of warnings.

"Take your pleasures as you will," he reminded them as they slowly ascended the wide sweep of the palace steps—still not entirely sure of just how their bodies should align in the act, testing the cold marble through their shoes. "But remember how fragile these creatures are. Spill not their blood. Draw not their notice."

His gaze lingered upon Ulla too.

Through two high, narrow doors they passed, into a

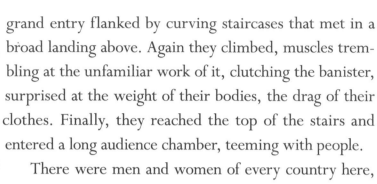

grand entry flanked by curving staircases that met in a broad landing above. Again they climbed, muscles trembling at the unfamiliar work of it, clutching the banister, surprised at the weight of their bodies, the drag of their clothes. Finally, they reached the top of the stairs and entered a long audience chamber, teeming with people.

There were men and women of every country here, swathed in lace and rich silks, jewels at their cuffs, little gilded heels on their shoes. Ulla marveled at how different they were from the Hedjüt with their broad shoulders and bent backs, their thick knuckled hands and weather-ravaged faces. These were the soft, perfumed bodies of people who did not work.

Silence fell as the sildroher passed, and Ulla found it hard not to laugh at the thought of Kalle's warning. There was no way their party could avoid drawing notice. Despite their tentative steps, the sea folk moved as no human could, their lithe bodies drifting in a liquid sway, their limbs graceful as seagrass.

As they'd been instructed, they made their bows and curtsies to the human king, who greeted the royal brothers warmly. And well he should. For though their clothes might be peculiar and their accents strange, each year the sildroher brought such treasures as the human king had never seen. Kalle gestured to his servants, who carried forward three chests of pearls. The first were white and luminous as snow, the next the silvery gray of storm clouds, and the third chest of pearls glittered blacker than a moonless night. There were chests of coin too, jeweled swords, heavy trenchers made of gold. Ulla watched the mortal king smile and preen and pour wine into a silver cup, little realizing that this treasure had come from wrecked ships, gifts from dead men, their bones rotting at the bottom of the sea. What did mortals care? Treasure was treasure.

But as the eyes of the human court were focused on each new gem and bauble, Ulla saw that one young man did not gawk or marvel. He stood behind the king's throne, beside a bearded man who wore the sash and smoky-blue sapphire of a seer. The boy's clothes were black, his hair blacker still, and he was looking directly at Ulla, the weight of his stare heavy ballast. Ulla returned his gaze, expecting him to glance away. He did not, and though she knew it was impossible, she had the strange sensation that she'd met him before.

The king clapped his hands. The doors to the feasting hall were thrown open, and the nobles moved forward in order of rank. But as Ulla drifted through the doors of the audience hall to the strange smells of human food beyond, she looked back and saw the boy in black still watching.

They feasted. They danced. They lifted cups of wine to their lips for the first time. They laughed and stomped

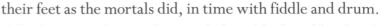

their feet as the mortals did, in time with fiddle and drum. The humans clustered around the sildroher, blood suffusing their warm cheeks, chests rising as if they couldn't quite catch their breath, eyes moist and glittering with desire, and by evening's end, Roffe had one mortal girl on his knee, another tucked close against him.

Ulla could not see the pain in Signy's face, but she saw the effort her friend took to hide it.

"You knew why he wanted us here," Ulla reminded her, as gently as she could.

Not for love but for magic, for what they might help Roffe accomplish onshore.

Signy shrugged one gleaming shoulder. She had drawn her hair back from her face with two sapphire combs and changed into a corseted blue gown that curled like a wave over her breasts and left her white shoulders bare. How many times had Ulla seen Signy's shoulders? Why, now that they were framed by silk, did they seem like something entirely new?

"He's meant to have his fun," Signy said with ease that did not ring true.

"You should have some, too," said Ulla, and took Signy's hand, drew her back into the dance, let the heat of human bodies, the brief, wild flutter of mortal life surround them.

Later, when the candles burned low, and

Ulla toed her pinching slippers from her feet, when she'd bound her damp hair in a braid, marveling at the moisture that beaded at the nape of her neck, when the wine fizzed happily in her blood, and the shadowed corners were full of ardent gasps and low laughter, she leaned back against the wall, shoved another body away, and wondered why she did not feel the pull the others did.

The sildroher went to shore to taste human language, to sample the decadence of their world, but also to sample *them*. It was a means of easing their longing, controlling their temptations. Always, the sea folk have been drawn to mortals, to their solid bodies and brief lives, the way they strive and toil and quiver with endeavor. So why did Ulla feel no desire? Why could she not be like Signy swaying slowly, clasped in mortal arms, or Roffe plucking kisses from each eager human mouth? Was she doomed to sit at the edge of the world here as she had below the waves?

It was only then that she saw the black-clad boy crossing the room toward her. The shadows seemed to shift as he passed, pulled along by him like a tide. Ulla took in the familiar angles of his face, the slash of his dark brows, and felt fear coil in her stomach. She touched her tongue to her teeth, already imagining the song she would raise to defend herself. Such music would doom her—sildroher magic was

221

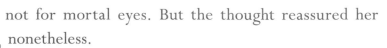

not for mortal eyes. But the thought reassured her nonetheless.

"I remember you," he said when at last he reached her. His eyes were gray agate.

That isn't possible, she thought to say, but instead asked, "Who are you?"

"The seer's apprentice."

"And can he really tell the future?" she asked, her curiosity getting the best of her.

"He can tell the king what he wants to hear, and that's more important than knowing the future."

Ulla knew she should say her good nights, put distance between herself and this odd creature, but she'd had too much wine to heed caution. "Why do you say you remember me? And why do you watch me like a black-backed gull seeking prey?"

He leaned forward slightly, and Ulla could not help drawing back.

"Come to the Prophetic's Tower tomorrow," he said, voice cool as glass. "Come, and I'll tell you all you wish to know."

"To the library?" She could not read. Only the sildroher royal family could, trained in the ways of diplomacy and treaties.

"I do not expect you to read," he said as he

slipped past her without a sound. "Any more than you expect me to breathe underwater."

Ulla slept badly that night. When the sun had set, the cold had crept into her bones, and she shivered beneath the covers. She could not get warm or purge the scent of sweat and tallow and roasting meat from her nose. She couldn't get used to the feeling of the bed beneath her, the sense that her heavy body might sink right through the sheets. Then there was the painful pressure that had pushed at her abdomen until at last she remembered the chamber pot and what she was meant to do with it. When at last she dozed, she dreamed of her parents, of her father's cold eyes and her mother's sorrowful hands tugging at her hair as if, were she only able to pull hard enough, she might change its color.

Ulla woke early, filled the basin nearly to the brim, and plunged her face into the cold water, letting the silence fill her ears, trying to remember herself. Her few belongings had already been placed in her dressing room, and she quickly checked the contents of her locked trunk, making sure the sykurn blade was safely bundled in the folds of her scales.

She could not quite settle. Her skin smelled sour, wrapped tight and stiff around her frame. Her stomach growled. She ran her hand over the bed's embroidered coverlet, drew off her slippers, and felt the cool stone floors through the soles of her feet. She plunged her toes into the soft furs that had been laid before a vast hearth. Though the summer air was warm, the palace was all cold rock and high ceilings, and the remnants of a fire smoldered in the grate. She had been too tired to realize it was there the previous night. But now Ulla knelt before it, felt the heat radiating from it against her palms, and had to keep herself from reaching for those glowing embers. She had studied the songs and artifacts. She knew the idea of fire. She'd been taught about it, sung the word. But *seeing* it—so close and so alive . . . It was like having a little sun to keep all for herself.

The chamber had tall, pointed windows that looked out over the royal gardens and the forest beyond, and on the table set before them was a gray glass ewer full of what Ulla thought might be roses, heavy-headed things, their smell sweet and strange, their pale, dawn-pink petals slightly darker at the center. She touched her fingers to the place on her neck where her gills had been before the song of transformation, then inhaled deeply, the scent of the flowers filling her nose and lungs and making her dizzy. She plucked a petal and laid it thoughtfully on her tongue. When she chewed, the taste was disappointingly bitter.

She was grateful when a maid arrived bearing

a tray of tea and salt fish, followed by servants carrying pails of steaming water. Though Ulla had been told about bathing, she'd never been properly dirty before, and she was shocked at the dust that washed from her body in a gritty cloud, the slip of sweet oils that coated her. But nothing was more startling than the sight of her funny little toes curled over the tub's edge, the tender bones of her ankles, the smooth incrustations of her claws—*nails*. The water felt too slick on her skin, flat and saltless as the rivers she had explored with Signy and Roffe on cloudy afternoons.

Once Ulla was clean and dry and patted with powder, the maid helped her into a gown and laced her tight, then vanished out the door with a nervous glance over her shoulder. Only then, in the silence of her room, did Ulla finally see herself in the mirror that hung above her dressing table. Only then did she realize why she'd drawn so many stares from the sildroher—and from the humans as well. Away from the blue depths of the sea, the sallow gray-green tinge of her skin was gone and she glowed burnished bronze as if she had tucked sunlight beneath her tongue. Her hair was black as it had always been, but here in the bright light of the human world, it shone like polished glass. Her eyes were still dark and strange, but dark like a midnight path that might lead somewhere wonderful, strange like the sound of a new language.

She left her room, the palace silent around her,

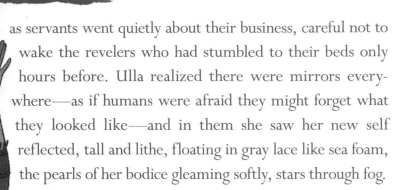

as servants went quietly about their business, careful not to wake the revelers who had stumbled to their beds only hours before. Ulla realized there were mirrors every-where—as if humans were afraid they might forget what they looked like—and in them she saw her new self reflected, tall and lithe, floating in gray lace like sea foam, the pearls of her bodice gleaming softly, stars through fog.

The apprentice was waiting at the base of the tower stairs.

Without a word, they began to climb, Ulla clinging to the banister as they rose higher, the air thick with dust that glittered in beams of early morning sun.

Books had a scent, she realized, as they passed level after level of libraries and laboratories, shelves lining their round walls, packed with brightly bound volumes in tight rows. The books meant nothing to her. The sildroher had no pen and paper; no parchment survived beneath the waves, and they had no need of it. Their histories and knowledge were held in song.

At each level the apprentice named another sub-ject: history, augury, geography, mathematics, alchemy. Ulla hoped they'd wind all the way to the top of the tower, where she knew they'd find the famous observatory. But instead, when there were still many floors above to discover, the apprentice led her from the spiral stairs to a dimly lit room set with long tables and tall glass cabinets. They were full of odd objects—a golden hoop spinning continuously on its axis, stuffed birds with scarlet feathers and glossy beaks, a harpoon made of what looked like volcanic glass. One entire shelf was taken up by hourglasses of different sizes and filled with varied colors of sand, another contained flats of insects pinned to boards, and still another was crowded with many-legged specimens floating in sealed jars of amber fluid.

Ulla drew in a breath when she glimpsed a sykurn knife, wondering who it had belonged to and what possible reason its owner could have for relinquishing it. But she forced herself to move on, conscious of the apprentice's observant gaze.

They passed a vast mirror, and Ulla saw their shapes reflected in the gloom. The girl in the glass waved.

Ulla leapt back and the apprentice laughed. His reflection joined him, though the pitch was not quite the same.

"I can hear him," Ulla said, clutching the edge of the table. It was as if the boy in the glass was simply another boy in another part of the room, as if the frame were an open doorway.

"It's an illusion, nothing more," the apprentice said, and his reflection gave a dismissive wave of his hand.

"A powerful one."

"A useless one. It's a frivolous object. My master's predecessor made it while attempting to find a way

to place a soul in the mirror so that the old king might live forever once his body was gone. All he managed was this."

Ulla peered at her reflection, and the girl in the glass smiled. No wonder others shied away from her. There was something sly in the mirror girl's expression, as if her lips might part and show an extra row of teeth.

"It's impressive nonetheless," she managed.

"It's a waste. The reflection has no soul, no animating spirit. All it can do is echo. The new king brings it down for parties to charm the guests. You'll see at the ball. They put it in the main hall as a diversion. You can even have a little conversation with yourself."

Ulla could not resist such a temptation.

"Hello," she said tentatively.

"Hello," the mirror girl answered.

"Who are you?"

"Who are *you*?" There was that smile again. Did Ulla imagine it or had the girl's inflection changed?

Ulla sang a soft note, not a spell, just a sound, and the girl opened her mouth, joining Ulla in harmony. Ulla couldn't help the delighted laugh that sprang from her, but the mirror girl flushed when she saw the apprentice's bemusement.

"It seems I am as easily entertained as the king's party guests," said Ulla.

His lips quirked. "We all love novelty."

The apprentice's gaze slid to their reflection, and he squared his shoulders so that he and Ulla stood side by side, much the same height, their hair as black and gleaming as deepwater pearls.

"Look at that," he said, and his reflection lifted a brow. "We might almost be blood relations."

He was right, Ulla realized. It was not just the hair, or the slender-reed build that they shared. There was something in the shape of their faces, the sharp cut of their bones. She touched her fingers to her scalp as if she could still feel her mother's hands tugging, tugging at her braids, hear her doleful song withering their garden and filling Ulla with regret. The apprentice was offering her an answer, an oyster pried open, a jewel upon a plate. She need only reach for it.

She said nothing.

"Why are you here in Söndermane?" he asked, and his reflection remained quiet as if waiting to hear the answer too.

Ulla ran her thumb over the table. Her reflection blinked rapidly, looking far more flustered than she would have liked. "I came for the cool weather," she said lightly. "You came here to study?"

"No," said the apprentice. The gray eyes of his

reflection narrowed. His voice was like the cold pull of a glacier. "I came here to *hunt*."

Beneath the waves, small creatures survived by hiding when a predator was near, and everything in Ulla longed to cower, to tuck herself into some scrap of shadow and escape his gaze. But there was nowhere to hide here on land, and the sildroher did not shrink from humans. She had song and he was only a mortal.

Ulla turned to the apprentice, made herself meet his gaze without flinching. "Then I wish you good fortune," she said. "And easy prey."

He smiled, the same sly, dangerous smile she'd seen on her own face in the glass. Ulla had come for answers, but why should she believe this boy knew anything about her? For all she knew, his mysterious words had been nothing but an empty lure. Best to get away quickly. Besides, even in that long ago time, Ulla knew a bad bargain. Maybe this boy held secrets, but whatever knowledge he might possess would not be worth the price. She turned her back on him and forced herself not to run as she began the long, winding journey down the stairs.

Despite the apprentice and his threat, for a time Ulla was happy. They all were in their own ways. Roffe took his pleasures; Signy suffered but drowned her longing in a tide of human lovers; and Ulla let herself be carried away too, far from the clutter of ardent hearts, into the wilds of the wood, where the pines made a green cathedral and the air was thick with the smell of sun-warmed sap. She watched for deer and beaver, stained her lips with berries, marked the sun on its path as it set beneath the horizon, then rose again to color the whole world.

At night, she feasted with the others, watched Signy hope, and Roffe charm, and all his golden brothers hold court. The beauty that had revealed itself in Ulla when she came to land earned her gifts of jewels and poetry, posies left outside her door, even a proposal. Nothing could tempt her, and this only strengthened her allure. The steady beat of mortal fascination made her weary.

She would sit for hours as the great hall emptied, listening to the human musicians, studying their fingers on the frets of an oud, giving herself over to the thump of the drum, the pull of the bow, until the last note was played. There were legends of instruments enchanted by sildroher and gifted to human favorites. Finger cymbals that made the dancer more graceful, harps that would play themselves when their strings were wetted with blood. But for Ulla there was only music.

Some nights, when Signy had taken no lover, she would come to

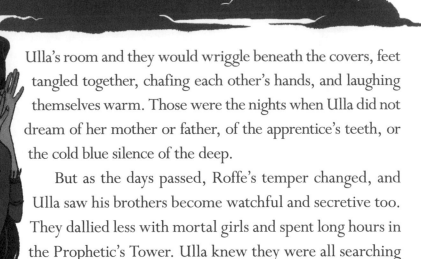

Ulla's room and they would wriggle beneath the covers, feet tangled together, chafing each other's hands, and laughing themselves warm. Those were the nights when Ulla did not dream of her mother or father, of the apprentice's teeth, or the cold blue silence of the deep.

But as the days passed, Roffe's temper changed, and Ulla saw his brothers become watchful and secretive too. They dallied less with mortal girls and spent long hours in the Prophetic's Tower. Ulla knew they were all searching the pages of human books for mortal magic, for a gift they might bring back to their father—the thing that might change their fortunes forever.

As Roffe's mood grew darker, Signy became restless and skittish too, endlessly twining her bright hair around her nervous fingers, her teeth worrying her lower lip until it bled in tiny garnet beads.

"You must stop," Ulla told her beneath the blankets, dabbing the blood away with the sleeve of her nightgown. "Your misery won't fix this for him. He'll find his way. There's still time."

"When he does, he'll seek you out."

"Both of us," said Ulla.

"But you are the composer," Signy said, pressing her feverish forehead to Ulla's. "You are the one he needs."

"He needs us both for any song of worth."

The tears came then and Signy's voice broke. "When he truly understands your power, he will want you for his bride. You will leave me behind."

Ulla held her close, wishing she could shake Signy from these thoughts. Neither of them were fit to be a princess, no matter how powerful their song. "I will never leave you. I have no wish to be his bride."

Signy's laugh was bitter in the dark. "He's a prince, Ulla. He will have what he wants."

As if Signy's own small hands had set a secret clock ticking, Roffe approached Ulla the next day. It was late afternoon, and a long, languorous meal of cold fowl and chestnuts with citron had been served on the terrace overlooking the gardens. Chilled bottles of yellow cherry wine had been emptied and now, as the servants cleared the table, humans and sildroher drowsed in leafy alcoves or chased one another through the turns of the hedge maze.

Ulla stood at the terrace's edge, looking down at the gardens, listening to the bees hum. Her mind had already begun to build a song that might transform a corner of the undersea garden she and Signy had raised for the royal family into a maze like this with a whirling

pool at its center. It would be a trick of the eye, of course, a gesture toward human fountains, but she thought fish could be made to swim in a circle if she could simply build a strong enough pattern into the melody.

"I need a gift like Rundstrom's tiger," said Roffe, coming up beside her and leaning on his elbows. "A horse. A great lizard if I could find one."

The tiger was a legendary gift, but it was no simple spell. The creature had to be enchanted to breathe underwater, to endure the cold, and then to obey its master. Rundstrom's tiger had survived barely a year beneath the sea. Long enough to make a second son a king.

"You'll have to do better than that," she murmured, the sun warm on her shoulders. "Or you'll look no better than a cheap imitation."

"Kalle and Edvin have already found their gifts. Or so they say. But still I falter. An elixir of strength from the alchemist? A bird that sings beneath the waves?"

Ulla huffed out a breath, a human gesture she'd learned to enjoy. "Why does it matter? Why do you even want to be king?"

"I thought you of all people would understand."

Hungry Ulla. Maybe she did. A song had made two lonely girls friends. A prince's favor had made them worthy of notice. What might a crown do for that prince?

"You want to spend your days negotiating with the other sea folk?" she asked. "Your nights in endless ritual?" She bumped her shoulder against his. "Roffe, you can barely be counted upon to rise before noon."

"That's what advisers are for."

"A king cannot simply rely on advisers."

"A king bows to no one," Roffe said, his blue eyes trained on something Ulla could not see. "A king chooses his own path. His own wife."

Ulla shifted uneasily, wishing she could be weightless for just a moment, caught in the saltwater arms of the sea. Was Roffe making the very offer Signy had feared?

"Roffe—" she began.

But as if sensing her discomfort, Roffe continued, "A king chooses his own court. His own singers."

How easily princes played. How easily they spoke of dreams they had no business offering. But Ulla could not help the yearning she felt as Roffe bent his head as if to whisper endearments.

"I would raise you so high, Ulla. No one would gossip about your birth or your wayward mother ever again."

Ulla flinched. It was one thing to know what others thought, another to hear it spoken. "They will always gossip."

Roffe smiled slightly. "Then they will do it far more quietly."

What might a crown do for a prince? What might a king do for a girl like her?

Signy's laughter floated up to them from the maze below. She was easy to spot, her hair burning like banked embers, a red banner of war streaming behind her as a mortal boy pursued her down the row. Ulla watched her let the boy catch her, spin her around.

"You want to win the throne and impress your father?" she asked Roffe.

"You know I do."

Signy tossed back her head and threw her arms wide, her face framed by curls like living flame.

Ulla nodded. "Then bring him fire."

As soon as she said it, Ulla realized her foolishness, but from then on, the prince could think of

nothing else. He left off chasing human girls entirely, clois-tered himself in the Prophetic's Tower, barely ate or drank.

"He will drive himself mad," said Signy as they shivered beneath the covers one night.

"I doubt he has the focus for it."

"Don't be unkind."

"I don't mean to be," said Ulla, and she thought that it was true.

"Could the mirror be a gift for the king instead?" Signy asked. Ulla had told her of the strange mirror and the room full of odd objects in the tower.

"He might be amused by it." For a time.

"Roffe thinks only of fire, day and night. Why did you put such a thought in his head?"

Because he made me dream of things I cannot have, she thought, but said, "He asked and I answered. He should know better than to think it's possible." It was one thing to bring a crea-ture of the land beneath the sea and make it live and breathe for a time. That was powerful magic, yes, but not so radi-cally different from the enchantments that allowed the sildroher to walk on land. But to toy with the elements, to make a flame burn when it had no fuel to do so . . . It would require greater magic than the song that had

created the nautilus hall. It could not be done. "He must turn his mind to something else."

"So I've told him," Signy fretted. "But he will not listen." She tugged gently at Ulla's cuff. "Perhaps the king's seer might help. Or the seer's apprentice. He's been friendly to you. I've seen it."

Ulla shivered. The apprentice had left her in peace since that day in the tower. He seemed to have his own work to attend to, but she was aware of him always, sitting silent at table beside his master, walking the grounds, the spilled ink of his black clothes moving from shadow to shadow.

"Talk to him," insisted Signy. "Please, Ulla." She took Ulla's hands in hers. "For me. Won't you at least speak to him? What harm could it do?"

Quite a lot, Ulla suspected. "Perhaps."

"Ulla—"

"Perhaps," she said, and rolled over. She did not want to look at Signy anymore.

But when her friend took up a dreaming song, low and sweet, Ulla could not help but join her. It wove a warm glow around them as it rose and fell.

Ulla did not know which of them fell asleep first, only that she dreamed she stood at the center of the hedge maze wearing a mantle of fire,

238

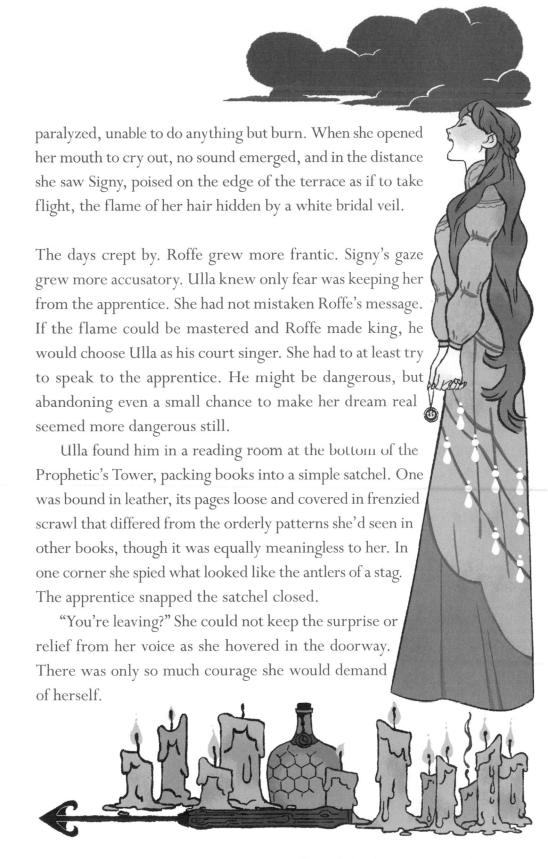

paralyzed, unable to do anything but burn. When she opened her mouth to cry out, no sound emerged, and in the distance she saw Signy, poised on the edge of the terrace as if to take flight, the flame of her hair hidden by a white bridal veil.

The days crept by. Roffe grew more frantic. Signy's gaze grew more accusatory. Ulla knew only fear was keeping her from the apprentice. She had not mistaken Roffe's message. If the flame could be mastered and Roffe made king, he would choose Ulla as his court singer. She had to at least try to speak to the apprentice. He might be dangerous, but abandoning even a small chance to make her dream real seemed more dangerous still.

Ulla found him in a reading room at the bottom of the Prophetic's Tower, packing books into a simple satchel. One was bound in leather, its pages loose and covered in frenzied scrawl that differed from the orderly patterns she'd seen in other books, though it was equally meaningless to her. In one corner she spied what looked like the antlers of a stag. The apprentice snapped the satchel closed.

"You're leaving?" She could not keep the surprise or relief from her voice as she hovered in the doorway. There was only so much courage she would demand of herself.

"I can never stay in any one place too long."

She wondered why. Had he committed some crime?

"You will miss the ball," she noted.

A bare smile touched his lips. "I do not care for dancing."

But Ulla had not risked this visit for the sake of idle conversation. She flexed her toes in her slippers. There was nothing for it but to ask. "I seek . . . I seek a flame that might burn beneath the sea."

The apprentice's gray eyes skewered her like a pin through a moth's body. "And what possible use could such a thing have?"

"A frivolity," Ulla said. "Like the mirror. A trifle for a king."

"Ah," mused the apprentice, "but which king?"

Ulla said nothing.

The apprentice tightened the clasps on his satchel. "Come," he said. "I will give you two answers."

"Two?" she said as she followed him up the spiral stairs.

"One to the question you asked, and one to the question you should have asked."

"What question is that?" She realized he was leading her back to the room of strange objects.

240

"Why you are not like the others."

Ulla felt the cold settle in her bones, the night rushing in, vaster than the sea. Still she followed.

When the apprentice opened the door of the glass cabinet beside the trick mirror, she thought he would reach for the sykurn knife. Instead he held up a bell that she hadn't even noticed, the size of an apple and tarnished from neglect.

As he lifted it, the clapper struck—a high silvery sound— and Ulla released a cry, clutching at her chest. Her muscles seized. It felt as if a fist had squeezed itself tight around her heart.

"I remember you," he said, watching her, the same words he'd spoken when he'd approached her at the first night's feast.

"That can't be," she gasped, breathless from the pain, the ache receding only as the sound of the bell faded.

"Do you know why your voice is so strong?" the apprentice asked. "Because you were born on land. Because you took your first breath above the surface and bawled your first infant cry here. Then my mother, *our* mother, took up the bell your father had given her, the bell he'd placed in her hand when he realized she carried a child. She went down to the shore and knelt at the waters and held the bell beneath the waves. She rang it once, twice,

and a few moments later your father emerged in the shallows, his silver tail like a sickle moon behind him, and took you away."

She shook her head. *It cannot be.*

"Look into the mirror," he commanded, "and try to deny it."

Ulla thought of her mother's long fingers combing through her hair tentatively, then grudgingly, as if she could not quite bear to touch her. She thought of her father who had raged and warned of the temptations of the shore. *It must not be.*

"I remember you," he repeated. "You were born with a tail. Every summer I've come here to study and watch the sea folk, wondering if you might return."

"No," said Ulla. "No. The sildroher cannot breed with humans. I cannot have a mortal mother."

He gave a slight shrug. "Not entirely mortal. The people of this country would call her drüsje, witch. They would call me one, too. They play at magic, read the stars, throw bones. But it's best not to show them real power. Your people know this well."

Impossible, insisted a shrill, frightened voice inside her. *Impossible.* But another voice, a voice sly with knowing, whispered, *You have never been like the*

242

others and you never will be. Her black hair. Her black eyes. The strength of her song.

It cannot be true. But if it was . . . If it was true, then she and this boy shared a mother. Had Ulla's father known the girl he'd laid down with was a witch? That there might be a price for his dalliance, one he would be forced to look upon every day? And what of Ulla's sildroher mother? Had she been able to bear no child of her own? Was that why she had made a cradle for some unnatural thing, fed her, tried to love her? *She does love me.* That voice again, wheedling now, feeble. *She does.*

Ulla felt the hurt inside her winnow to a hard point. "And did your witch mother care at all for the child she abandoned to the sea?"

But the apprentice did not look troubled by her harsh words. "She isn't one for sentiment."

"Where is she?" Ulla asked. A mother should be here to greet her daughter, to explain herself, to make amends.

"Far to the south, traveling with the Suli. I'll meet with her before the weather turns. Come with me. Ask her your questions, if you think the answers will bring you comfort."

Ulla shook her head again, as if such a gesture might erase this knowledge. Her limbs had gone weak. She grasped the lip of the table, tried to stay standing, but

it was as if with the ringing of that bell, her legs had forgotten what they were meant to do. Ulla slid to the floor and watched the girl in the glass do the same.

"You claimed you were hunting," she said, a flimsy kind of protest.

"They say the sea whip roams these waters. I want to see the ice dragon for myself. Knowledge. Magic. A chance to forge the world anew. I came seeking all those things. I came seeking you." The apprentice knelt beside her. "Come with me," he said. "You needn't return with them. You needn't belong to them."

Ulla could taste the salt of her tears on her lips. It reminded her of the sea. Was she crying then? What a human thing to do. She could feel herself splitting, dissolving, as if the apprentice's words had been a spell. It was like the cut of the sykurn knife, being torn apart all over again, knowing that she would never be wholly one thing or another, that the sea would always be strange upon her, that she would always carry the taint of land. Nothing could transform her. Nothing could make her right. If the sildroher ever learned what she was, that the rumors were not just rumors but true, she would be banished, maybe killed.

Unless she was too powerful to abandon. If Roffe became king, if Ulla found a way to give him what he wanted, he could protect her. She could make herself unassailable, indispensable. There was still time.

"The flame," she said. "Tell me how it's done."

He sighed and shook his head, then rose. "You know very well what it requires. You are creating a contradiction. A flame must be made and remade from moment to moment if it is to burn beneath the water."

Transformation. Creation. This would be no mere illusion. "Blood magic," she whispered.

He nodded. "But the blood of the sea folk will not be enough."

At this, Ulla's heart gave a frightened hitch. There were few rules the sildroher were bound by on land. They might trifle with the humans, break their hearts, steal their secrets or their treasures, but they could not take a mortal life. *Remember how fragile these creatures are. Spill not their blood.* The sea folk had too much power over the people of the shore as it was.

"Human blood?" Even speaking the words felt like a transgression.

"Not just blood." Her brother bent and whispered the requirements of the spell into the shell of Ulla's ear.

Ulla shoved him away and scrambled to her feet, stomach roiling, wishing she could unhear the words he'd just uttered.

"Then it cannot be done," she said. She was lost. Roffe was lost. It was that simple. That final. She brushed the tears from her eyes and smoothed her skirts, wishing they were scales. "The prince will not be happy."

Her brother laughed. He touched his finger to the silver bell that still sat on the table. "We were not made to please princes."

You were born on land. . . . You took your first breath above the surface and bawled your first infant cry here.

And she'd been crying out since. She did not want the apprentice's knowledge, not of her birth, not of the ways of blood magic. She did not want this tower with its rotting books and pillaged treasures. She turned and fled toward the stairs.

Then the bell tolled, sweet and silver, the sound a hook that lodged in her heart. Her muscles contracted and she felt herself turning as the bell drew her back, just as it had once compelled her father.

Ulla seized the doorjamb, forced her muscles to still, refusing to let her traitorous legs carry her

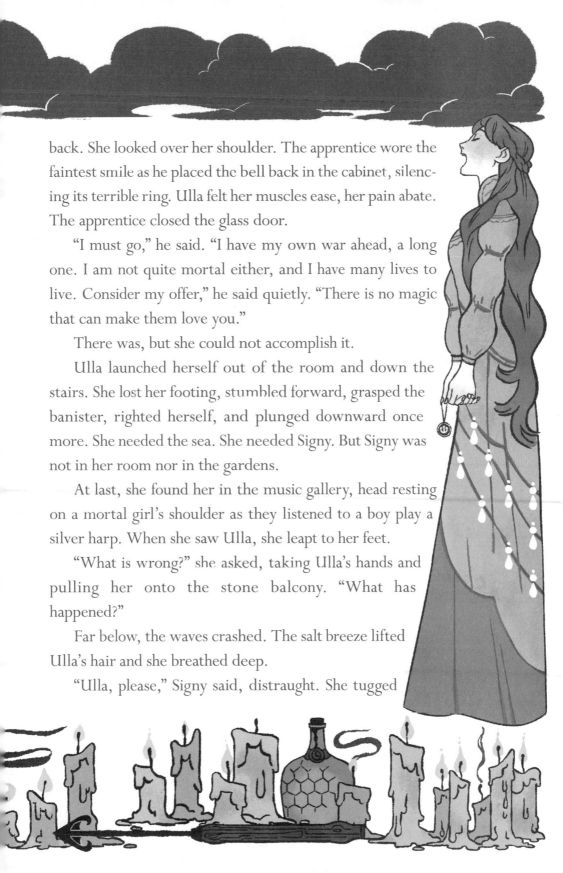

back. She looked over her shoulder. The apprentice wore the faintest smile as he placed the bell back in the cabinet, silencing its terrible ring. Ulla felt her muscles ease, her pain abate. The apprentice closed the glass door.

"I must go," he said. "I have my own war ahead, a long one. I am not quite mortal either, and I have many lives to live. Consider my offer," he said quietly. "There is no magic that can make them love you."

There was, but she could not accomplish it.

Ulla launched herself out of the room and down the stairs. She lost her footing, stumbled forward, grasped the banister, righted herself, and plunged downward once more. She needed the sea. She needed Signy. But Signy was not in her room nor in the gardens.

At last, she found her in the music gallery, head resting on a mortal girl's shoulder as they listened to a boy play a silver harp. When she saw Ulla, she leapt to her feet.

"What is wrong?" she asked, taking Ulla's hands and pulling her onto the stone balcony. "What has happened?"

Far below, the waves crashed. The salt breeze lifted Ulla's hair and she breathed deep.

"Ulla, please," Signy said, distraught. She tugged

Ulla down beside her onto a marble bench. Its base was carved to look like leaping dolphins. "Why these tears?"

But now that she was here, now that Signy's arm was around her, what could Ulla say? If Signy shrank from her, showed even the slightest sign of revulsion, Ulla knew she couldn't bear it. She would be undone.

"Signy," she attempted, eyes on the far blue plain of the ocean. "If the stories . . . what if the stories about me were true? What if I was not sildroher, but mortal too?" Drüsje. Witch.

Signy expelled a disbelieving laugh. "Don't be silly, Ulla. No one ever really believed that. They were just children being cruel."

"Will you not answer?"

"Oh, Ulla," Signy chided, drawing Ulla's head onto her lap. "Where is this nonsense coming from? Why this misery?"

"A dream," she murmured. "A bad dream."

"Is that all?" Signy began to hum a calming song, one that wove between the stray notes that drifted out to them from the harp.

"Will you not answer?" Ulla whispered again.

Signy ran a gentle hand over the silk of Ulla's

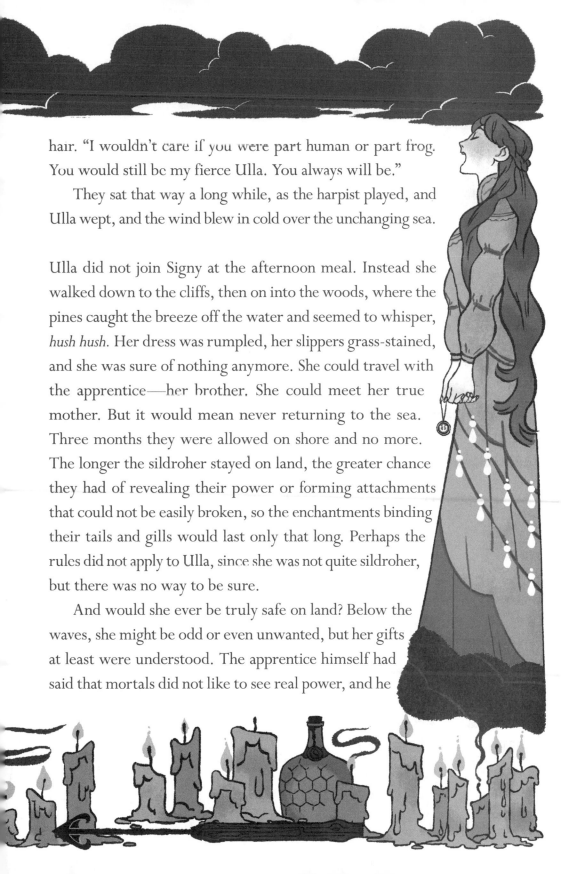

hair. "I wouldn't care if you were part human or part frog. You would still be my fierce Ulla. You always will be."

They sat that way a long while, as the harpist played, and Ulla wept, and the wind blew in cold over the unchanging sea.

Ulla did not join Signy at the afternoon meal. Instead she walked down to the cliffs, then on into the woods, where the pines caught the breeze off the water and seemed to whisper, *hush hush*. Her dress was rumpled, her slippers grass-stained, and she was sure of nothing anymore. She could travel with the apprentice—her brother. She could meet her true mother. But it would mean never returning to the sea. Three months they were allowed on shore and no more. The longer the sildroher stayed on land, the greater chance they had of revealing their power or forming attachments that could not be easily broken, so the enchantments binding their tails and gills would last only that long. Perhaps the rules did not apply to Ulla, since she was not quite sildroher, but there was no way to be sure.

And would she ever be truly safe on land? Below the waves, she might be odd or even unwanted, but her gifts at least were understood. The apprentice himself had said that mortals did not like to see real power, and he

had little idea of what her song could do. She sensed that, perhaps, it was best that he didn't know.

Ulla thought of the spell's requirements and shuddered. She could not give Roffe and Signy what they wanted. No one could.

And yet, when she found Roffe in the gardens and explained what the apprentice had told her, he did not put his face in his hands and admit defeat. Instead he leapt to his feet and paced, back and forth, crushing green leaves beneath his boot soles.

"It could be done."

Ulla lowered herself to the grass in the shade of the alder tree. "No, it could not."

"There are prisoners in the palace dungeons, murderers who will face the gallows anyway. We'd be doing no one any harm."

That was a lie she would not indulge in. "No."

"You needn't sully your hands," Roffe pleaded, going to his knees like a supplicant. "All you need accomplish is the spell."

As if that was some small thing. "It cannot be, Roffe."

He placed his hands on her shoulders. "I have

been a friend to you, haven't I, Ulla? Don't you care for me at all?"

"Enough to keep you from this wickedness."

"Think of what our lives could be. Think of what you might accomplish. We could build a new palace, a new concert hall. I would make you court singer. You could have your own choir."

The dream she'd held close to her heart for so long. There was no place for her on land or on sea, but Roffe was offering her the chance to make one. A chance to forge the world anew. With a choir at her command, she would have her own army, and who would dare challenge her then?

The want in her was an animal, scratching at her resolve, fretting its claws and saying, *Why not? Why not?* Safety, respect, companionship, a chance at greatness. What feats might she accomplish, what new music might she make, what future might she lay claim to—if she would only take the risk, pay the bloody price?

"No," she said, finding the anchor's chain within her. She had to keep steady. "I will not make this bargain."

Roffe's brow lowered. Weeks in the sun had turned his skin gold, his hair white. He looked like a petulant

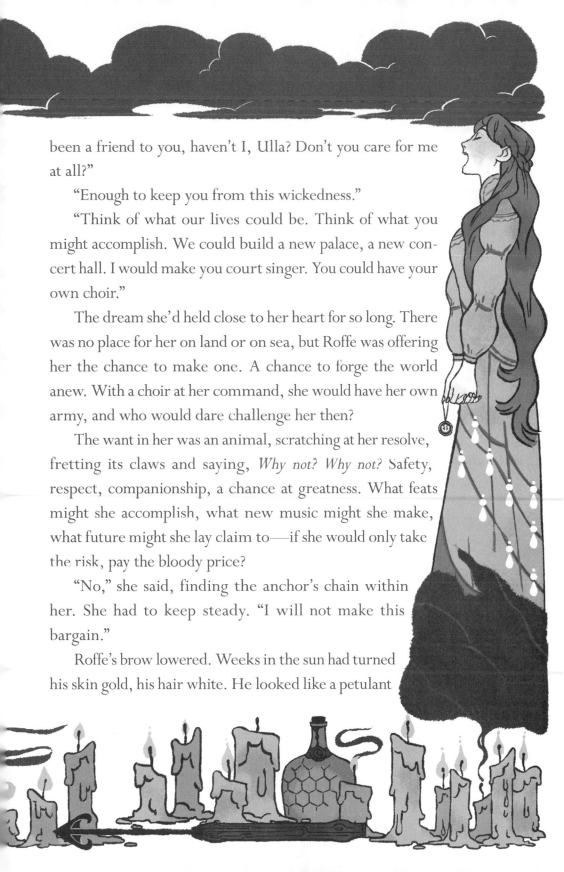

dandelion, gathering breath to throw a tantrum. "Tell me what you want, Ulla. Tell me and I will give it to you."

She closed her eyes. She had never felt so weary. "I want to go home, Roffe. I want the quiet and the weight of the water. I want you to give this up and stop worrying Signy sick."

There was a long silence. When at last Ulla looked at Roffe, he had rocked back on his heels and was watching her, his head cocked slightly to the side.

"I could make Signy my queen," he said.

In that moment, Ulla wished that she and Signy had chosen a humbler song when they had first performed for Roffe, that they'd never raised the royal gardens, or drawn his notice, or come to this place. Cunning Roffe. She should have known he would not be so easy to refuse. Had he always known the truth of Signy's heart? Had he enjoyed the steady light of her longing? Cultivated it?

"Do you love her at all?" Ulla asked.

Roffe shrugged and stood, brushing grass from his breeches. The sun behind him set his bright hair aglow.

"I love you both," he said easily. "But I would break her heart and yours to take my brother's crown."

I will not do it, Ulla vowed, watching Roffe stride across the gardens. *He cannot make me.*

But he was a prince and Ulla was wrong.

The beginnings of the spell crept into Ulla's dreams that night. She could not help it. Even as she'd denied Roffe, she'd started to hear the shape of the music in her head, and though she tried to quell the melody, it found its way to her. She woke up humming, a dull warmth in her chest. The flame would have to be built in her body and be born on her breath. But then what? Could it be transferred into an object?

No.

As she came fully awake, she sat up in her bed and tried to shake the echo of the song and the delicious pull of those questions from her head.

She could not do what Roffe asked. The risk was too great and the price too high.

But at breakfast, Roffe filled Signy's water glass himself instead of leaving it to a servant. At lunch he peeled the orange on his plate and fed her one of the slices. And when they went down to dinner, he turned away from the human girl on his left and spent the night making Signy howl with laughter.

It was a careful campaign he waged. He found ways to make sure he was seated next to Signy at meals. He rode beside her on every hunt. He lavished his golden smiles on her—tentatively at first, as if he was unsure of their reception, though Ulla knew that shyness was a ruse. Roffe watched Signy now as she had once watched him. He let her catch him looking. Each time, her cheeks flushed pink. Each time, Ulla saw new hope flare within her. Bit by bit, moment by moment, in a thousand small gestures, he made Signy believe he was falling in love with her, and Ulla could do nothing but observe.

The night before the great ball, the last of the parties before they would return to the sea, Signy slipped under the covers of Ulla's bed, glowing with the hope Roffe had kindled inside her.

"When we said good night, he pressed his lips to my wrist," Signy said, placing her own lips to the blue veins where her pulse beat. "He took my hand and placed it against his heart."

"Are you sure he can be trusted?" Ulla asked, so gently, so carefully, as if she were trying to hold broken glass.

But Signy recoiled, clutched her kissed hand to her chest like a talisman. "How can you ask that?"

"You are not noble—"

"But that's the magic of it. He doesn't care. He's grown weary of noble girls. Oh, Ulla, it is more than I could have hoped. To think he could want me above all others."

"Of course he could," Ulla murmured. *Of course.*

Signy sighed and flopped back against the pillows, slender hands pressed to her brow, as if she suffered from headache. "It cannot all be real. He cannot possibly mean to make me his wife." She bounced her dainty heels against the sheets, kicking the way humans did when they were trying not to drown. She had never been more beautiful. Ulla tasted poison in her mouth. "Do you think I might make a passable princess?" Signy asked.

Charming Roffe. More clever than Ulla had ever imagined. If Ulla did as the prince asked, he would give Signy all she wanted, or at least the illusion of it. If Ulla did not, he would break Signy's heart, and Ulla knew it would destroy her friend. It was one thing for Signy to have loved Roffe from afar, but how deeply had she let herself fall now that he'd given her permission to love him? The dam had broken. There was no calling back the water.

So it was decided.

"You would make a passable princess," Ulla said. "But a far better queen."

Signy seized Ulla's wrists. "You spoke to the apprentice? You've found a spell for the flame?"

"A song," Ulla said. "But it will be dangerous."

Signy pressed a kiss to her friend's cheek. "There is nothing you cannot do."

And nothing I will not do to protect you, Ulla vowed. *The bargain is made.*

Signy was all joy the next day, asking Ulla to sing her a dress for the ball, laughing that she cared for mortal clothes no longer.

Ulla prayed Roffe would make Signy happy. Though he might not make a great king, he would at least be a cunning one. Besides, she would be there at his right hand to make sure he kept to their bargain. Now she knew she was not just sildroher but something else too. She had witch's blood in her veins. Roffe would make Signy a queen and treat her as such, or Ulla would bring the roof of his palace down on his kingly head.

Signy brought one of her mortal dresses to Ulla's room. They threw open their trunks and chose the best pearls and beading from their wardrobes and sang them together into a gown of copper fire that made Signy look like a living conflagration. A good reminder for Roffe. When they were done, there was little left for Ulla, so she plucked a clutch of irises from the garden, and from them and a slender scrap of silk she sang a purple gown hemmed in gold.

They ascended the great stairs and passed the landing where the clever mirror had been set to entertain the guests, who were already clowning before it. Their reflections waved to them, then preened in their fine clothes.

Up to the grand ballroom Ulla and Signy climbed, and there they joined the celebration.

Ulla danced with anyone who asked that night. She had not bothered with slippers, and her nimble feet peeked from beneath her skirts as she whirled and leapt on the marble floor. But she took no pleasure from the perspiration on her skin, the rapid keening of the fiddles. For all its wonders, she'd grown weary of the human world and the constant press of mortal desire. She longed for the sea, for the mother she knew, for the barely broken quiet.

She would have been happy to return now, before midnight struck, but there was still work to be done on land—work that would secure all their fortunes.

Ulla saw Roffe disappear from the crowd. She saw his brothers drinking and dancing on this the last night. And then the clock was striking the eleventh hour.

She found Signy in the crowd and pressed her palm to the damp small of her back. "It's time," she said.

Hand in hand they left the ball and went to meet Roffe outside Ulla's chamber.

When Ulla pushed open the door, she could already feel the wrongness that had settled there. The chamber had become familiar to her, dear to her in its own way despite her homesickness. She was used to its smells, stone and wax and the pines far below. But now there was something—someone in her bed.

In the moonlight, she saw the body laid out upon the covers.

"I do not wish to do this here."

"We're out of time," said Roffe.

Ulla drew closer to the bed.

"He's young," she said, a sickness growing in

her gut. His hands and feet were bound. His chest rose and fell evenly, his mouth hanging open slightly.

"He's a murderer. Sentenced to hang. In a way, this is a kindness."

This death would be painless, private. No wait in a prison cell, no walk up the gallows steps or crowd to jeer him. Could that be called a kindness?

"You drugged him?" Signy asked.

"Yes, but he'll wake eventually, and the hour of return comes on. Hurry."

Ulla had told him they would need a vessel of pure silver to capture the flame. From a case by the window, Roffe drew a square silver lantern. Into its side, the symbol of his family had been cut—a three-pronged triton. There was little other preparation to be made.

Ulla had worked the spell again and again in her mind, practiced snippets of it separately before she would try to piece together the whole. And if she was honest, she'd had the sound of it with her since she'd first made the suggestion to Roffe in the garden. He had pushed her to this moment, but now that they were here, some shameful part of her thrilled to the challenge.

She knelt to face the hearth and set down the

silver lantern. Signy settled beside her, and Ulla lit the
white birch branches that she'd lain in the grate. The night
was far too hot for a fire, but the flame was required.

"When do I—" said Roffe.

Without turning, Ulla silenced him with a raised hand.

"Watch me," she said. "Await my signal." He might be
a prince, but tonight he would follow her orders.

She kept her hand in the air, her eyes on the flames, and
slowly, she began the melody.

The song built in easy phrases, as if Ulla was stacking a
different kind of kindling. The melody was something
new, not quite a healing song, not quite a making song. She
gestured to Signy to join. The sound of their twined voices
was low and uneasy, the striking of flint, the hop and
crackle of sparks.

Then the song jumped like fire catching. Ulla could
feel it now, a warm glow inside her, a flame she would
breathe into the lantern and, in one bright moment,
make a future for them all. The price was the boy on
the bed. A stranger. Little more than a child. But
weren't they all children really? Ulla kept to the
melody, pushed the thoughts from her head. *The
boy is a murderer*, she reminded herself.

Murderer. She kept that word in her head as

the song rose higher, as the blaze in the hearth leapt wild and orange, as the discord sharpened and the heat in her belly grew. *Murderer,* she told herself again, but she did not know if she meant the boy or herself. Sweat broke over her brow. The song filled the room, so loud she worried they might draw someone's attention, but all were below, dancing and feasting.

The moment came, a high crescendo. Ulla dropped her hand like a flag of surrender. Even above the sound of their voices, she heard a horrible wet *thunk*, and the boy cried out, woken from his sleep by the blade piercing his chest. She heard muffled moaning and knew Roffe must have a hand on the boy's mouth as he cut.

Signy's frightened gaze flicked to the bed. Ulla told herself not to look, but she couldn't help it. She turned and saw Roffe's back, hunched over his victim as he did his work—his shoulders too broad, his gray cloak like the pelt of a beast.

Ulla turned her eyes back to the fire and sang, feeling tears slide down her cheeks, knowing they had crossed a border into lands from which they might never return. But there was nowhere else to look when Roffe knelt beside her and slipped two fresh, pink human lungs into the pyre.

This was what the spell required. Breath. The fire

demanded air just as humans did. It would need to breathe for itself beneath the sea.

The flames closed over the wet tissue, fizzing and spitting. Ulla felt the magical heat within her bank, and for a moment she thought both fires would simply go out. Then, with a loud *snap*, the flames roared up in the grate as if they had a voice themselves.

Ulla fell backward, fighting the urge to cry out as the blaze in her gut tore through her, up through her own lungs, her throat. Something was horribly wrong. Or was this the pain that creation required? Her eyes rolled back in her head and Signy reached for her, then cringed backward, as flames seemed to flicker beneath Ulla's skin, traveling her arms, lighting her up like a paper lantern. Ulla smelled burning and knew her hair had caught fire.

She released a wail and it became a part of the song as flames poured from her throat and into the silver vessel. Signy was weeping. Roffe had his bloody hands clenched before him.

Ulla could not stop screaming. She could not stop the song. She seized Signy's arm, pleading, and Signy reached forward to slam the silver lantern shut.

Silence. Ulla crumpled to the floor.

She heard Signy cry her name and tried to answer, but the pain was too great. Her lips were blistered; her throat still felt as if it was burning. Her whole body shook and convulsed.

Roffe held the silver lantern in his hands, the shape of his family's triton glowing with golden light.

"Roffe," said Signy. "Go to the ballroom. Get the others. We need to sing healing. My voice won't be enough."

But the prince wasn't listening. He walked to the dressing table and upended the basin, dousing the lantern. The flame did not even sputter.

Ulla moaned.

"*Roffe!*" Signy snapped, and some part of Ulla's heart returned at the anger in her friend's voice. "We need help."

The clock began to chime the half hour. Roffe seemed to return to himself.

"It's time to go home," he said.

"She's too weak," said Signy. "She won't be able to sing the transformation."

"That's true," Roffe said slowly, and the regret in his words set Ulla alive with fear.

"Roffe." Ulla gasped his name. Her voice was a shattered thing, barely a rasp. *What have I done?* she thought wildly. *What have I done?*

"I'm sorry," he said. Are there any words so cursed? "The lantern must be my gift only."

Despite the pain, Ulla wanted to laugh. "No one . . . will believe . . . you worked . . . that song."

"Signy will be my witness."

"I will not," Signy spat.

"We will tell them you and I forged the song together. That the lantern is a sign of our love. That I am a worthy king and you are a worthy queen."

"You took a human life . . ." Ulla gasped. "You spilled human blood."

"Did I?" Roffe said, and from his cloak he drew Ulla's sykurn knife. He'd wiped it mostly clean, but the wet remnants of blood still gleamed on its blade. "You took a boy's life, an innocent page who caught you working blood magic."

Innocent. Ulla shook her head, and fresh pain flared in her throat. "No," she moaned. "No."

"You said he was a criminal," cried Signy. "A murderer!"

"You knew," said Roffe. "Both of you knew. You were as eager as I, as hungry. You just wouldn't look your ambition in the eye."

Signy shook her head. But Ulla wondered. Had either of them bothered to look closely at the boy's soft hands? At his clean face? Or had they simply wanted this enough that they'd been willing to leave the ugly work to Roffe?

Roffe dropped the blade at Ulla's feet. "She cannot return now. The blade is sacred. It can touch nothing human or be corrupted. It's useless."

Signy was sobbing. "You cannot do this. You cannot do this, Roffe."

He knelt, and the flame of the lantern caught the gold of his hair, the deep ocean of his eyes. "Signy, it is done."

That was when Ulla understood. It was Signy who had asked her to unlock her chest to make her a gown.

"Why?" she rasped. "Why?"

"He said he needed the knife to secure your loyalty." Signy wept. "In case you changed your mind about the spell."

Oh, Signy, Ulla thought as her eyes filled with fresh tears. *My loyalty never wavered, and it was never his.*

"It is done," Roffe repeated. "Stay with Ulla and live in exile, pay the price with her when the humans discover her crime. Or. . ."—he shrugged—"return to the sea as my bride. It is cruel. I know it is. But

kings must sometimes be cruel. And to be my queen
you must be cruel now too."

"Signy," Ulla managed. Her name hurt more to speak
than any other word. "Please."

Signy's tears fell harder, splashed over the knife. She
touched her fingers to its ruined blade.

"Ulla," she sobbed. "I cannot lose everything."

"Not everything. Not everything."

Signy shook her head. "I am not strong enough for this
fight."

"You are," Ulla rasped past the tortured flesh of her
throat. "We are. Together. As we have always been."

Signy brushed her cool knuckles over Ulla's cheek.
"Ulla. My fierce Ulla. You know I was never strong."

My fierce Ulla. She saw then what she had been to
Signy all along—a shelter, a defense. Ulla had been the
only rock to cling to, so Signy had held on, but now
the seas had calmed and she was slipping away to seek
other shelter. She was letting go.

Ulla found that she was tired. The pain had
devoured her strength. *Rest*, said a voice inside
her. Her mother? Or the witch mother she'd
never known? The mother who had left her

to the mercy of the waves. If Signy could leave her behind so easily too, maybe it was best not to try to hold on.

Ulla had made a vow to protect Signy, and she'd done it. That had to mean something. She released her friend's hand, a final kindness. After all, she was the strong one.

"Leave the knife," Ulla croaked in her broken speech, and prayed that death would close over her like water.

But Signy did not pick up the knife. Instead she turned her eyes to Roffe—and in the end, this was the thing that doomed all of Söndermane. Ulla could forgive betrayal, another abandonment, even her own death. But not this moment, when after all her sacrifice, she begged for mercy and Signy sought a prince's permission to grant it.

Roffe nodded. "Let it be our gift to her."

Only then did Signy place the blade in Ulla's hand.

Roffe took up the lantern, and without another word, they were gone.

Ulla lay in the dark, the sykurn knife clutched in her fingers. She felt the stillness of the room, the cold grate, the chill presence of the hollowed corpse on the bed. She could end her life now. Simply, cleanly. No one would ever know what had happened. She would be buried in the ground or burned. Whatever they did to

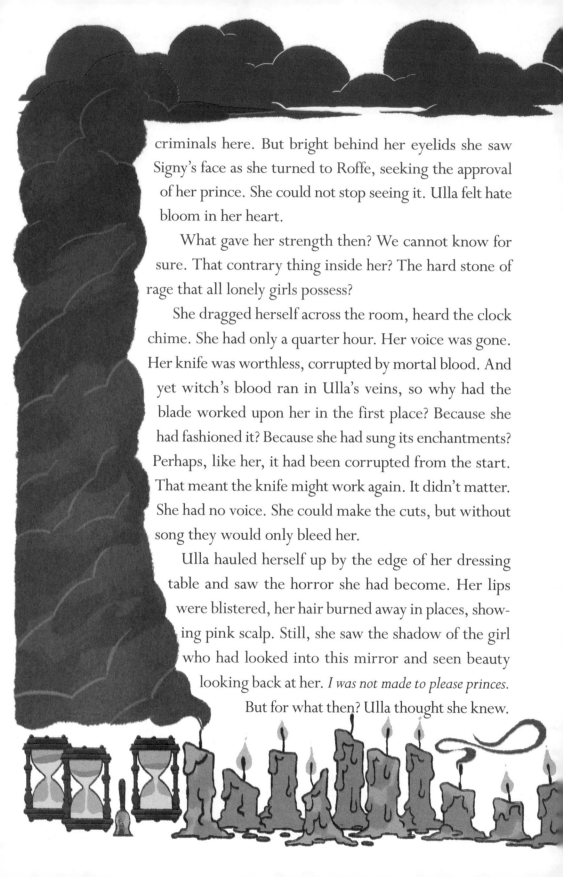

criminals here. But bright behind her eyelids she saw
Signy's face as she turned to Roffe, seeking the approval
of her prince. She could not stop seeing it. Ulla felt hate
bloom in her heart.

What gave her strength then? We cannot know for
sure. That contrary thing inside her? The hard stone of
rage that all lonely girls possess?

She dragged herself across the room, heard the clock
chime. She had only a quarter hour. Her voice was gone.
Her knife was worthless, corrupted by mortal blood. And
yet witch's blood ran in Ulla's veins, so why had the
blade worked upon her in the first place? Because she
had fashioned it? Because she had sung its enchantments?
Perhaps, like her, it had been corrupted from the start.
That meant the knife might work again. It didn't matter.
She had no voice. She could make the cuts, but without
song they would only bleed her.

Ulla hauled herself up by the edge of her dressing
table and saw the horror she had become. Her lips
were blistered, her hair burned away in places, showing pink scalp. Still, she saw the shadow of the girl
who had looked into this mirror and seen beauty
looking back at her. *I was not made to please princes.*
But for what then? Ulla thought she knew.

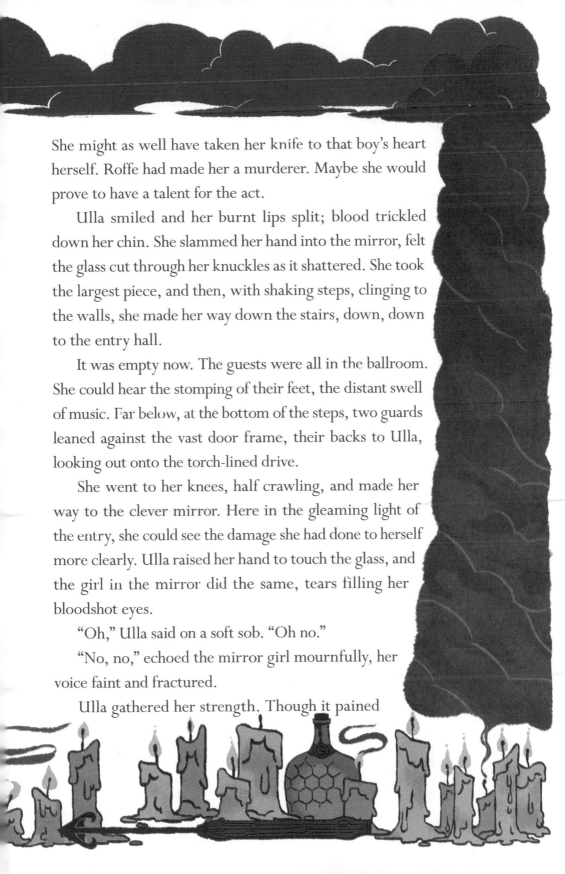

She might as well have taken her knife to that boy's heart herself. Roffe had made her a murderer. Maybe she would prove to have a talent for the act.

Ulla smiled and her burnt lips split; blood trickled down her chin. She slammed her hand into the mirror, felt the glass cut through her knuckles as it shattered. She took the largest piece, and then, with shaking steps, clinging to the walls, she made her way down the stairs, down, down to the entry hall.

It was empty now. The guests were all in the ballroom. She could hear the stomping of their feet, the distant swell of music. Far below, at the bottom of the steps, two guards leaned against the vast door frame, their backs to Ulla, looking out onto the torch-lined drive.

She went to her knees, half crawling, and made her way to the clever mirror. Here in the gleaming light of the entry, she could see the damage she had done to herself more clearly. Ulla raised her hand to touch the glass, and the girl in the mirror did the same, tears filling her bloodshot eyes.

"Oh," Ulla said on a soft sob. "Oh no."

"No, no," echoed the mirror girl mournfully, her voice faint and fractured.

Ulla gathered her strength. Though it pained

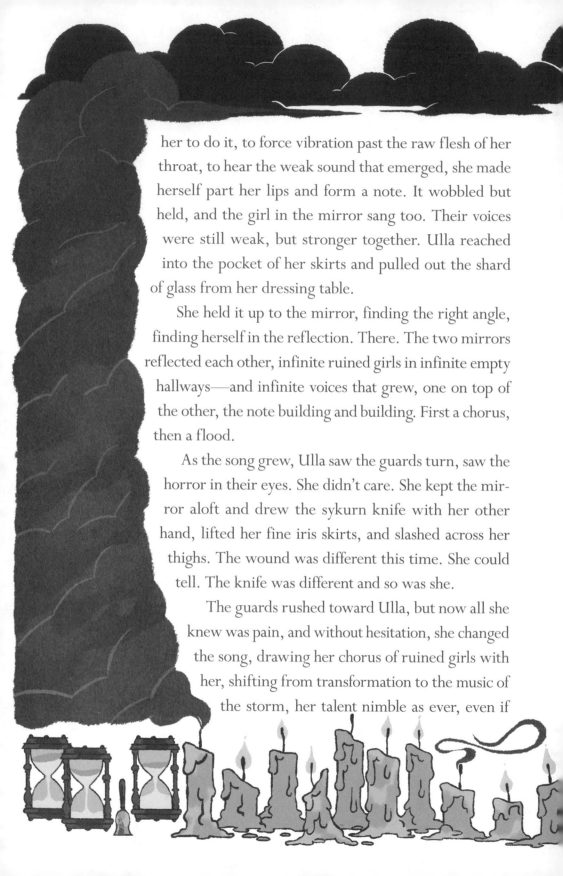

her to do it, to force vibration past the raw flesh of her throat, to hear the weak sound that emerged, she made herself part her lips and form a note. It wobbled but held, and the girl in the mirror sang too. Their voices were still weak, but stronger together. Ulla reached into the pocket of her skirts and pulled out the shard of glass from her dressing table.

She held it up to the mirror, finding the right angle, finding herself in the reflection. There. The two mirrors reflected each other, infinite ruined girls in infinite empty hallways—and infinite voices that grew, one on top of the other, the note building and building. First a chorus, then a flood.

As the song grew, Ulla saw the guards turn, saw the horror in their eyes. She didn't care. She kept the mirror aloft and drew the sykurn knife with her other hand, lifted her fine iris skirts, and slashed across her thighs. The wound was different this time. She could tell. The knife was different and so was she.

The guards rushed toward Ulla, but now all she knew was pain, and without hesitation, she changed the song, drawing her chorus of ruined girls with her, shifting from transformation to the music of the storm, her talent nimble as ever, even if

her throat bled around the notes she demanded. Thunder cracked, shaking the palace walls, hard enough to drive the guards down the stairs.

Storm magic. The first she had learned. The first they all learned, the easiest, though impossible to accomplish on your own. But Ulla was not alone; all these broken, betrayed girls were with her, and what a terrible sound they made.

Onward Ulla drove the song, weaving the two melodies together, sea and sky, water and blood. With a crack of lightning, the transformation took hold. Her hair rippled from her scalp, and in the mirror she saw it billowed and curled like dark smoke. Her skin was hard stone and bloomed with lichen, and when she looked down, she saw her thighs binding. But the scales that emerged were not silver, no, they were not scales at all. Her new tail was black and slick and muscular as an eel.

On and on the voices rose, and now Ulla thought she could hear the sea moaning, calling out to her. *Home.*

A great wave slammed against the side of the cliff with a tremendous *boom*. Another and another. The sea climbed with Ulla's song. Water roared over the cliff and rushed into the palace, smashing the windows, pouring over the stairs. Ulla heard people screaming,

a thousand mortal cries. The water reached her, embraced her, tore the glass from her hand. But it didn't matter. This was blood magic, and the song had a life of its own.

The tempest that raged that night broke the land from the northernmost tip of Fjerda and formed the islands that the men of the land now call Kenst Hjerte, the broken heart. The sands turned black and the waters froze and never warmed again, so now all that exist there are whaling villages and the few brave souls who can bear such empty places. Söndermane, its treasures and its people, the Prophetic's Tower and all the learning it contained, vanished into the sea.

The storm tore the palace of the sildroher kings from the seabed and wrecked the gardens Ulla and Signy had once built, leaving nothing behind. When at last the waters calmed and the sea folk found one another once again, Signy and Roffe and their silver lantern had survived it all. After an appropriate time had passed, he became king.

As it happens, Roffe did stay loyal to Signy. Perhaps he loved her all along. Perhaps she knew

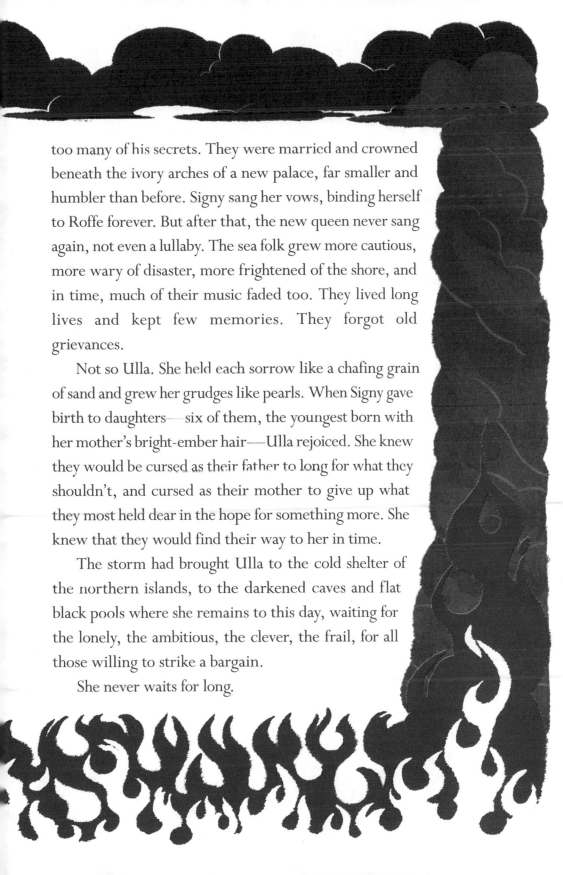

too many of his secrets. They were married and crowned
beneath the ivory arches of a new palace, far smaller and
humbler than before. Signy sang her vows, binding herself
to Roffe forever. But after that, the new queen never sang
again, not even a lullaby. The sea folk grew more cautious,
more wary of disaster, more frightened of the shore, and
in time, much of their music faded too. They lived long
lives and kept few memories. They forgot old
grievances.

Not so Ulla. She held each sorrow like a chafing grain
of sand and grew her grudges like pearls. When Signy gave
birth to daughters—six of them, the youngest born with
her mother's bright-ember hair—Ulla rejoiced. She knew
they would be cursed as their father to long for what they
shouldn't, and cursed as their mother to give up what
they most held dear in the hope for something more. She
knew that they would find their way to her in time.

The storm had brought Ulla to the cold shelter of
the northern islands, to the darkened caves and flat
black pools where she remains to this day, waiting for
the lonely, the ambitious, the clever, the frail, for all
those willing to strike a bargain.

She never waits for long.

THE WANDERING ISLE

THE BONE ROAD

JELKA

VILKI

OLEFLIT

NOVYI ZEM

WEDDLE

THE TRUE SEA

REB HARBOR

EAMES HARBOR

SHRIFTPORT

EAMES CHIN

COFTON

KETTERDAM

BELENDT

KERCH

LAND BRIDGE

SOUTHERN COLONIES

Map Illustration by Keith Thompson

ISENVEE

KENST HJERTE

ELLING

OVERÜT

AVFALLE

FJERDA

ELBJEN

DJERHOLM

PERMAFROST

TSIBEYA

PETRAZOI

THE UNSEA

RAVKA

KRIBIRSK

OS KERVO

OS ALTA

KERAMZIN

TSEMNA

DVA STOLBA

SIKURZOI

KOBA

BHEZ JU

SHU HAN

AHMRAT JEN

AUTHOR'S NOTE

Back in 2012 during the lead-up to the release of my first novel, my publisher asked if I would write a prequel story for *Shadow and Bone*. I was game, but the idea that came to me had little to do with the characters of that book. Instead, it was a tale that the characters might have heard when they were young, my own take on a story that had troubled me as a child—"Hansel and Gretel."

My favorite version of that particular story was the creepily titled *Nibble Nibble Mousekin* by Joan Walsh Anglund, and it wasn't the cannibal witch who bothered me. It wasn't even the selfish stepmother. For me, the real villain was Hansel and Gretel's father, a man so weak-willed, so cowardly, that he let his wicked wife send his children into the woods to die twice. *Don't go back*, I would whisper as we approached the inevitable final illustration—happy father reunited with children, evil stepmother banished—and I was always left with a feeling of unease as I turned the last page.

In many ways, that unease has guided me through these stories, that note of trouble that I think many of us hear in familiar tales, because we know—even as children—that impossible tasks are an odd way to choose a spouse, that predators come in many guises, that a prince's whims are often cruel. The more I listened to that note of warning, the more inspiration I found.

There were other influences, too. The horrible legends of Tarrare's polyphagia found their way into Ayama's first tale in far gentler form. The childhood trauma visited on me by *The Velveteen Rabbit* and the distressing idea that only love can make you real took a different shape in "The Soldier Prince." As for my mermaids, while Hans Christian Andersen's original tale served as a point of departure, it's worth mentioning that Ulla is the Swedish diminutive of Ursula.

I hope you enjoy these stories and the world they populate. I hope you read them aloud when the weather turns cold. And when your chance comes, I hope you stir the pot.

ACKNOWLEDGMENTS

Sara Kipin's illustrations grace nearly every page of this collection, and I am grateful for each bold brushstroke and surprising detail.

Many wonderful people at MCPG and Imprint worked tirelessly to bring this project to life—particularly my magical editor Erin Stein; Natalie Sousa and Ellen Duda, who gave this book its beautiful cover and guided the design of its interior art; my genius publicists Molly Ellis and Morgan Dubin; the relentlessly creative Kathryn Little; Raymond Ernesto Colón, who helped manage the complicated production process of a two-color printing; Caitlin Sweeny; Mariel Dawson; Lucy Del Priore; Tiara Kittrell; the entire Fierce Reads team; Kristin Dulaney; Allison Verost; and, of course, Jon Yaged, who keeps indulging me for some reason. Thanks also to Tor.com for publishing the three Ravkan tales that appear in this book and to Noa Wheeler who edited them so thoughtfully.

I somehow landed in the field of clover that is the New Leaf Literary family. Many thanks to Hilary Pecheone, who always finds a way to deliver on the impossible; Devin Ross; Pouya Shahbazian; Chris McEwen; Kathleen Ortiz; Mia Roman; Danielle Barthel; and, of course, Joanna Volpe, who nurtured the dream of this collection from the start.

Endless gratitude to my army of witches and queens who give generous feedback and ferocious support: Morgan Fahey,

Robyn Kali Bacon, Rachael Martin, Sarah Mesle, and Michelle Chihara. Along with Dan Braun, Katie Philips, Liz Hamilton, Josh Kamensky, and Heather Joy Rosenberg, they also helped name this collection. That nice lady at the party helped too. I think she was a landscape architect. It was a team effort all around.

Sarah Jae-Jones advised on musical terminology. Susan Dennard educated me on marine biology and the existence of moon jellyfish. David Peterson helped me name my mermaids and my knives. Marie Lu, Sabaa Tahir, Alex Bracken, Gretchen McNeil, Jimmy Freeman, and Victoria Aveyard kept me laughing. Rainbow Rowell sustained me with joyful teas and sound advice. The Golden Patties kept me in glorious shade. Hafsah Faizal delivered elegant graphics in a snap, as did Kayte Ghaffar, who has been known to dabble in sorcery. Hedwig Aerts helped me sort Nachtspel revelry, and Josh Minuto puts up with texts that begin with things like, "Hi, how are you? I have a funny pain in my chest. Should I go to the hospital?"

As always, I want to thank my family: Emily, Ryan, Christine, and Sam; Lulu, who let me read whatever I liked so long as I was reading; and my grandfather, who never tired of telling me the story of the monster at the door.

And a special thank-you to my readers, who were willing to follow me into a thorny wood.